STATE OF WAR

IAIN KELLY

By the Same Author

The State Trilogy

A Justified State

State Of Denial

State Of War

State Of War

© Iain Kelly, 2020

First Published 2020

Independently Published.

All Rights Reserved

The moral right of the author has been asserted.

All characters in this publication are fictitious and resemblance to real persons, living or dead, is purely coincidental.

www.iainkellywriting.com

ISBN – 9798636825258

They say a good soldier fights a battle, never a war. That's for civilians.
        - John Steinbeck, The Winter of Our Discontent

And now, instead of bullets wrapp'd in fire,
To make a shaking fever in your walls,
They shoot but calm words folded up in smoke,
To make a faithless error in your ears:
Which trust accordingly, kind citizens,
And let us in, your king, whose labour'd spirits,
Forwearied in this action of swift speed,
Crave harbourage within your city walls.
        - William Shakespeare, King John, Act I, Scene 2

PROLOGUE

Sand and dirt swirled around her, kicked up by the persistent breeze that hadn't relented for days. She thought about the chemicals contained in the particles that covered her. How many radioisotopes from the nuclear attack that wiped out Billings and Columbus was she exposed to? The fallout had spread down the central spine of the continent, leaving the west and east cut off from each other by a wasteland in the middle. Gabriella imagined the microscopic cells attacking her body, evolving and decaying, sparking a cancerous invasion. She glanced at the needle on the Geiger counter. It flickered in the white safe area of the dial. She didn't trust it. She pulled up the thick scarf to cover her mouth and nose, the rough cloth irritating her skin. She wiped the sight on her rifle and peered through it. Most army snipers preferred the modern augmented digital scopes, but Gabriella preferred the old-fashioned telescopic sight. Through the haze she saw her target. It was a huge building, impossible to miss, towering above the small town of Idyllwild. For the last fifteen minutes she had watched soldiers of the Axis Powers unloading military hardware. They were setting up a base. The locals had been gathered into groups, separated into men, women and children.

Static crackled in her ear. 'Command to Outpost. Do you have a visual?'

Gabriella pushed the send button, 'Affirmative,' she whispered and waited for a response.

'Are we clear to proceed?'

'Negative. I repeat, negative. Civilians in close proximity.'

There was a long pause. Gabriella imagined the urgent conversation between the commanders. When the response finally came it was the voice of Lieutenant-Colonel Phillips who spoke.

'How many civilians? Over.'

'Between one-fifty and two hundred being used as a human shield.'

Again a long pause, then, 'Affirm this is definitely an enemy sighting.'

'Affirmed. One battalion with heavy equipment and residual support.' They couldn't be contemplating going ahead, the rules of engagement were explicit: if there was a threat to civilian life, no bombing could take place. If they wanted to attack this Axis base they would need to call in the infantry, or a tactical automated unit. The longer static buzzed in her ear, the more nervous Gabriella became.

Phillips came back over the radio, 'Light up the target. The drone is beginning its run.'

'Repeat. Civilians in close proximity.' Had they not heard her correctly?

'Received, soldier. You have your orders.'

'Sir, they will be killed. I repeat, civilians will be killed.'

'This is a direct order from State command, soldier.' The voice was firm. 'Light it up.'

***

The night before had been her first chance for uninterrupted sleep in a fortnight.

Gabriella had arrived at base camp in the early evening, debriefed the Camp Commander and a posse of other officers, grabbed dinner in the mess and found a free TouchScreen to check for messages. There was no word from home. Her parents, born in the European Union, had migrated to the State before Gabriella was born. Now they were being held in a detention centre, waiting to be processed and facing deportation. Gabriella had found a solicitor to help them. They launched an appeal against the decision. There was no word if the court had decided to re-hear their case. A daughter serving with distinction in the State Forces was given as one of the mitigating circumstances, but the odds were stacked against them. The State had been removing all immigrants for years, determined to relieve the overpopulation situation and to clamp down on illegal refugees and terrorists. It was a political show. No one would have remotely considered her parents a threat.

Operations Specialist Ivan Fleming found her and invited her to the camp bar for drinks. They were both rotating off duty the next morning, with a month of furlough back home to look forward to. Gabriella would use the time to deal with her parents' situation. Fleming was in the mood to celebrate the prospect of a month of freedom.

Gabriella declined. Instead she left him to join the others and found a bed to slump into. The mission to Red Rock Canyon that day had turned out to be a damp squib. Increasingly the intelligence they were responding to was sketchy and unverified, and often completely false. Reports of Axis soldiers and machinery as far inland as Red Rock Canyon had to be checked, but Gabriella had never believed they would be true. Unsurprisingly, all they had found was bare red rock. On the plus side, it had been a welcome respite away from the frontline. Sixty kilometres north and west of the base camp, Santa Monica and Pasadena were being obliterated by another Axis onslaught. As Gabriella lay on the thin mattress, she could hear the thud of heavy artillery exploding in the distance.

She drifted off to sleep. This time tomorrow she would be somewhere over the ocean heading back to the State for a month of rest and relaxation.

It was Fleming who woke her, kicking her leg that hung over the edge of the bed.

'Rise and shine. We're up.'

Through narrow eyes she squinted up at her fellow specialist 'We're off duty as of this morning.' She rolled over and closed her eyes again.

'We're off duty at zero-nine hundred hours. It's only six-thirty, which means we still have to do their bidding, and intel just came in of Axis activity that needs checking out. Your beauty sleep will have to wait, let's go.' Fleming grabbed the side of the bedframe and tipped it up, sending Gabriella sprawling onto the floor.

'Goddamn it, Fleming.'

'Language, soldier, that could get you court-martialled. Briefing room in five.' Fleming walked out of the tent smiling. Gabriella flipped a middle-finger at his disappearing back and pulled herself up. They had spent too long in each other's company.

They sat in the front row. At the table in front of them stood their commanding officer, Major Falconer, and another officer with the stripes of a Lieutenant-Colonel on his uniform. Gabriella had a feeling she had seen the tall man with short dark hair before. Behind them on a large screen was the familiar map of the Civil American States, or what was left of them. On the left-hand side was Laramidia, the strip of land along the coast of the Pacific Ocean, where what was left of the Civil American States' military combined with the State and continued to try and repel the might of the Zhonghuan army. To the east was the red-shaded block of the exclusion zone, the dead area where radioactive fallout from the First Strike attack was lethal. Even now, forty years since the nuclear missile had destroyed the city of Billings in Montana, the land and atmosphere around the centre of the impact area was considered unsafe. The Civil American States had quickly blamed the Zhonghua Republic for the attack and retaliated with force, and the First Strike War had begun. No one could have predicted the fighting would still be continuing all these decades later. Many of the soldiers, like Gabriella and Fleming, had never known peace in their lifetime. Further east from the exclusion zone was Appalachia, the other side of what remained of the Civil American States. There, the Allies were represented by the African and European Union forces, who were embattled against the Union of Soviet Socialist Republics.

They sat in silence until the tent flap opened and Decker, the American drone pilot, entered and took a seat next to Fleming.

'Good,' said Falconer, 'now we can begin.'

'We're due to rotate out in two hours,' Gabriella cut in before they could progress any further.

'I'm well aware of that, Marino. If you wish to consult the regulations after the briefing you are free to do so. You will find that firstly, any furlough can be suspended if circumstances dictate it and secondly, until furlough has officially begun, any soldier is liable to be commandeered as required. May I continue?'

It was a rhetorical question. Their previous six month tour of duty was not going to be taken into consideration. It was the military way.

Falconer drew his eyes from Gabriella and began his briefing. 'Significant intelligence tells us the Axis Powers have found a route behind our lines to here,' he touched his TouchScreen panel and the image on the wall zoomed into an area of forest and mountains. 'The San Jacinto region, specifically a small town called Idyllwild.'

Fleming interjected, 'All due respect, sir, how solid is this intelligence? We just got back from one wild goose chase, and this seems unlikely.'

It was the Lieutenant-Colonel who answered, 'The intel is solid.'

Falconer did the introductions. 'This is Lieutenant-Colonel Phillips, Special Forces. He will be running the operation.'

Something chimed in the back of Gabriella's mind. The name Phillips wasn't right. She tried to picture where she had seen him before. She recalled a den somewhere, a camp's mess perhaps, drinking shots with her unit, banging the glass down on the bar top. He had been there, but he wasn't called Phillips then. When had that been? A year ago, or longer? Time was difficult to track in the middle of a war zone. He hadn't been a Lieutenant-Colonel either. He had been a private, one of the infantry. There had been more of a human presence in the battalion back then, before the mechanised forces had begun to replace the soldiers. Now there were more mechanical units than humans in the expeditionary force. That meant less human casualties, which always went down well back home where the politicians had to justify the war to the citizens. The grunts on the front line had mixed feelings. They didn't yet trust the technology that was replacing them, but at the same time, those that had seen the worst of the fighting were happy for machines to bear the brunt of the violence instead of them.

She remembered they had been playing cards, poker probably, that was their game of choice. They were celebrating some sort of success, who knows which one, there had been so many missions now, and they all rolled into one confused memory. There was a lot of drink, which was standard in the army camps even though alcohol was banned in the State. The officers liked to keep their personnel happy. Gabriella had been drunk. Had she done anything she shouldn't have with him? It wasn't uncommon, although it was frowned upon. Gabriella had slept with a few of her fellow soldiers. It meant nothing to any of them, it was just a way to escape the war for a few moments. But she was sure she would have remembered if she had done anything with this guy. She knew they had chatted, but she couldn't recall the subject. She remembered there had been something different about him, like he was holding back, calculating something, watching his fellow comrades. The next day, hangovers shaken off, they had all moved on to their separate details. Gabriella had transferred to another post along the front line and had thought nothing more about the young man. He was just another of the many soldiers she had shared a passing moment with in the ongoing war.

So how had the infantry grunt changed his name and become a high-ranking officer in a couple of years? The only explanation, if it was the same man, was that he had been recruited by the State Security Forces, the intelligence arm of the State Forces. Gabriella watched him now with darkening suspicion.

'I've been told you are the best sniper team in the unit,' Phillips addressed Fleming and Gabriella, 'that's why I requested you. This incursion represents a significant change in Axis tactics. They thought they would be able to roll over the top of us, but we've held up well. We've stalled them at the coast. Now they are endeavouring to outflank us and attack inland. We need to stamp out that possibility.'

'How did they get there?' Decker asked. 'They can't sneak an army around our surveillance.'

'Intel suggests they flew in over the exclusion zone and landed somewhere to the south before marching up through the mountains to San Jacinto.'

'But that's illegal. No forces are allowed inside the exclusion zone, including flying through it.'

'I'm well aware of that,' Phillips replied. 'It appears our enemies are willing to ignore the international laws of combat.'

Falconer returned to the mission briefing, 'We're too stretched along the Pacific front to spare any manpower so our best option is a tactical airstrike. Captain Decker will be in control of an ST-568 drone, armed with laser-guided ST-CC missiles. Due to the heavy forest cover, we need eyes on the ground. Specialists Fleming and Marino will make a stealth insertion through the forest to provide missile guidance.'

'You make it sound so easy,' Gabriella said.

'Nothing we can't handle, sir,' said Fleming.

'Be ready to roll in twenty minutes. Lieutenant-Colonel Phillips and I will run the mission from Base Command.'

An hour later Fleming and Gabriella made the low-level parachute jump from the ST-568 drone and landed on the southern tip of the San Jacinto forest. They split up and moved in a parallel formation through thick foliage and rough terrain until they crested a ridge. Below them lay the town of Idyllwild.

'Toss you for it,' said Fleming as he joined Gabriella.

'No way, it's your turn.'

'You can't count Red Rock, there was no one there.' Fleming smiled and took his lucky coin from his pocket – an old State sestertius, with the head of former Chancellor Anthony on it. It was over a hundred years old. Anthony was the last ruler of the State to have his image on currency before coins and notes were abolished.

Fleming flipped it into the air and caught it on the back of his hand, covering it with the other.

'Heads,' called Gabriella.

Fleming revealed the coin. The image of the State coat of arms – a dove flying over a bull – faced them. 'Tails it is. Enjoy the trip, I'll be having a nice lie down here until you get back.'

'F--- you, Fleming,' Gabriella punched him on the arm.

'You love me really,' he grinned as Gabriella set off down the slope and disappeared into the thick forest of trees.

It had taken her an hour to find a vantage point through the trees which overlooked the main centre of Idyllwild. Like most towns in Laramidia, the war had taken its toll on the settlement. Buildings were shabby and ill-repaired, overgrown weeds and grass were reclaiming roads and pavements, which were cracked and pitted. A few townsfolk milled about without purpose, wandering along deserted streets. It looked like most civilians had left town already. It had an empty, tumbleweed feel to it. At first Gabriella thought the intel had been wrong again. There was no obvious sign of enemy forces. She skirted round the town centre and reached the far end of the main street.

It was the sound that alerted her. Beneath the rustle of tree branches waving in the breeze, she picked out the ugly noise of machinery: engines powering tracks across rough ground. She pinpointed where it was coming from and moved nearer, creeping through the woods. As she got closer she could distinguish other sounds: voices calling out to each other, tools being used, heavy footsteps that could only be made by soldiers marching in unison.

She found a ridge in the forest and, lying on her stomach, she crawled to the top of it. She peered over and saw the large, iron warehouse that must have once been a hangar or barn. Coming in and out of it were soldiers of the Zhonghuan Army. She tried to count how many she saw and how many drone tanks and planes they had. There was no doubt they could not have travelled unnoticed from the coast. Phillips's intelligence was right. They must have flown through the exclusion zone in military cargo planes. They would have been undetected because no one watched the airspace. It was too dangerous to fly through – but the Axis Powers had done just that, and they had brought a full battalion with them.

Alongside the Zhonghuan soldiers, lined up by the warehouse and around the clearing, were the men, women and children of Idyllwild.

***

'You have your orders, light up the target.' The voice in her ear was louder now, she could hear the anger rising. Decker was ready to fire his missiles but had reported back that he could still not detect any target for them to lock onto. Phillips was shouting 'This is an order from State Command, soldier. Light up the target.'

Gabriella aimed her laser rifle at the large metal structure. If she didn't select a target they would use unguided weapons and the damage would be even worse. She was a soldier of the State and these were her orders. If there were any repercussions they would not fall on her. She would just have to live with what she had done. She squeezed the trigger.

'Target is lit, sir,' she spat the last word into the mic.

'Copy that, I have it,' answered Decker's voice. 'Missiles one through ten are away.'

Gabriella heard the rising scream as the warheads descended from the sky, converging on their target. It was too late for her to do anything. She buried her head into the ridge of earth and waited as the shrieking drew closer. In a split second before the impact she heard cries from the soldiers who recognised the fury that was racing towards them. Some looked to the heavens and saw the sleek, silver cylinders arrowing downwards. The civilians did not know what was about to hit them until the first missile impacted.

The explosions made the earth shake around Gabriella. She sank back down the ridge and rolled away, covering her ears with her hands. Boom. Boom. Boom. The rain of thunder struck, ten missiles within a minute. Then an eerie silence. Her eardrums recovered, the ringing in her head slowly clearing to be replaced by human cries from injured soldiers. There was a crackling noise too, flames of fire licked at the trees around the massive crater that now occupied the space where a warehouse and an army battalion had been moments before.

'Status report.' It was Falconer in her ear.

Gabriella crawled back to the top of the ridge and looked over. She would never be able to forget what she saw: burnt human flesh, charred remains mixed with mangled metal. The images were seared into her brain forever.

'Direct hit.'

'Copy that. Fall back to the rendezvous point for extraction.'

'All civilians killed. Repeat. No civilian survivors.' She was answered only by static.

She climbed back out of the valley to where Fleming was waiting for her. He watched her approach along the path.

'Looked like a success from up here. Quite a display of force.'

'They killed them all,' Gabriella muttered.

'Why so sad? You did your job.'

'There were children there, civilians. The people we are supposed to be protecting. They didn't care.'

'We just do our duty, that's all. It's not up to us to question their decisions.'

He couldn't understand, he hadn't been there.

'Then who should question them?' she asked bitterly.

The gunshot rang out across the rocky mountains at the same time as Fleming threw himself forwards and pushed Gabriella to the floor. Gabriella spun as she fell. She drew her sidearm and aimed as she landed. The Zhonghuan soldier, covered in blood from a wound on the side of his head, pointed his gun at her. She pulled her trigger first. She shot him through the chest, then through his forehead. He collapsed to the ground.

She picked herself up and walked over to the body. She kicked the lifeless form.

'Must've followed me all the way from the town. I should have noticed him tracking me.' She hadn't been thinking straight, her anger had clouded her concentration. She turned back to Fleming and saw him lying on the ground.

His eyes were wide open, staring at her. She would never forget the look of shock on his face. It burned into her conscience alongside the charred remains of the townsfolk of Idyllwild. From the neck wound, his dark blood streamed onto the grey-brown rock, congealing with the earthy dust.

Military Operations Specialist Gabriella Marino emerged from the San Jacinto forest carrying her fallen comrade at dusk. The ST-568 drone was waiting to pick her up. She fell into the aircraft, exhausted by the weight she had carried over the rough terrain. She refused to leave Fleming's body behind. His head rolled from side to side in her lap with each pitch of the aircraft. By the time she had returned to base camp, Lieutenant-Colonel Phillips had disappeared. Gabriella found Falconer and informed him that she was now on furlough. There was a cargo plane leaving for the State that evening and Gabriella was aboard it. She did not inform Major Falconer that she intended to use her furlough to resign from the State Military Force and would not return to the front line. She had done her mandatory five years' service. She had seen enough of the war, and she was finished taking orders from the State military.

THE WANDERER

He clambers over the debris: piles of rubble constructed to form a barrier, or fallen there when the buildings had been bombed. The streets are strewn with boulders of grey concrete, metal poles, cables and loose wiring – the infrastructure of a city lying in ruins, dirt and dust covering the remains. A carpet of glass shards crunches underfoot, few window panes survive intact. He treads cautiously. Worn, tattered shoes will do little to protect the soles of his feet. On the partial walls that still stand, her face, daubed in paint. He remembers her name: Maxine Aubert. He was there the day she was murdered. The day the war began.

He reaches the end of a street. It opens out onto an empty square. He realises where he is. The main square of the city. The parliament building once stood along one side. It was gone, one of the first victims of the war, reduced to a mound of shapeless granite, and scoured with black streaks of fire damage. Shelling and artillery brought it to its knees. Which side did it? The State military or the rebels? Does it matter? Surrounding statues lie in pieces – fallen idols with limbs and heads smashed asunder, State Chancellors ripped from their plinths by defiant citizens using only bare hands and brute force.

On this exact spot it had begun. After that nothing had been the same. Three years ago, four? How many seasons had passed? The rains were due again any day now, the hot and dry summer was over. The snows would follow. He could not face another winter, this would be his last. The cold weather would bring another virus season. The vaccines that had once banished the annual plague of coronaviruses and respiratory diseases were no longer available. Another generation of elderly and weak citizens would be decimated through exposure to another epidemic. His body is too weak, he feels his lungs wheeze with every breath. He remembers when he took pride in his appearance. His crisp, clean uniform, his short, neat haircut, his trained and trim body. Now his limbs are thin, nothing more than skin and bones. His hair is long, hanging in patchy, straggling clumps. His beard is unkempt and lice-covered, stretching down to his chest. His fingernails are gone, his hands are cracked and bleeding. His skin is scarred and blistered, boils of infected pus cover him. He is malnourished and dirty, his clothes nothing more than rags.

He stumbles on, seeking shelter before the sun goes down. There is peace over the city tonight, no bombing or gunfire. It is a while since he has been to this part of Central City. Once it had been his home, now he wanders from one coast to the other and back again. Scavenging, surviving, crossing the city from east to west and west to east. Once he had ventured north, like so many other citizens, seeking escape in the wilderness beyond the city walls. Some chose to stay there, adapting to a different life. Most returned, unable to acclimatise to the natural world. He chose the city. His city. The place he knew, even if parts of it were no longer familiar to him. Those that chose to stay did so knowing they were in the heart of a war zone.

The peace was pierced by a feral howl. Several wild dogs charged across the square. He crouched and watched. Wild-eyed, skinny brutes with scabious coats, barking with their loose jowls flapping, covered in saliva. Packs like this ranged across the city. Before, there had been no stray animals. Now they came in from the wilderness searching for scraps of sustenance, part of nature trying to reclaim this urban landscape. It wasn't just dogs, he had seen deer, cats and wolves.

His thoughts turn to his aching stomach. It had been months since his last proper meal. A dog would feed him for days. The meat would be tough and taste foul, but it would be nourishing. Too late, they were gone. He didn't have the energy to pursue them.

He leaves the main square behind, heading south. Soon he arrives at the cold and forbidding river. Once the water had been a glorious turquoise. He walks along the north bank. The bridges are gone, destroyed in the war. He passes what is left of the arch bridge. Once it was called the Citizen's Leap. The elderly, the tired and the depressed had jumped from here into the water below. The bridge was gone, death remained.

There is no way for him to cross the water. He meanders on. The sun starts to fade, darkness descends. There are no artificial lights to illuminate his way. In the distance, a volley of artillery fire, the first of the night. He tries to pinpoint it. Somewhere to the east, not a full scale assault, perhaps a State Military patrol stumbling upon a band of rebels. Or vice versa. It doesn't concern him, he is invisible. A ghost. One of the forgotten majority of citizens trapped between the two sides, forced to live in the middle of the violent battle that envelops them. There is no escaping it. So many dead and injured from the bombs and the bullets. They had been abandoned by the State and betrayed by the rebels. No one cared about them. They were the lost citizens of Central City.

An orange flicker ahead. Firelight. Silhouetted figures surround it. He hides in the shadows. It could be soldiers or it could be fellow survivors. Both options present danger. Even if they are like him, they may not welcome him - another mouth to feed, another body to house and provide warmth to. He has encountered this situation many times before. The selfish will to survive turns citizen against citizen. He has lost faith in humanity. Too often he has seen its ugly side, even before the war.

He could wait to see if they dispersed. They may leave food scraps or dying embers. There were three of them, all women he thinks, though it is hard to tell in the gloom. Poverty and hardship obscure gender appearance. He sees boxes and blankets arranged in rough beds forming a camp. They will not be moving on. He no longer stays in one place for more than one or two nights. Inevitably they will be discovered by someone – mercenaries, rebels, soldiers or thieves.

By the light of their ramshackle brazier he sees a nearby building. The roof and upper levels have gone, one wall has crumbled. Pock-marked and battered, the other three sides remain. The chill wind blowing in from the river convinces him. He skirts round and enters from the side. It is pitch black, there is no guarantee he is alone here. But he is weak, he needs to lie down and he needs shelter for the night. He has no choice. Finding a corner, he settles down. Dull thumps of heavy artillery and rapid strafes of gunfire are distant. Somewhere more people are dying, but not him, not tonight. Tomorrow he will need to find water and food, tonight he just needs to rest.

The chatter of the three women by the river fades. They too have bedded down for the night. It gives him some comfort to have these neighbours. It is a small contact with the living world that he rarely finds. His eyelids close, a shivering, disturbed sleep takes hold.

Suddenly he awakes. He has no idea of the time. How long has he been asleep? There it is again, a faint, light noise. Rats scurrying through the rubble? No, too slow, too measured. Footsteps, barely audible. A larger animal? In the wall above his head, a gap, a shattered window. He creeps underneath it and rises, his eyes peer over the parapet. At first he sees nothing. The clouds break, moonlight adds a dim shine. He sees the movement rather than the person. A shadow moving among the blackness that surrounds it. Then another. How many are there? He can't be certain as they move past him. If they see him they do not stop for him. He is a ghost, he is not important. Then they are gone, like a black shimmer, a breeze, barely noticed. Was there ever anyone there? He can no longer trust his mind. Perhaps he imagined them. He hears a faint splash, something dropping into the river. Then another one.

He looks one last time, searching along the river. He sees nothing and shrugs. His eyes settle on the huge chimneys of the State arms factory. He remembers. They tower over the city, just as they did before the war. There are some lights there, windows in the darkness.

Retreating, he hunkers back down into his corner. He must rest. He feels the first drops of rain, large, heavy drops falling slowly at first. They land on the dirt and dust, turning them into a veneer of mud. He has nothing with which to cover himself so he presses himself harder into the corner. His dishevelled hair is soon dank and matted, raindrops fall from his head over his eyes. The rains have arrived. Existence becomes a still greater challenge. He closes his eyes, unsure if they shall ever open again, uncaring about his fate.

1

The rain was unwelcome but changed nothing. In fact it helped to give some cover as they rowed across the river in the small inflatables, disguising the ripples they carved into the murky black water. The clouds closed in and cloaked the moonlight. As they made progress towards the southern bank, Danny lost sight of the other craft. He wiped his brow and the end of his automatic machine gun. He swept the approaching edge of the river, swinging the gun barrel round, looking for any movement. If they were spotted at this point, the mission was over. They were relying on surprise. He saw nothing. Rodrigo steered them close to the sheer brick wall, a remnant of the long forgotten dockyards that once gave the city its character. Standing on the prow, Danny reached out and grabbed hold of an iron rung, cemented into the brickwork. He slipped a rope through it and tied it off, securing the inflatable to the wall. He was first to climb up the ladder and emerge at the top. Rodrigo and Verona followed him, Kyle stayed with the boat.

    Danny crouched low until the others had joined him. He signalled them to follow him. They started to creep forward along the edge of the river. If things had gone to plan those from the other boat should be waiting for them fifty metres further along. There was little natural cover in the exposed concrete walkway they followed, the darkness was their only concealment. Danny counted down the paces, then raised a clenched fist and stopped. Rodrigo and Verona came to a halt behind him. They heard a sharp hiss to their left. Just beyond the edge of the walkway there was a low wall and some sparse foliage. Danny signalled again and they moved swiftly and silently towards the source of the noise. They reached the wall and jumped over, landing next to three more people. Guns were pointing at them, but once identities had been established they were lowered. Gabriella, one eye covered by a black eye-patch, gave Danny a nod. Lachlan and Zeb were with her. So far, so good. They had got this far. Now they were six. Gabriella took point, she was the natural leader, Danny had no complaints.

The rain made the black make-up on his face run. He could taste it on his lips and wiped his mouth with a gloved hand. The rain got harder, they could hear its constant patter on the concrete around them. They stole forward another fifty metres, which brought them to a tall perimeter wall. They pressed against it. Danny watched as Zeb, the tall, bulky figure behind Gabriella, removed his backpack. With fluid, well-drilled motions, he unpacked a rope ladder. Danny leaned back and peered up into the black, soaking night sky. The chimney towers loomed above the wall, stretching upwards for what seemed like kilometres, disappearing into the low clouds. Much of his life had taken place in the shadow of those looming towers, landmarks of his city. He remembered when he used to walk past them every day. Little remained of that life. His family, his career, Central City – all had been destroyed, but the towers of the State arms factory still stood, unyielding. Until tonight, he thought. If all goes to plan, they would destroy another piece of his past. He would not miss this piece, he would not mourn for this piece.

Zeb stepped backwards, away from the wall, and raised a large cylinder to his shoulder. There was a muted thump as he fired. The grappling hook was invisible as it arched into the sky. There was a metallic clang as it hit stone. Zeb pulled on the end of the rope ladder, testing to see if the hook had made its mark. Satisfied, he took a rubber mallet and hammered pegs into the ground to secure the bottom of the ladder. He retreated into the shadow of the wall and tapped Gabriella on the shoulder. Without hesitation, Gabriella swung her machine gun onto her back, raced to the bottom of the ladder and began to ascend the rungs. Verona detached herself from the cover of the wall and followed her. The others waited.

In the darkness all Danny could hear was his own breathing and the internal beating of his heart. On the other side of the wall the factory lay silent. It hadn't functioned for the last couple of years, not since the rebels, the Independents, had seized control of it from the State Forces. As they had been forced to retreat and surrender the factory, the State Forces had blown up the generators that were needed to power it. The Independents had managed to take control before all the equipment could be destroyed. Had they been able to utilise the munitions factory, the war may have taken a different path, but they had been unable to find sufficient energy supplies to run the assembly lines. They had made full use of the weapons they discovered in the factory and it had boosted their war effort for a few months, until the resources had dwindled away to nothing.

Danny peered upwards again, waiting for the signal from Gabriella and Verona. He saw the lights emanating from a few windows on the side of one of the towers. It was this which had forced them to act. The Independents were now retreating at an alarming rate, ceding ground they had spent years claiming from the State, including the arms factory. The State had the infrastructure to get power back to the factory. The lights shining in a few rooms were the first signs of this. Within days the State would have a fresh source of weapons ready to dispense more misery and death, unless they could be stopped.

A low whistle, the signal that told them it was safe to proceed. Rodrigo and Lachlan swiftly climbed. Zeb would stay and secure the rope ladder ready for their escape. Danny followed the others. He reached the top and lay on the narrow wall, scanning the ground in front of him, before swinging his legs down and falling through the air, landing with bent knees on the concrete three metres below. Remaining crouched, he hustled across the empty space, reaching a brick wall against which the others were pressed. Verona worked on the lock of a door. If the factory was fully functioning, if the State surveillance cameras were operating, if the security drones were active, then they would already have been spotted. In the days when the State ran and controlled the city this infiltration would have been impossible, but times had changed. The civil war had levelled the playing field. Technology could no longer be relied upon to guard and protect. The war had become about human resources, endeavour, skill and tactics. It was a mistake not to have deployed any soldiers to provide a secure perimeter around the factory. In twenty seconds the door was open and they slipped through. Danny closed the door behind them.

They stood in a utility room, exactly as the floorplan of the factory had described. Lachlan flipped a fallen table up from its side and placed it in the middle of the floor. Verona flicked on a wind-up torch and placed it on the table. They arranged themselves around the dimly-lit workspace. The rain drummed on the roof and windows outside. No instructions were necessary, each knew their role. Each unbuckled a utility belt from their waist and unpacked their equipment. They started with the three lumps of mouldable clay, removing the packaging from the Semtex carefully. Then they pressed charges into the clay. Gabriella picked up her timer and waited for the others to catch up with her.

'Fifteen minutes.' She watched their shadowed faces to make sure they all agreed and turned dials to the allotted time. 'We regroup here in ten minutes. Anyone not here by then is assumed lost and left behind.' Again, grim nods of agreement. 'Mark.' Each of them simultaneously clicked their timer to start the countdown. The digital red figures started descending.

Lachlan was first to the door and opened it. Verona, Gabriella and Rodrigo exited, back into the dark night. Lachlan followed them with a nod to Danny. Danny was the last to leave and again closed the door behind him.

By the time he turned into the driving rain, the four other members of their small infiltration unit were gone. Each had their destination, strategic points at which to deposit their explosives. Gabriella had the furthest to travel to get to the far side of the complex and the second of the chimney towers. Verona and Rodrigo headed to the south side of the main building, where a large hangar stored the raw materials required to feed the factory. Lachlan should have been a few paces ahead of Danny as he turned and moved along the wall, heading to the north side, nearest the river. Here, Lachlan would find the generators that fed the factory its independent power source. They had sat idle for the last few months, but the few lights in the offices and towers above them suggested they were once again producing electricity. Danny saw the hulks of cylindrical metal that comprised the generators, three of them lined up along the edge of the water. He could not see Lachlan, but he assumed he was there, planting his primitive bomb.

Danny kept close to the walls. His target was the first tower. It did not stand alone, rising from the ground, but grew from the roof of a small rectangle building at its base. He crossed an area of overgrown vegetation, feeling the wet grass make his boots and trousers damp. He saw the door he must enter and headed straight towards it. There was no time for subtle lock picking now. As he got within two paces of the door he turned his shoulder into it and crashed through it. The rotten wood splintered easily and with little noise. Inside the building the corridor was where he expected it to be. He rushed along it, fifty metres at a sprint. The spiral staircase was at the end of it. Now Danny climbed. Five levels up and he reached the point where the building ceased and the circular tube of the tower continued upwards. Now he removed the plastic explosives from his belt once more. They had stayed dry, the charges were still in place. He planted each of the clay lumps equidistantly around the circumference of the tower wall. From each he trailed a wire into the centre of the circle. He took out the timer and looked at the clock. The seconds continued to countdown. He had five minutes to complete his mission and get back to the others. He took the three individual ends and wrapped them together to create one combined wire. The volatile nature of the explosives and the consequences of a misplaced connection did not enter his mind. He pressed the wire into the bottom of the timer and quickly screwed it into place. There was no way to check the connection, he had to trust his handiwork. He checked that each of the charges was still buried in the

Semtex, then he turned and ran. He took the steps three or four at a time, leaping downwards in a dizzying vortex. He hit the ground at the bottom and sprinted along the corridor. He could see the opening of the broken door in front of him, and he could see the torchlight shining through it.

Danny did not decrease his pace. He unslung the machine gun from his back and released the safety. If it came to it, he would have to risk the sound of gunfire. Drawing closer he could make out a hand and arm swinging the torch around the broken door, inspecting the unexpected breach. He could make out the detail of the State Military uniform. His luck was in, the soldier was facing the other way, looking out into the rain-filled night, seeking an answer to the damaged door they had stumbled upon. Danny willed the soldier not to turn towards him. He tried to run lightly, but the heavy boots he wore made it impossible. As he got to within three metres of the doorway, the soldier heard him. Surprise came to Danny's rescue, the shock of seeing an on-rushing opponent careering towards them meant the soldier was a fraction too slow in raising their gun. By the time it was level with Danny's chest, Danny was leaping through the remaining space between them, raising his machine gun and crashing the butt of it into the head of the soldier. His momentum carried them forward. Together, they battered through the remains of the stricken door. The soldier ended up sprawled on the cold, wet ground, with Danny straddled on top of them.

The torch rolled out of the soldier's hand and pointed towards them from the ground. By the light of the torch, Danny could see the face of the soldier for the first time. She was young, perhaps only seventeen or eighteen. She had blonde hair, braided into a ponytail.

She looked too innocent to be dressed in State army fatigues. Dazed by the sudden assault, she mumbled and rolled her head from side to side. Danny did not hesitate. He punched her on the side of her skull. One blow was enough. She was unconscious, but he could not bring himself to leave her there, under the shadow of the tower that was set to blow up in less than ten minutes.

'Shit,' he muttered. He realised this is what made him different from others in this bloody conflict. His conscience. He could not leave her to die, he would not stoop to their level, he would do what he could to avoid committing murder. He sized up the soldier. She was no taller than one metre seventy and she was thin. He reckoned she must weigh no more than sixty kilograms. He pulled her inert body up by the arms and swung her onto his back, her slight frame lying across his shoulders. He started running, no longer being cautious to remain low or to search for the shadows. As he advanced the weight across his back seemed to increase. He turned the corner and passed the generators. There was no sign of Lachlan. Without a free hand to wipe his face, the rain started to blind him as it drove into him. He saw the perimeter wall ahead. In the darkness he could not make out anyone or any movement. He reached it and started moving along it, hoping to stumble across the end of the rope ladder. He began to think he had gone too far and had missed the meeting point when he heard a sharp call above his head. He looked up from under his human cargo and saw the barrel of a gun pointing down at him. At the other end of the barrel was Gabriella.

'It's me,' he called up in a loud whisper.

'What the hell?' Gabriella muttered and holstered her weapon. She turned and gave a sharp whistle to the other side of the wall. In ten seconds she was joined by the hulking presence of Zeb on the narrow ledge. The rope ladder was thrown down.

'How long?' Danny shouted upwards.

'Less than five,' came the reply. 'Come on.'

They had time, Danny thought, calculating his chances. He dropped the soldier and wrapped the end of the rope ladder around her midriff, tying it loosely. Without pause, he scampered up the rungs of the ladder. As he neared the top, Zeb and Gabriella reached down, grabbed him by the arms and hauled him up.

'We don't have time for this,' Gabriella hissed at him. Danny sensed her anger. Gabriella was ex-military. For her, war was clear cut, the enemy did not deserve any mercy.

Danny looked to Zeb, ignoring her warning. 'Help me pull her up.' Zeb took one side of the rope ladder, Danny the other, and together they hoisted the inert woman up the side of the wall. With Zeb's extra strength it did not take them long. Gabriella had already dropped down the other side of the wall. Zeb took the soldier and tossed her onto his shoulders like she was a feather before jumping down. Danny followed.

'Two minutes,' it was Verona who took the rear now, pushing Danny ahead of her. 'Move.' The others had already gone. Danny could see them as the clouds cleared and moonlight provided some illumination. There was no point in remaining in a controlled formation now, each of them was sprinting across the open ground to get back to the river as fast as they could.

Kyle emerged from behind the low wall as they approached. He saw it was his comrades and lowered his weapon. Wordlessly the group split into two. Verona, Rodrigo and Danny followed Kyle down the iron rungs of the river wall into the boat moored at the bottom.

Further along the bank, at the next ladder, Gabriella, Lachlan and Zeb, still shouldering his extra passenger, descended into their vessel. Once they were in their boat, Danny could no longer make out the other inflatable through the murk. Kyle untied the rope. Verona and Kyle took the oars, Rodrigo manned the tiller.

'One minute,' growled Verona. The oars swept into the water. Danny felt the boat surge away from the wall and out into the open. They should just make it to the other side. He looked back at the chimney towers, looming above them, the random pattern of rectangular lights climbing their sides. There may be people behind them, members of the State Forces, or citizens just like them. Gabriella had been confident there would be no one working in the building at this time of night. They could not afford to wait, the factory had to be destroyed, there was no ideal time. Danny had run into one soldier on a security detail, he was certain she would not have been there alone.

The far side of the river drew near. Kyle and Verona pressed on. The front of the inflatable boat hit the brick wall that rose up from the water. They were all thrown forward. At the exact same moment the first explosion ripped through the night sky. Kyle managed to regain his footing and stepped to the bow of the boat. He reached out and grasped a passing iron rung. The boat steadied. The four passengers turned to look back at the factory.

There were four more loud explosions, all in quick succession. The cumulative noise was deafening, it left Danny with ringing in his ears. Each detonation was accompanied by an orange fireball that burst out from the base of the factory complex. Metal, brick and concrete debris launched into the sky. Some fragments landed in the water with heavy splashes. The river started to swell as waves were created. The last pieces of wreckage settled with bangs and clatters. There was a moment of quiet, a settling. They stood in the boat, transfixed. Then there was a new noise, a loud creaking as tonnes of plastic, metal, fibre glass and concrete started to sway and crumble. Both the towers began to sway above the burning inferno at their base. The one furthest away, the one that Gabriella planted her bomb in, was the first to collapse. It folded in on itself, the top remaining intact as it dropped down, engulfed by dust and rubble that bloomed into a rising cloud. The second tower, the one that Danny was responsible for, was doing something different. It seemed to hang for a moment, deciding which way to topple. Too late, Danny realised which way it was falling.

'Get out now!' he screamed and pushed Verona forward. Kyle was still holding on, attaching the boat to the side of the wall. Verona scrambled up the wall, one rung at a time, Rodrigo followed her. 'Go!' Danny screamed at Kyle, while watching the tower. The swaying structure began to give way, collapsing not straight down like the first tower, but leaning to one side, heading straight for the river in a long, tumbling arc. As Kyle left the boat, a swell pushed the inflatable down river, Danny dived instinctively forward and his flailing hand managed to grip a ladder rung at water level. He felt the boat disappear from beneath him as it was swept away. With the support gone Danny was suddenly submerged in the freezing, murky water. His head went under for a moment. It happened so quickly he sucked in a lungful of water. Holding tightly, he pulled his head up, emerging with a cough and splutter. There was an almighty crash as the tower hit the water, bridging the full width of the river, its top pummelled into the river bank a hundred metres from where Danny clung on. The crash was followed by a whooshing roar. River water was sent into the air in a white, broiling spray. A tsunami of displaced water rushed down the river towards Danny. He could not pull himself far enough up the ladder in time. The wave crashed over him, ripping at his body, determined to prise him away from the ladder and send him tumbling into the black depths of the deep river.

The power was immense as the force of the water threatened to drag him to a certain death. He felt his fingers uncurling from the metal. He fought back. His lungs felt like they would explode. He needed air. He would not let the river claim him. Not like it had Rosa. Perhaps she was waiting for him in the black depths, waiting for him to come and join her, waiting for him to rescue her. He felt he was about to black out. He had nothing left, no energy, no strength, no oxygen.

Then the force relented. The wave subsided. He gasped as he was able to raise his head above the water. Another swell hit him, but it was weaker. The power of the initial wave had dissipated. He pulled his free hand through the water and managed to cling onto the metal rung. Instinct kicked in and he found himself climbing the ladder, his leg and arm muscles working on adrenaline alone. He reached the top of the river wall and hands grabbed his soaking clothing, hauling him over the edge. He collapsed, rolling onto his back, coughing up water mixed with vomit. Rodrigo and Kyle pulled him to his feet. Instantly, the other team joined them, they needed to retreat before the place became swamped with State personnel. Danny grabbed Gabriella's shoulder as she passed. 'The girl?'

'She's safe.'

They ran. Danny gulped in fresh air. After a few steps he was able to brush Kyle and Rodrigo aside and carry on himself. They followed the route agreed upon. Each of them knew the city well. If they did not meet any obstacles they would be back at their camp beyond the city walls well before daybreak. Danny returned to his position at the rear of the column, relieving Verona of her duty. As they ran, he looked back over his shoulder. The rain had not been able to dampen the roaring inferno they had left behind. Orange flames licked the night sky, rising thirty metres from the ground. Through the patter of heavy rain he could hear the crackle and hiss of fire. Where the two towers had once stood there was a void in the skyline. Another piece of the city had disappeared. Since the start of the civil war much of the world he once knew had been destroyed. His childhood had been burned and blown away, the physical memories of the love he had once had and lost had all gone. The towers were part of those memories. For all the citizens of Central City, they represented the technological and industrial power of the State. The spell they had cast had finally been broken.

2

The next morning he could still see the rising smoke down by the river. Danny was the first to wake as the sun broke through the tree cover. He threw off his blanket and dressed in a t-shirt and fatigue trousers. His clothes from last night lay in a wet pile. He gathered them up and took them outside, where he wrung out the water from them, twisting them into a tight knot. Then he hung them over a low-hanging branch, letting the morning sun dry them. No one else stirred in the camp. Lachlan was on sentry duty a kilometre away. Danny let the others sleep, there was no reason for them to be up early today. It had been three o'clock in the morning when they had returned, after the long, uphill trek out of the city and into the hills.

Their camp was just outside the old boundary wall of the city, in a wooded area on the crest of a hill that overlooked the valley below. Central City sprawled out before them as far as they could see. The secluded camp sat in a clearing between six oak trees. Branches from the trees stretched into the middle of the space, creating a natural covering that protected their dwellings from rain and snow in the winter, from searing heat in the dry summer, and from surveillance drones and satellites all year round. The leaves had recently fallen from the branches, covering the forest floor in a damp, orange-yellow carpet. In the centre of the clearing was a campfire, with stones gathered round it for seats. A collection of mismatched tins, pots, plates and cooking utensils were gathered in a pile, still to be cleaned after their meal the previous evening. Danny picked up a metal pail and walked across the clearing. A hundred metres through the woods was a small burn that flowed down the hillside. It eventually joined with other streams and flowed into the river, heading towards the sea. Danny heard a steady trickle through the trees, the heavy rain the night before had swelled the flow of fresh water. His feet shuffled through the fallen leaves, he kicked pine cones as he wandered along. In the peace of the forest he could have forgotten they were overlooking a war zone.

Danny reached the stream and bent down, careful not to lose his footing on the slippery bank. He dipped the bucket into the river and water rushed into it. Once full, he heaved it out and stood. He looked along the stream, following its path until it dropped out of view on its journey down the hillside. Beyond, he saw the expanse of the valley open up below. He picked out the river and looked along it to the spot where the chimney towers of the arms factory had stood the day before. In their place he saw plumes of smoke. The rain during the night had extinguished the large fires, leaving just burning embers among the rubble.

It had been Gabriella who had pushed them to do something about the factory. She had learned that the retreating rebel forces had left in such haste that they had failed to destroy the works. Within days the State would have had it functioning again. Would they have taken the same course of action if the rebels had been close to getting the factory up and running? Danny was sure he would have done the same, and he was sure Gabriella would have been in agreement. The others he was not be so sure about. Zeb and Rodrigo had once been part of the rebel movement, members of the Independents as they called themselves. They still believed in the core principle of the rebellion: to overthrow the corrupt Central Alliance Party that ruled the State. They would have preferred to see the weapons factory utilised against the State Forces, but as it had fallen back into the State's hands, they were eager to see it destroyed.

Danny walked back to their encampment over the uneven ground, spilling water as the bucket swayed in his hand. He hung the pail over the remains of the campfire. Next to the fire was the wood store, a small wooden box with a sheet of tarpaulin covering it to keep the contents dry. He pulled the tarpaulin back and discovered only a handful of chopped logs and sticks. Cursing under his breath, and casting blame on whoever was supposed to have filled the store the previous day, he set off to find more wood. He picked up a small hand axe as he walked back into the forest. In truth he did not mind the manual labour. After the exertions and stress of the previous night, he found pleasure in the simple act of collecting wood. It was something he had discovered during the war. He liked to be distracted by simple endeavours. The more convoluted and violent the war became, the more he liked to preoccupy himself with uncomplicated tasks. Gabriella was the opposite. She was constantly scrutinising the war, speculating the next move either side might make, planning what role they should play and thinking what more they could do to help those trapped in the city.

He found a tree with low branches and set to work with the axe. The exercise loosened off the muscles in his shoulders. The ache brought back the feeling of the powerful water rushing over him and his desperate effort to cling on to the iron rung in the river wall. Once he had chopped an armful of logs, he gathered them up and walked back to the camp. He dropped them into the store. With what dry wood he had, he set about making a small fire that would suffice for cooking breakfast.

Sitting on one of the stones, Danny prodded the fire with a metal poker. There was movement in Verona's tent, a shuffling of canvas as she extracted herself from her sleeping bag and dressed. The door unzipped and she peered out, giving Danny a sleepy wave and smile. She slipped on her boots, without bothering to tie the laces and came to join him. The sun had fully risen now, it was a moist, cool autumn morning. Verona patted him on the shoulder as she joined him, sitting on the rock next to his. As they spoke, faint clouds of breath left their mouths. It would not be long before night time frosts would arrive and living in the woods would become much less comfortable.

'No one else up yet?'

Danny shook his head, 'Just me and the birds.'

Verona yawned, 'Feeling okay?'

'Good.'

'Some night.'

'Sure was.'

They both watched the small flickering flame for a moment.

'I'll find something for breakfast.'

Verona moved off towards the storage pit they had dug behind one of the oak trees. Danny watched her go. Her slight frame looked childlike, belying the fearsome tenacity she possessed. Unlike Gabriella, who had the physical appearance of someone who had served in the military, Verona had been a school girl when the war had broken out, an average citizen caught up in extraordinary circumstances. She had taken no part in the war, nor had she joined the avid peace movement that grew alongside the escalating conflict. Along with the vast majority of the millions of citizens crammed inside the boundary walls of Central City, she was simply present as the bloodshed unfolded around her. For two years she concentrated on survival, her own and that of her family. They had scraped out an existence, bartered and traded for enough food and money to keep going, learning to live without electricity and the modern comforts of life they had become reliant on. They lost their home and had found themselves in one of the huge refugee camps set up around the city. Many in the camps were radicalised by the Independents. Verona's brother was one such person. He joined the rebel movement and was killed in a skirmish with State troops. Verona decided she had to do something, she could no longer be a passive victim. She left her parents in the refugee camp. She had heard of the small bands of unaffiliated groups within the city, mercenaries who supported neither the State nor the rebels, but who were determined to try and protect the citizens caught up in the conflict.

It was Kyle who had found her, lost, starving and alone. He listened to her story and brought her back to the camp. Gabriella had been furious with him for trusting a stranger and bringing her into their midst. Danny understood why Kyle had done what he did. Kyle had lost a daughter in the conflict, she would have been about Verona's age. Gabriella's anger subsided in the following weeks, helped by the aptitude Verona showed for the fight. Gabriella had taken the girl under her wing, teaching her and training her. Danny watched her preparing breakfast for the camp, no longer the innocent girl she had been at the start of the conflict, now a soldier, a mercenary, at the age of twenty-one.

The metal door to the largest dwelling around the campfire opened. It was a wooden hut that Zeb and Rodrigo shared. The large figure of Zeb emerged, squinting as the sunlight breached the bare, leafless branches. Danny was amazed that Zeb managed to retain his bulky figure, despite the scant rations they lived on. Danny himself was leaner than he had ever been. The middle-aged paunch he had developed when he had lived in the city had long gone, there was not an ounce of fat on his body. He didn't suit the look, when he shaved the face that looked back at him from a broken mirror was gaunt and drawn. The war had aged him. Zeb must have been born with the over-developed muscles that still bulged in his near two metre tall frame. He grunted towards Danny, then staggered off to the latrine that was situated fifty metres away from the clearing.

The surrounding forest stirred now that more humans had disturbed the slumber of nature. Danny continued to prod the small flame until it was strong enough to heat the water in the bucket. In a minute he would be able to clean the collection of pots and dishes. He rested his stubbled chin in his free hand and contemplated their actions of the previous night. What consequences would it have for the war? How would both sides react? They had not set upon destroying the factory for the benefit of one side or the other. They wished to destroy as many weapons as possible to protect innocent citizens. They had achieved their goal. It remained to be seen if there would be wider ramifications. That was the risk with every action in the war. The State Military may choose to take retribution for the loss of such a valuable commodity.

A flap of tarpaulin lifted from the bivouac that was propped up against the side of Danny's small shack. The familiar head of short, tousled dark hair emerged. Gabriella stood in her fatigue trousers and boots. The olive skin of her torso and chest glowed in the sun as she slipped a white vest over her head. She pulled the garment down and walked towards Danny. He still couldn't get used to the black eye patch that covered the damaged remains of her left eye. Around it, the olive skin was an angry pink, scarred down the side of her face and across one side of her neck, the result of being caught too close to an exploding grenade. Her good eye glinted at him, matched by a broad smile on her face. She was in a celebratory mood after their night's work. They had been through a lot together since the day the war started, they no longer needed to say much to each other to understand what each was thinking.

They had been caught between the two opposing factions from the start, both wanted by the State, charged with murder and on the run. The leader of the Independents, their one-time comrade Phillips, also wanted them dead because they knew the truth about what he had done. They did not belong to either side. When the journalist Maxine Aubert had been killed by Phillips as part of his plan to start a civil war, they had been thrown together, two outcasts thrust into an unlikely partnership. Before that day, Danny did not trust Gabriella. He knew her as an assassin for hire, an ex-soldier who had murdered a Central City politician and the Chief Commander of the city police force. Then she had escaped, disappeared, only to reappear alongside Phillips as part of his band of rebels seeking to disrupt the State elections and bring down the ruling Central Alliance Party. Only at the last moment did Gabriella understand the full extent of Phillips's plan. She was betrayed by him. It was not something that Gabriella would ever forgive.

She sat next to Danny. The water was warm now and together they began putting the dirty utensils in the bucket. Danny picked up an old brush and began scrubbing. As he finished each item he handed it too Gabriella, who dried it with an old cloth.

Gabriella watched him as he scrubbed the next plate. Her scarred skin tingled. She scratched it. It was not sore this morning, the cold air helped. The warm summer irritated it more and gave her a constant pain down one side of her face. She had learned to live with it.

'How's the arm?' she asked.

Danny had needed his arm rebuilt after being shot when he was a police officer. It rarely caused him any pain these days, but last night had put a lot of stress on it. 'Fine, hadn't even given it a thought.'

'We need to talk about the girl,' she said as he handed her a plate.

Danny had known she would bring it up. 'I couldn't leave her.'

'It could have cost you your life. A moment longer and we would have gone and left you on the wrong side of the wall.'

'I made it.'

'There would have been others. She wouldn't have been on her own.'

'I know that.' Danny stopped scrubbing, 'but I didn't see them. I saw her. I knocked her out. I couldn't just leave her there to die.'

'You put us all at risk.'

'I'll apologise to everyone.'

Gabriella let the silence fall between them. She was angry with him, but she knew nothing she said would make him change. He was not like her, he was not a soldier. Perhaps that was why she remained with him.

She remembered the first time she had met him. He had looked a lot different then. She was on the run from the State at the time. She had worked freelance since leaving the State Military, hired to take out specific targets for a certain price. She didn't ask questions, she didn't worry about motives. She had done work for the State and for private individuals and companies. Then she had taken a job in Central City. With hindsight she realised returning to work in her home city was a bad move. She killed a politician, a State City Consul. The fallout changed everything. Detective Daniel Samson was the police detective investigating the murder. He was middle-aged, going to seed. He had tracked her down in the wilderness while she was being pursued by a State hit squad. His gun had been pointed at her. She would have killed him had Phillips not intervened. Danny and Phillips saved her from the State soldiers, then took her back to the city to question her about murdering the city consul Donald Parkinson. After she had escaped from police headquarters she fled south with Phillips. They had learned the truth about Parkinson and why Gabriella had been paid to kill him. She had no great connection with the city cop who had arrested her, she did not see or hear of Danny for three years until she returned to Central City. It had been Gabriella's turn to save Danny's life this time, freeing him from a State jail as he was about to be murdered. He had changed. He had survived in the wilderness during the intervening years. He was physically and mentally harder, leaner, less naïve. It was Gabriella who had been naïve this time. Danny had warned her not to trust Phillips, cautioned her that he was up to no good, but she hadn't listened until it was too late. Maxine Aubert had been killed because she had not listened to Danny, the path towards civil war in the city was set, and Phillips had left both of them for dead.

They had stayed together because each had no one else. They hid in the city, reacting as the war unfolded. They saw the violence spread, they saw the innocent citizens killed, wounded and displaced. They saw families and lives torn apart. For Gabriella it was a familiar sight. She had seen similar things during her time in the military, serving the State in the First Strike War. For Danny it was a new kind of hell. He had been through his own personal hell – twins that died at birth and his wife who could no longer live with the pain. This was different. He had only heard stories about the First Strike War and seen the sanitised reports on State media. Now he witnessed the raw horror at first hand. Gabriella helped him survive it, he helped her navigate around the city he had lived in for forty years. She changed him, hardening him against the onslaught of war, but he would never be like her. He was too emotional, he could not keep his feelings in check, he cared too much.

They decided they would stay in the city. They would fight for the citizens, for those caught up in the conflict with no one on their side, for those who had no one else to turn to. They started small, scavenging their first weapons by stripping the bodies of dead soldiers. They moved around a lot, staying in the shadows, watching the war unfold.

The Independents took the early initiative against an unsuspecting State army. The sleeping giant of the State military eventually awoke and fought back with greater firepower. The battle for the city swayed one way and then the other. It became a war of attrition. Thoughts of an easy victory for one side or the other faded. A year passed and there was no end in sight. Through perseverance, the rebels began to take hold of the city, for a time it seemed like Phillips and his Independents would win. They controlled most of the territory. Then the war spread. The HighLand City to the north was engulfed. Phillips's forces became spread too thin, trying to fight the war on two fronts. The State exploited this lifeline. The military clawed their way back into Central City, pushing the rebels north and east. By the third year of the war the Independents were clinging on to a small enclave in the east of the city, but much of their strength had dissipated. It seemed only a matter of time before the State would claim victory in Central City.

Gabriella and Danny picked their targets carefully: munition dumps, supply lines, transport vehicles. Danny always pleaded caution, looking for targets with the least probability of casualties. Gabriella was strategic, looking to find targets that brought the most disruption and tactical value. They made sure they targeted the rebels and the State Forces equally. Both were driven to help the citizens, but to different degrees. For Danny they were all he cared about, while Gabriella had other motivations. She had history with the State military and she had history with Phillips. She wanted to see them both defeated. One side or the other winning the war was not a satisfactory outcome for her, they both had to be destroyed, if it meant she took each of them apart one piece at a time. Danny wanted the war to end and the citizens to have their city back again.

They rescued Kyle from an abandoned military base where he was being held as a prisoner of war, accused of spying for the rebels. He had been tortured. When the army had retreated under rebel fire, they had left him to die. Gabriella found him the next day while searching for supplies in the abandoned base. Lachlan joined them soon after, a farmer who had lost everything. By the end of the second year Verona, Zeb and Rodrigo had joined their unconventional unit. The seven of them moved out of the city as the State secured more ground. They retreated to the hills and set up their camp at the start of the year. It had been a comfortable home through the spring and summer. They would soon have to decide if they could survive another cold winter in the forest or if they would need to find shelter in the city.

Danny noticed Gabriella scratching the scarred skin on her neck.

'Sore?'

'No more than usual. Better now it's getting cooler.' He had nursed her through the trauma of her injury. It was the first time either of them had been seriously wounded. Danny had been fifty metres away from the explosion, searching through crates of unused weapons. He heard the grenade land on the wooden floor with nothing more than a sharp click, then it had rolled across the planks. He looked towards the sound just in time to see Gabriella jump back. She reacted a split-second too late. The blast slammed her against a wall. Danny ran towards her through the settling dust and debris. He ripped his shirt off and used it to pat out the fire on her hair and face. The skin was blistered and bleeding, her left eye had gone, but he couldn't risk taking her to the hospital. He hauled her out of the building and carried her on his shoulders into the night. She did not scream once. They had never found out who threw the grenade.

Verona nursed Gabriella in the camp. Danny gave up his shack to let her have a comfortable bed, he slept in her bivouac. That had been five months ago. Within a week Gabriella was back on her feet. Now only the scars and the eye-patch recalled the trauma. She managed to style her short hair to hide the area where it no longer grew.

The incident proved to Danny what he had already known: they were a family, tied together by a bond forged in warfare. Danny felt the weight of the women he failed to protect in his past: Cassandra Ford, his friend in the police force; Montana Childe, the witness to State corruption; Maxine Aubert; and his wife Rosalind most of all. He carried the loss of his children, Hanlen and Isla, too, so young he had barely met them. So much loss, could he survive losing anyone else? He knew Gabriella operated with a soldier mentality, she would die for him because her code of honour told her to act in that way. But did she think of him as family? He doubted it. She had that cold, emotionless, taciturn personality that she wore like armour. He had never seen her cry or complain. She was a soldier without an army.

They finished the dishes. Zeb returned from the latrine. Kyle and Rodrigo emerged from their beds when Verona called out that breakfast was ready. They all sat and ate around what was left of the small fire. Mostly they sat in silence, each having their own thoughts, enjoying the simplicity of a meal eaten in good company on a fine autumn morning. Once the meal was over they began to talk. They each had recollections from the night before to share. Then they had chores to attend to. Rodrigo headed off to relieve Lachlan at the lookout and allow him to return to camp and get his breakfast. Gabriella and Kyle walked to the area behind Danny's shack and brushed aside a carpet of leaves and dirt that camouflaged a metal panel. It was secured with a padlock. Gabriella opened it. They both jumped down into the cramped metal room that was dug into the forest floor. Inside, arranged on tidy shelves, was their armoury. It amounted to a small collection of mismatched weapons, collected at various times. They spent the morning stripping, cleaning, greasing and re-assembling the guns used the night before, and stowed them on the shelves.

3

Phillips pulled the binoculars away from his eyes and handed them to Casper. The first report had reached him in the early morning. Despite the risk of venturing into territory occupied by the State Forces, he had to see for himself. If the reports were true then he knew it was over.

Casper took his turn to look through the binoculars. 'It's gone,' he muttered as he scanned the rising plumes of smoke and the rubble by the river. 'Both chimney towers, one on top of the rest of the buildings, the other into the river.'

Phillips didn't respond.

'At least the State doesn't have it either,' the young man offered consolation to his leader.

Phillips stared ahead, looking along the valley. They were at the top of a bombed out building, one of the few high-rise office buildings that had existed before the war had started, and one of only a handful that still stood. There were gaping holes in the sides of the building, revealing dusty offices that had lain undisturbed for years until stray artillery shells and missiles had ploughed into the structure. They stood on the top floor, looking out through a gap where a wall had once been.

His lieutenant was right: if there was a silver lining, it was that the State Army would be unable to build more weapons to use against them, but Casper was missing the bigger picture. Without the arms factory, there was little reason for them to stay and fight for the city. He had held out a small hope that they could claw back some territory, establish a foothold once more, and with luck and determination, perhaps be able to claim back the prize of the arms factory. More than anything else, the Independents needed more weapons to be able to match the vastly superior resources of the State. Now, the only sensible decision left for Phillips was retreat. He knew it was the right thing to do. Head north, regroup in their HighLand stronghold, and live to fight another day. War was a battle of attrition: who could stomach the fight and survive for the longest? Who could take the loss and pain? Who believed in their ultimate goal the most?

His training, his instinct and his mind all told him what to do next, only his heart disagreed. Phillips was not an emotional person, but he had fought for this city with all that he possessed. He fought for the citizens, he wanted to free them, to show them the true nature of the corrupt State and its leaders. Phillips had been part of the corruption once, when he had served in the State Military and then as an agent in the State Special Forces. The army had been a family to him. He had turned his back against his family when he had learned what the Central Alliance Party and the State Forces were capable of. He had seen civilians murdered in war. He had seen torture, violence and death. Some of it he had accepted as part of the cruelty of war. For a long time he had sought to rationalise and justify it. If losing those lives was the price it cost to win the war, then they had to be prepared to pay it.

Then he had discovered what the Party was doing in Central City: a medical trial where innocent newborn babies were being murdered to control population numbers. The final straw had come when he had learned the truth about the First Strike War, the global conflict fought by the Allies against the Axis Powers for over fifty years on a false premise. There had been no First Strike, only an accident, a stray nuclear missile, a self-inflicted apocalypse by the Civil American States. It was their own missile that had obliterated the city of Billings and the nearby town of Columbus. Millions had died. The cover up had started before the radiation cloud had started to spread across the land. The Civil States blamed the Zhonghu Republic, their long-time rival and the only superpower that could threaten their domination in the world. The allies of the Civil American States, including the State, had gone along with the cover up. They had retaliated with nuclear missile strikes on Zhonghuan cities. Those were the truly innocent victims, those who burned to cover up a political and military disaster. The stage was set for a global conflict, and the profiteers, the large multinational companies and wealthy businesses began to circle as the government spending boom increased economic growth. War was good for business. The politicians saved face and shared in the profits. The tragedy became an opportunity for many countries to restrict rights, assume new powers, close borders and control populations under the cover of national emergencies.

Phillips had tried to tell the citizens of his own country what their politicians had done. He hired the journalist Maxine Aubert to write about the Central Alliance Party's policy on infant euthanasia in Central City. The citizens had read the truth, but they had not been convinced. Phillips had killed Maxine, shot dead by Casper on his command. He needed a martyr to start a war, he wanted to start a revolution. He needed to make the State pay, he needed to make the corrupt leaders of the Party pay. He wanted blood, he wanted them to lose everything. He wasn't to know that after half a century, the citizens had little desire for conflict left. The First Strike War had started so long ago, did it even matter why they were still fighting?

At the start he had underestimated the response his rebellion would spark. His small army of mercenaries and volunteers, armed with antique and homemade weapons, were overrun as battalions of State Army soldiers and equipment were rushed north to Central City. The Independents survived on belief and spirit. They held out and gradually their numbers grew. They scored some small victories which enabled them to commandeer more sophisticated, deadlier weapons. The fight became a fair one. His swelling forces began to claim territory in the city. They had a foothold. After the first year they had the momentum. Phillips thought back to that time. If only the rest of the citizens of Central City had been persuaded to join them. In that moment they could have swept the State Forces out of Central City. They could have held the city walls and established their own independent territory. The HighLand City would have followed them. Those from the south would have risen up to their cause. MidLand City had suffered in the same way as Central City and HighLand City. Perhaps even the Capital City would have begun to see the truth. Phillips had no desire to rule over the entire State. Land and territory were not his concern. Freeing the citizens and bringing down the corrupt leaders of the Central Alliance Party were all that he was interested in.

The chance had passed. No matter how many battles they won, they ran short of weapons. They could not match the resources of the State Military in terms of combatants, technology or armoury. It happened slowly, but Phillips could see where it would end. They lost the territory they had gained. State Forces pushed them east. They held on to the arms factory as long as they could, it became a detached enclave surrounded by the State army on all sides, before finally falling.

Now they existed only in the extreme eastern corner of the city. The surrender of the city was almost complete. The last hope had vanished, blown up in a fireball. What Phillips was looking at was more than the rubble of fallen towers and crumbled buildings: it was the death of his dream.

He felt the anger burning inside him, a bitterness that ate away at him. All those who had died, all those brave soldiers he had lost. Their fellow citizens had betrayed them. They had refused to join the fight. They had betrayed the Independents. He did not see these citizens as victims or innocents. They were traitors to the cause. If they had only had the courage to join the fight, they could have won.

'Why would the State blow it up? They could have used it for themselves.'

Casper's question brought Phillips back from his dark thoughts. He had to remain focused. He had to react calmly, without emotion. The city was lost. It was a setback, a major one, but the war was not yet over.

'The State didn't destroy it.'

'Who then?'

Before Phillips could answer they heard the sound of a drone approaching. The transceiver in Phillips's hand burst into life with a crackle of static.

'UAV coming over,' Harley's voice shouted through the radio. Casper and Phillips ducked behind the remains of the building wall. They knew it would be a State

Unmanned Aerial Vehicle, the Independents had lost the last of their drones months ago.

'It's a hot one,' Harley's voice informed them, meaning it was a weaponised drone rather than just a surveillance one.

Phillips spoke into the radio, 'Get away. Make your own way back to base. We'll meet you there.'

'Ten-four.' Harley signalled his understanding. Pressed with his back against the wall, Phillips could hear the drone circling the building. Unlike the larger State Reaper drones that flew at higher altitudes, this was a medium sized one, capable of flying through the streets and between the buildings of the city. It wasn't an innocent fly past, it was hunting for them. He was sure no one would have given away their location, perhaps a glint of light on the binocular lenses had betrayed them, or perhaps they were just unlucky.

He thought about Casper's question. Who would destroy the arms factory? Who would want to do it and who would have the ability and daring to do it?

It was them, he knew it could only be them. Gabriella and Samson. Of all the small bands of resistance groups out there, Gabriella was the only one with the military knowledge, skill and balls to pull off something like this. It was audacious, risky and brave, but it had succeeded. It had to be her.

The buzzing of the drone grew nearer.

***

He knew they were out there somewhere.

Phillips saw Gabriella as he had last seen her, standing in the middle of the road, the car hurtling towards her. At the last minute she had jumped out of the way. Phillips had looked in the side mirror as Casper had driven past. He saw her staring after him. He saw the look of hatred in her green eyes. He regretted losing her. Danny Samson he had no time for, he was just an ex-cop he hardly knew. They had worked one murder investigation together. He had saved Samson's life. At the time it had been the right thing to do, but Samson was insignificant. Later, Phillips had used him in order to expose the State and the crimes they had committed. Then he had no further use for him, he no longer cared what happened to Danny Samson. He was a nobody, just another one among the millions of civilians that had refused to join him.

Gabriella was different. He had known her briefly when they had served together in the State Army. Their paths had crossed on a few occasions, he had been impressed with her and had followed her career until she had quit. He knew why she had left, he understood her reasons. Fate brought them together again in Central City. He was a State Special Agent sent to liaise with the police investigation into a politician's murder, she was the assassin who had killed him. When they learned the truth about the State's murder of innocent children, they headed south together to the Capital City and found the politicians responsible: the Defence Secretary and the Vice-Chancellor of the State. They killed them, one each. They were complicit, and bound together. They fled the State to let the dust settle. They travelled around the rest of the world, together for most of the time. Phillips had done some digging, learned some truths about his State and the Central Alliance Party. He had heard rumours and found confirmations. He had uncovered a bombshell that very few knew about, that no one would admit to on the record and that no one would believe - the First

Strike War was a con, a swindle, a lie. He kept the revelation from Gabriella. He knew what he had to do, he knew she would not play his game. She liked direct action, she liked to find the person accountable and make them pay. That wouldn't work for this. This needed something more cunning, Phillips needed to play the Party at their own game. He brought Gabriella back to Central City with him on the eve of the decennial elections. He put plans and people in place, he used old military contacts, he started gathering volunteers, and set up a base. He told Gabriella it was about being able to defend themselves. She believed him and trusted him.

Maxine Aubert died from a single sniper bullet to the head. He could have used Gabriella to do the job, but he knew she would never have agreed to it. Casper was not as good a shot, but he was good enough, and he was young, impressionable and in need of a leader. Maxine had been standing in front of a State SuperTank, blocking its path, trying to protect protesting citizens. It was framed as State-sanctioned murder, government brutality against its own people. Phillips's volunteer army seized the moment. Primitive firebombs ignited a civil war. Casper and he had left the scene. As they reached the car they saw Gabriella and Samson. They all knew what had occurred. He should have killed them both then. Perhaps he thought one day they would join him, perhaps there was too much happening to allow for further complications. Perhaps he was just too fond of Gabriella. They drove away and left them in the street. Phillips saw her staring after him. He saw the look of hatred in her eyes. He knew that one day they would meet again and that one of them would die. Gabriella would not rest until she had confronted him.

The war had erupted. In all the time since, he had never seen Gabriella or Samson, but he knew they were out there. He heard rumours and sketchy intelligence reports about bands of mercenaries who took no side in the war, who protected the citizens caught in the crossfire and helped refugees flee the country. He wondered if she thought of him. He knew the answer. He had betrayed her, and she would not stop until she had her revenge. The arms factory was one piece of that revenge, one step along a long and bitter road. Her hatred for him was matched only by her hatred for the State, for which they had once served alongside each other. The destruction of the factory was Gabriella's work, he was sure of it.

***

'We have to move, sir,' Casper's urgent voice brought him back. The buzzing sound of the drone was closer, it was on the other side of the crumbling wall. In seconds it would skirt round the side and find them. The artillery guns that it carried would exterminate them in a hail of rapid fire. The top of the staircase that they had climbed up was on the opposite side of the room.

'You go first,' Casper said. 'I'll cover you.'

Phillips made no comment, just nodded. Casper had grown a lot in these last few years. He had been too young to ever be called up to the State military, but he had become an outstanding loyal soldier under Phillips.

'On three.' Casper counted with his fingers. As the third finger rose they sprang forward.

The drone rounded the corner of the wall at the same moment. Phillips sprinted for the opening that led to the top of the stairs. Casper was a pace behind him, shielding him from the firing line of the drone and turning to face it. He fired his heavy rifle before the drone had a chance to compute what its camera was seeing. Bullets sparked off metal. The drone ducked back behind the cover of the wall giving them enough time to make it to the doorway. They were hurtling down the first flight of stairs when they heard the hail of bullets crash into the empty room they had just left. The drone stopped firing after thirty seconds. Bricks and dust settled. The top floor of the building that had been there half a minute earlier was gone, only the cratered floor remained. The drone scanned the debris and found no targets had been eliminated. It began descending to ground level. They would have to emerge at some point. The drone could wait, it was in no rush.

Phillips reached the fourth floor landing and kept low, crouching in the corner. The noise of the drone was below them now. It was the one weakness they could exploit - a drone was noisy and that noise meant it could be heard. Casper arrived two seconds behind him and set to work straightaway. He flipped the compact launcher from his shoulder and in three swift moves had it assembled. From his utility pack he took the small armour-piercing missile and loaded it into the dull-green tube. So long as the drone camera wasn't looking straight at them, Casper would have time to aim and fire. Without hesitation he moved over to the opening in the wall. Phillips watched him take one breath to calm himself, his cheeks puffed out and then deflated. It was hard for Phillips to remember that Casper was still only a boy. He was unsure of his exact age. Eighteen? Nineteen? Barely a man. When Phillips had been that age he had only just handed in his application to join the State Forces, an eager innocent ready to do his duty in the First Strike War, proud to serve the Party and the State against the evil of the Axis Powers. Casper had already seen three years of war, violence was all he knew.

The boy stood and turned, his eye to the sight of the launcher, the end of the launcher pointing out of the window. There was an imperceptible 'click' as he pushed the trigger button, followed by the whoosh of the missile leaving the tube at a hundred and fifty metres per second. One second later it hit the target. The explosion rocked the fragile building. Casper had crouched down to avoid any unintended blast damage from the impact of the projectile. He loaded a second missile into the launcher. After a moment he stood again and looked out of the window, launcher at the ready.

'Clear,' he said. He was like a robot, as all well-trained soldiers should be. He had no compassion, he showed no emotion. He did what was needed, what was ordered. Phillips had been like that once too. He sometimes longed to return to that state of being, but he had seen too much of the world, and the evil that existed in it.

'Let's go.'

They knew the drone would have been sending live updates of its mission back to a headquarters somewhere. State officers would have been watching its progress, analysing it and feeding it instructions. If it had been able to get a picture of Phillips's face then they would know they were actively hunting the leader of the Independents. And if they knew that, they would have been sure to have scrambled reinforcements. The drone's demise would have triggered an alarm. More drones would be on the way, followed by back-up automatic tanks and infantry. This was no time to hang about and fight a one-sided battle. They had to be gone before any supplementary State Forces converged on their location.

They exited the building and kept running, dodging over and round the rubble that cluttered the streets. Harley had taken the transport carrier, as he should have. Phillips and Casper would have to make the full journey back east on foot. Phillips did a quick calculation. It was about twenty kilometres to the outskirts of their base. Uninhibited they could cover that distance in two hours, but they would have to run evasively. They would have to be alert and look out for other drones or State air support. They would need to hide and detour. It would be nearing evening before they would make it back.

Casper's youth meant he had the edge on Phillips for pace. He knew he was getting too old for this sort of warfare, no matter how well he looked after his body. Central City was lost and he no longer had the energy required to take it back. He no longer had the men, the weapons or the desire. It was gone. They would have to retreat to the north. There was still the HighLand City. It had become the Independents stronghold. They would regroup there and then he could decide what to do next. Phillips had no great love for Central City, it was not his home, it was merely the place where he had chosen to fight his rebellion. An idea stirred in his mind as he chased after Casper. He had lost the battle, but he had no intention of leaving the field to the State.

The rain began to fall again. Now that the rains had arrived, every day would experience a heavy downfall until the snows came. It did nothing to brighten Phillips's mood. He bared down, gritted his teeth against the elements and pushed on.

THE WANDERER

Bright, white light metamorphosed into blinding orange, red. The sun was eating the earth, swallowing it, enveloping it. And so the world burned. He felt the heat. Was he delirious? He was losing touch with the real world, no longer able to trust his own mind.

But this was no hallucination, this was real. He had been woken by a huge explosion. It was still night but the dark had been vanquished. He sat up and peered out of the gap in the wall. A fireball engulfed the sky. The initial roar grew louder. His ears screamed with pain. He covered them with his hands. What was he seeing? The end of the world? The roar declined, replaced by a low rumble. The towers fell, one collapsing in on itself, the other crashing down sideways. It came towards him, across the river. It seemed like it would land on top of him. He didn't scream or react. He was frozen, accepting of whatever fate this fury had in store for him.

It missed him. In the blinding furnace he could not judge how near or far he had been from death. A wave of water hurried along the river. The dust cloud engulfed him. He pulled his tattered shirt up to cover his mouth and nose. With stinging eyes he tried to see. The dust cleared and the dark night reclaimed its territory. The orange glow receded, confining itself to the far side of the river. Through the motes dancing around him he heard footsteps. The shadows returned, black against orange. They didn't see him. They passed without a word. They left something behind. A body, dumped next to the remains of the building that sheltered him.

He waited and watched. He had learned to always be cautious. The State knew he betrayed them, they will kill him if they find him. But they can't because he has become invisible. He is not the man he once was. His crimes are insignificant now, compared to the destruction around him. Faces from the past haunt him, dancing in front of his eyes. Looking at the fire burning in the night sky, he saw them again.

She is all around him, painted across the city. The journalist they killed at the start of the war. He was there when she died, in a nearby building. He should have protected her. But it is the other one that visits him more often. He wanted to kill her. She had killed his father. His memory is confused, their faces whirl around. He is losing his grip. He talks to himself, catches himself muttering names from the past.

He shook his head. All had gone quiet. He crept out from behind the wall into the open. He approached the body and saw the uniform of a State soldier. It was a young woman, a girl with blonde hair. She was bloodied and unconscious. He knelt by her side and placed a hand on her forehead. She moved. He jumped back. He looked round. They were alone. The women who had been camped by the river were gone. Perhaps they had scarpered as soon as the sky lit up red and angry, perhaps they had been swept away by the falling tower.

Somewhere inside him a feeling stirred. It told him what he must do. He must help. That is what he used to do. That used to be his job, to protect the citizens of this city, his city. She was one of them, even if she wore the uniform of the military. She needed to be saved, he needed to save her. He tried to lift her but he was weak. He managed to drag her across the cold, grey concrete back to the building. He sat with his back against the wall, her head on his lap. He tried to wipe the blood away from her face. She was like a child, delivered from the burning fires of the night. He would save her.

When he woke again it was daylight. He thought it had all been another of his dreams, his mind playing tricks on him again. He couldn't trust it anymore. He had to be cautious. But she was still there, her head resting on his lap. Gently he laid her head down and got up. The arms factory was reduced to a pile of rubble. He heard buzzing. Drones. They weren't looking for him. They were concentrating on the site of the wreckage. He should leave.

The girl was still unconscious, but she was breathing and the bleeding had stopped. She needed more help than he could give her. He had to get her to the hospital. Despite everything, he still knew his city. He remembered what used to be in the places that were now craters and bomb sites. The hospital was still there, no one attacked it. By convention or agreement he didn't know, he just knew it still stood. Holding her wrists, he pulled her up, her arms around his neck, her head flopping against his shoulder. The soldier was light, he could drag her like this, on his back. Her army boots scraped along the ground behind him as he walked. He could do this. He shuffled along, taking small steps. He could make it, he could save her.

Turning away from the river and heading back into the city, he retraced the way he had come the previous day. He was no longer invisible. If State Forces saw him carrying one of their soldiers on his back they would notice him. He had to stay hidden. He steered clear of the main streets, avoiding the main square he had crossed yesterday. He saw no soldiers. He was thinking clearly, a rare thing these days. Having a purpose, a task, had cleared the fog that shrouded his mind. He saw some citizens. An old woman stared at him, but no one said anything to him. Citizens had learned to mind their own business.

On he struggled. The rain started again. He had no idea how long it took him. The hospital was taller than the buildings that had been destroyed around it. As he got closer to it, he heard buzzing. Not drones, something louder. He panicked and tripped on debris, landing in the dust and dirt. The girl fell next to him, her head hitting the ground hard. He got up and pulled her across the concrete into a side alley. He looked up and saw a helicopter. It was a State military aircraft, but the green camouflage had a bright red cross in a white circle on it. It was a medical flight. He remembered they came every day with supplies for the hospital, mercy missions to allow the treatment of the injured and the sick. They were not looking for him, they were not searching for their missing soldier. The helicopter landed on the roof of the hospital, the blades kept turning. After ten minutes the engine pitch changed and it lifted off again, flying back across the sky, over their heads.

He stooped and picked up the girl, putting her on his back again. He remembered the entrance to the hospital, he used to visit it a lot in his past life. He got to the door, walking through concrete road blocks and barricades. He didn't see the guns that were trained on him as he approached, carefully watching his every move. The door wouldn't open. They kept it locked now.

There was a shout. He stumbled backwards, panicking again. A gun was pointing at him. He dropped the girl and fell on his back, his arms outstretched, pleading. He pointed at her, raising his arms in surrender. This had been a bad idea, they would capture him now, they would kill him. He was wanted by the State, they had not forgotten his betrayal. Two men rushed towards him. They picked up their fallen comrade and dragged her away from him, behind a wall of sandbags and through the doors of the hospital. He was sure they would come back to kill him, but they didn't. Only one guard, the one who first shouted, watched him, his gun still raised. He shouted something, gesturing with the gun, telling him to get the hell out of there. They do not know who he is. He is a nobody, a tramp, a citizen. He was free to flee. She was safe. He had saved her, his task was complete. No one would thank him for it, only he would know what he had done. He pulled himself up and ran, turning back to make sure he was not being followed.

And what now? He was without purpose again. His mind faltered. The same faces converged. The journalist stared down at him from the walls and rubble. Citizens avoided him. The other face emerged, the one he must kill if he ever saw her again. She killed his father, she could have killed him. She hadn't, why not? It was all too unclear. He walked on, destination undecided. He existed, that much he was sure of. It is still his city he walks through.

4

The alarm sounded through the forest on the fourth morning after the arms factory had been destroyed. Kyle, Zeb and Rodrigo had been out on a morning recce into the city, searching for any supplies they could commandeer. Gabriella and Verona were in the camp. Danny was walking around the perimeter of the wooded area, a sweep they usually carried out twice a day, but had had been doing every hour since their successful mission. Lachlan was at the lookout point that guarded the approach from the city. It was from there that the shrill whistle sounded.

Gabriella grabbed the nearest weapon to hand, an old shotgun she had been cleaning and assembling and glanced at Verona. She motioned her to go to the arms store. Verona understood and quickly moved. She unlocked the metal door and slipped inside, closing the lid on top of her. Gabriella stood still, shotgun raised, listening. She heard footsteps rushing towards her. She turned to face them and saw Danny crash through the trees, sidearm drawn and raised. She gestured towards the lookout where the alarm had come from. The whistle sounded again. Danny took off, heading towards the noise, but parallel to the main path through the trees. Gabriella continued to stand motionless, waiting and watching.

The sound of more footsteps came through the air. This time a group of people were approaching along the main path at walking pace. Wet leaves squelched and sticks broke as they grew nearer. Through the wet branches she saw bodies moving towards her. Rodrigo was in front, but he was followed by an unknown man. She counted six people in total. At the rear of the column she could make out Zeb, his bulk overshadowing those that walked in front of him. Rodrigo and Zeb had their weapons drawn. They did not trust those that came with them.

Gabriella had argued for them to strike camp and relocate further away until the dust had settled. The State was sure to want reprisals for the destruction of the arms factory and eventually they would come looking for them. The others had resisted. They had existed undiscovered in the woods for several months now. They had carried out other missions against the State and the Independents and no one had found them, nor had they seen any signs that they were being hunted. Gabriella disagreed. The extended stay at the camp was all the more reason to move on, stay mobile and not get comfortable. She had been overruled. Although they all looked up to her, they had agreed early on that no one person should be in charge of the group. Everyone's opinions were valid and taken into account when it came to any decision. The column approaching through the trees now proved to Gabriella that she had been right, but it was too late to start apportioning blame.

Rodrigo acknowledged her with a wary look as he emerged from the trees. He turned and waved his drawn pistol at the man that followed him, motioning him to sit on one of the rocks by the fire. He was a big man, with dark skin, dark eyes and dark hair. He wore old military fatigues, but they were not State uniform. His hands hung by his sides, not restrained and his manner was acquiescent. He did as instructed by Rodrigo without demurring. Behind him emerged another man, also in fatigues and similarly built. Kyle followed and sat him next to the first man. Gabriella kept her shotgun trained on the men.

When Kyle stepped to the side Gabriella saw the woman walking in front of Zeb. She had brown-blonde hair that hung around her face in messy clumps. She was thin and slightly below average height. Her eyes were downcast, making her seem even smaller next to the hulking presence of Zeb. She wore old fatigues as well, although they were ill-fitting and baggy, hanging from her slight frame. Zeb gave her a nudge on the shoulder to make her sit next to the other two men. Kyle and Zeb threw down the large backpacks they had been carrying on the floor in front of their prisoners.

'Lachlan?' Gabriella asked.

'At the lookout,' Rodrigo answered. They were a well drilled unit. Lachlan would remain in position to ensure no one else had followed this party up the hillside.

Rodrigo took off his own backpack.

'Anything?' Gabriella asked, wanting to know if they had found any supplies.

'Nothing,' Rodrigo answered. 'We only made it to the outskirts before we picked up the trail of these people heading in the direction of the camp.'

Danny had observed all this from behind the trees, covering the intruders with his sidearm as the group had made their way into the clearing. He had caught a glimpse of the prisoners as they were being marched along. The two men were familiar. He could not see the woman clearly, but he already knew who she was. Once they were sat in front of Gabriella, Danny stepped into the clearing and approached. Standing next to Gabriella, he looked at the woman, who turned her face up to stare at him. Danny placed his hand on the top of Gabriella's shotgun and gently pushed the barrel downwards until it was pointing to the ground.

'You know them?' Gabriella asked.

Danny stared into the blue eyes that had now risen from the ground to look directly at him.

'I know them.' His memory swept him back to the village in the wilderness, the last place he had known contentment. 'Eilidh,' he said.

'Hello, Danny,' Eilidh replied.

Danny pictured the same woman sobbing in the middle of a barren road as he drove away from her, taking with him her son, not knowing if either of them would ever see her again.

There was no emotional outburst, the atmosphere was restrained and tense. The others watched Danny, waiting for an explanation.

He turned to the two men sitting next to Eilidh, whom he also knew from the village in the wilderness. 'Hassan, Tyrell,' he greeted them. 'What are you doing here?'

Kyle answered before they could reply. 'We picked up their trail just outside the city boundary. A small fire had been burning overnight, footprints led away from the city. We thought we better follow them. They led into the forest, heading up the hill. We caught up with them after half a kilometre. They didn't resist, told us they were looking for Danny Samson. Said you would know them.'

'How did you know where to look for us?' Gabriella asked. No one replied. She raised her shotgun a fraction.

Hassan, the tall, dark man, answered, 'Quasimo.'

'Shit,' Gabriella looked to Danny, who shared her sentiment. 'We're blown.'

'We're blown,' Danny agreed.

Quasimo was a fellow resister of both sides in the civil war, but with very different motives to Gabriella and Danny. Originally from the Capital City, he had moved north when the fighting had started, seeing an opportunity to exploit. He was also a snitch and a double-crosser, quite happy to play either side off against the other for his own personal gain. They had used him before to gather information and supplies. He had not been a reliable ally. After a couple of satisfactory deals, his produce had become increasingly compromised. The ammunition he had delivered to them in one transaction had been spoiled by damp. Half of the bullets were useless, the other half were of the wrong calibre. Against their better judgement they had dealt with him again a few months later. This time he had agreed to sell them information they wanted: the route and time a convoy of rebel vehicles would pass through the city. Unbeknown to them, Quasimo also tipped off the Independents about the potential hijack and the rebels had changed their plans accordingly. Quasimo laughed off Danny's complaints. All was fair in war. He had wanted to work with them again in order to make amends, he claimed. Gabriella didn't trust him, so they backed off. It had been months since they had had any contact with him. He had never been brought to the camp and he didn't know their exact location, but he knew roughly where they were based. He was the sort of person who always seemed to have reliable information and sources.

Gabriella issued commands. 'Let's pack it up. We are leaving in thirty minutes. One bag each, essentials only. Anything we don't take we burn, including the shelters.'

She gave a sharp whistle that would bring Lachlan in from the lookout post. The others sprang into action, except Danny, who remained staring at the new arrivals. Sitting on the rocks they watched in confusion.

Gabriella ran to the armoury and hauled open the metal lid. Verona popped up, shouldering a machine gun.

'Forget it,' Gabriella told her. 'We're moving out. Start packing up all the weapons we can carry.'

Verona looked at the new arrivals and then ducked out of view without speaking. Now was the time to obey orders, questions could wait.

While the others busied themselves, Danny walked towards the ghosts from his past life that were now sat in front of him. Hassan stood and offered his hand. Danny didn't take it.

'Why are you here?' he asked again.

'We need your help,' Hassan answered him, withdrawing his proffered hand.

'With what?'

Hassan looked to Eilidh, who stood and looked at Danny.

'It's Lucas,' she said.

Forty minutes later they were moving through the woods, heading west along the ridge of the valley that overlooked the city. Each of them was laden with a backpack and as much weaponry as they could manage, including Hassan and Tyrell, who had been entrusted with utensils, tools and ammunition. Kyle and Verona were on point, while Zeb covered the rear. Everything that they had not been able to take with them was thrown into the metal pit.

The last thing Gabriella threw in was her collection of books. She had found them in the various burnt out buildings of the city. She loved to read. Her love of stories was something her father had instilled in her as a child. He would bring a selection of books home with him every few weeks. Gabriella had no idea where he managed to get them from. The Party, through Senate legislation, had started to restrict texts they found unacceptable at the start of the First Strike War. In an age where the State controlled the internet and no one bought paper books anymore, it was easy for them to delete, monitor and block literature. Somehow, Gabriella's father was always able to find old paper copies of books. He would read them to her, and then let her keep the copies, hidden in her room.

When the civil war started, Gabriella began finding books in the remains of citizens' houses. While the others searched for food or useful tools, Gabriella would look for books. It was surprising to discover how many citizens had shared in her illicit collecting. The citizens had been rebellious in their own quiet way long before the outbreak of violence. But the books were too cumbersome and numerous to take with them now that they were abandoning their camp and had to be mobile. She held the last book in her hand, having thrown the others into the pit one at a time: Harper Lee's *To Kill a Mockingbird*, William Faulkner, Muriel Spark, a treasured copy of Gibbon's *Sunset Song*. Now she held the last of them, her favourite: *For Whom the Bell Tolls* by Ernest Hemingway, a long-forgotten writer from the Civil American States. She had first heard the story when her father had read it to her as a child. Perhaps it had been that story of romance and war which had set her on the military path her life had taken.

She doused the pages of the book in lighter fluid, poured the rest of the canister into the pit and lit a match. The flame licked at the pages, burning the words and she tossed it into the pit with the rest of their expendable belongings. There was a whoosh as the lighter fluid caught fire. They turned their backs on their home and set off.

The terrain was challenging, especially with the baggage they were carrying. Underfoot the grass was slick and puddles of mud were frequent. The rain began to fall soon after they departed. Danny walked alongside Eilidh, Gabriella marched in front of them.

'How long have you been looking for us?' he asked.

'We left the village a month ago.' Eilidh answered. 'We had to trek down the country to get to the city. There was no transport we could use, so we had to walk the whole way through the mountains and round the lakes. We were fortunate, we only met fellow travellers along the roads, and we helped one another in any way we could.'

Danny had heard about the bandits that roved the countryside now, preying on those fleeing the war.

When he had left Central City, Danny had wandered in the wilderness for months. There had been a short stay on an island off the west coast, where he had lived with the strange cult and their leader Skylar, and had first met the boy called Casper. One winter he had stumbled into a valley that was home to a small settlement. They had taken him in. He had farmed the land with them and become part of their small community, living in the village for six months. Eilidh had been there and they had grown close. Her son, Lucas, had developed type-1 diabetes and needed care. Danny helped her, drawn by the opportunity to aid a mother and her child after he had failed to care so miserably for his own family. It could not last. Lucas grew sick and their supply of life-saving insulin dried up. His only hope of survival was at a hospital in the city. Danny volunteered to take the boy there. He had saved him by sacrificing his own new life, returning to the nightmare of his past.

Soon after, the civil war had started and Danny was caught in the middle of it with Phillips and Gabriella. He gave up any hope of ever returning to the village in the north.

'How is everyone?' he asked.

'It's not like it used to be,' Eilidh answered. 'There are so many refugees from the city. They come into the valley every day. Some move on, some stay. We try to house and feed them all, but there are too many. It has become a refugee camp. Jai Li left to join the rebels, along with Hansel and some of the others. They went to the HighLand City. We never heard from them after that. That was over a year ago.' Jai Li and Hansel had been two of the elders who ran the village.

'Do the State leave you alone?'

'Early on they came into the valley. They threatened to kill us all. Rona stopped them. They took her away instead. No one has heard from her since.'

Rona was the elder who had been in charge. Danny had no doubt she was dead now.

'Since then they have left us alone. We give them a solution, a place to house the citizens who have fled the war. It costs the State nothing and it uses up none of their resources.' Her voice trailed off in the pouring rain. She looked at him, anxiously. 'Have you seen Lucas?'

Danny thought about the boy he had carried into the city hospital in his arms. He had succeeded in delivering him to the doctors before he had been arrested by the State police.

'I haven't seen him since the day I left him at the hospital.'

'Have you heard anything about him?'

'Once, not long after the start of the war. He was at the hospital. They have an orphanage there. They took him in.'

'The hospital is still a safe place?'

'It's still standing.'

From the beginning of the war it was accepted that no side would attack the hospital. It was never declared a neutral zone or a safe haven, but the shred of humanity left on both sides of the bloody conflict had allowed the building to survive relatively unharmed. The medical staff who had stayed remained neutral, treating casualties on both sides, as well as innocent citizens caught in the crossfire. There had been occasions when stray artillery had damaged the building, but the truce had held. The State and the Independents had both accepted that medical supplies and equipment could be transported into the building by air drop. Nothing official was ever signed to secure these arrangements. Recently rumours had begun to spread that the hospital staff – still officially State employees – were favouring injured State soldiers, giving them the best treatment and care while letting the rebel casualties suffer. The State still ran the hospital. It had become militarised, with soldiers guarding fortified entrances. The soldiers decided who could enter and who could not. There were whisperings that the State was using some of the space as a base camp for army infantry. It was ideally situated to be used as an army barracks. State drones had been seen launching from the roof of the hospital, army vehicles had been seen entering the underground parking area. Rebels who had no choice but to seek medical attention were admitted into the hospital, but were never seen again. It was suspected that either they were shipped out to State prisoner camps in the south, or that part of the hospital was itself being used as a prison.

What Danny had discovered for certain was that the children kept in the orphanage were still there and were still being looked after in the early months of the war. Gabriella had been able to confirm this through contacts she still had within the State military and through other resistance fighters. As the war had dragged on, Gabriella's contacts within the State had dwindled away – injured, killed or shipped out. She had lost most of her human intelligence capabilities and it became increasingly difficult to get any hard information from either side, hence their reliance on people like Quasimo. And that was why he could tell Eilidh nothing more about her son.

'Do you think Lucas is still there?'

He didn't want to get her hopes up, but he saw her looking at him and felt as helpless as he had the last time he had promised he would save her son's life.

'There's no reason why he shouldn't be,' was his equivocal answer. 'That's why you've come all this way?'

'There's a rumour we heard from some people who arrived at the village. They said that in the European Union they have found a cure.' She paused, seeing if Danny understood the magnitude of what she had said.

Danny didn't respond. There had been a global remedy for the auto-immune disease many years before, but it was only effective if administered to a foetus still in the womb. Those born with the faulty gene that developed into type-1 diabetes continued to suffer and relied on insulin to treat the chronic condition.

Eilidh continued, 'Even without a cure, life over there is much better than here. How long can he survive in a war zone? If the medical supplies stop, if the hospital is bombed, if the State decides to stop providing insulin, then he will die.'

'You want to take him to the European Union?' Danny had stopped walking. Eilidh stopped two paces in front of him and turned back to face him.

'I want to save him. I let him go once, this time I will not walk away from him.'

'You know how difficult it is to get out of the State?'

'That's why we came to find you. We heard that you could help, that you knew a way.'

'Who told you that?' Danny was wary.

'Hassan brought word back to us that there was a group of fighters, not aligned to either side, who could help those that wished to leave the State get out safely.'

Danny shook his head and started walking again. They had helped some refugees leave the State in the past. Eilidh fell in step beside him.

'There is nothing safe about it,' he muttered.

They kept walking for most of the day, apart from a brief stop for a basic meal in an old abandoned warehouse that had once been part of the large agri-farms that had ringed the city. The land lay barren now, no crops had been planted since the outbreak of the war. Kyle and Rodrigo made a cursory sweep of the buildings and the surrounding area, but as expected anything worth pilfering had already been taken. Hassan and Tyrell began to speak with the others now that initial suspicions had been put to rest. Gabriella chose not to take part in the conversations that spread through the group.

They resumed their march until the sun began to set in the early evening, dipping below the horizon to the west. Then they halted and set up a camp to spend the night in. Without the shacks and bivouac they had left behind, the only accommodation they had been able to carry with them were the two single-person tents. It was agreed Eilidh and Verona would share one, squashing in next to each other and using the enforced closeness to create extra warmth through body contact. Hassan and Tyrell somehow managed to cram themselves into the other tent, despite protesting that they wished to help keep watch through the night. Gabriella dismissed the idea. Lachlan and Kyle positioned themselves further along the path and took it in turns to keep lookout. Zeb and Rodrigo did the same further back along the route they had walked to ensure no one was following them. That left Gabriella and Danny lying between the two tents, gathering as much shelter as they could from the unrolled blankets and survival bags they had brought with them.

'You heard why they came looking for us?' Danny asked Gabriella in a low voice when the chatter from the tents on either side of them had died down and only the sound of heavy breathing and the light patter of rain could be heard.

Gabriella grunted, 'I knew that kid would come back to haunt you.'

Danny said nothing more. He knew he couldn't force the issue.

Eventually she spoke again, 'You want to help them, don't you?'

Danny rolled over onto his back and looked up into the night sky. The rain that had fallen all day finally relented. There were small gaps in the thick, grey cloud cover. Tiny sparkles of light peeked out of the murky darkness.

'What else do we have to do?'

'You know how difficult it will be to get him out of the hospital?'

He didn't answer her. 'We can use Xavier again. He's still making runs across the sea. Our credit is still good with him.'

Xavier was a modern day pirate, a people trafficker who made his living transporting desperate refugees across the sea from the State to the European Union. He liked to think of himself as a trafficker with morals. He used his own boat and ensured safe passage, for the right price. He told anyone who would listen that he was not like the other traffickers who exploited the needy and sent them to their deaths on precarious rafts that stood no chance of surviving the rough crossing. He had taken refugees that Danny and Gabriella had helped to get to the coast before.

'You understand the risk we're putting them under?'

'We're their only option.'

They lay silently. Danny knew Gabriella was right. They had had no connection to the others they had helped escape from the State. They knew the odds were against the refugees making it safely over to the European Union, but they helped them because it was what the refugees wanted. They had no idea what future awaited them once they had made it to the shores of the new continent. If it didn't work out, it meant little to Danny and Gabriella.

This time would be different. Gabriella could read him too easily. She always had been able to, right from the moment he had pointed a gun at her in the forest all those years ago. She knew then that he would never have shot her. She knew now that taking these people to the coast and getting them out of the country was dangerous, but Danny had decided to do it no matter what she said.

She would help him. After all, this was the reason they had stayed in the city throughout the civil war. They stayed to help the citizens who had no one else to turn to.

She looked over at Danny. They had been through a lot together. It was a strange friendship that had evolved through necessity. After their first couple of encounters there had been a mutual distrust and dislike between them. It had taken a long time for those prejudices to erode away. He was hung up on the ghosts of his past, she was taciturn, not given to lowering her guard to anyone. They had grudgingly become friends and comrades. Gabriella was naturally a loner, she had no family left. Her parents had passed away in the European Union, expelled by the State because they were not born inside its borders. Danny had lost everything once before. They were brothers-in-arms, the only family either of them had left in the world.

'You realise this could get us all killed? Not just you and me, but her and the boy too.'

Danny didn't respond.

'You better be sure they're worth it.'

Gabriella rolled onto her side, her back to Danny, who said nothing and continued to stare into the dark space above them.

5

The signal was weak, the picture kept dropping out, cutting to a blank screen and then reappearing. The sound was better, and Phillips was able to listen to the transmission. He didn't need to see the picture anyway – the image being broadcast by the State News Channel was a familiar one. There she stood, State Chancellor Lucinda Románes, behind the lectern with the State crest emblazoned upon it, addressing the nation from inside the Palace. The consequences of what she was announcing could mean the end of his rebellion once and for all, but it had deeper ramifications. He could see what those in the Senate and at the top of the Central Alliance Party were doing. They were covering their tracks by rewriting history. They were ensuring their legacy would never be tainted by the truth that would never be revealed.

It had taken Casper and Phillips the entire day to return to their stronghold after the run-in with the surveillance drone. Although they often had to find cover until the coast was clear, they had managed to remain undiscovered. It had taken its toll on Phillips. In the days since, he had been suffering from a cold brought on by exposure to the cold autumn rain. After years of vaccines against such viruses, his body struggled to fight them off naturally. He would soon have to admit he could no longer put himself through such physical exertion, he was no longer a young military man in his prime.

But despite feeling under the weather, he knew he could no longer afford to delay. He had gathered the senior officers of his command around him and ordered the retreat. There was little argument, only reluctant acceptance. They knew it was the only option left to them. There was no time to waste. Over the past forty-eight hours they had begun pulling back from the frontline of their enclave. Phillips was surprised by the State's cautious response. Any decent commander would have pushed forward in a blitz, taking advantage of a weak retreating enemy and bombarding them into oblivion. The State was far too hesitant, hamstrung by bureaucracy in the chain of command. This would enable the Independents to withdraw in an orderly fashion, maintaining their line of retreat to the north and escaping with most of their personnel and materiel intact. The army in the northern city had been informed and were expecting them. Their retreat would at least bolster their forces in the HighLands and aid them in holding the one city they still controlled.

It was Harley who had brought him the TouchScreen, one of the few working units they had remaining and vital to their intelligence gathering capabilities as they became increasingly cut off.

'When did this happen?' Phillips asked his lieutenant, pointing at the stuttering image of Lucinda Románes.

'This morning, they keep running the speech over and over again.'

On the screen, the State Chancellor raised her hand in a cursory greeting to those gathered in the press room of the Palace. Lined up in front her were a series of officials. Phillips recognised the Vice Chancellor, the Defence Secretary Johnathan Sadiq, the Senate Leader and the Chairman of the Central Alliance Party. The presence of these heavyweights signalled the importance of the announcement.

On the far left of the screen, almost cut out of the camera frame were two more men. One, dressed in full State military uniform, was Field Marshall Harris Ellroy, the senior officer in the State Military, second in command only to the Chancellor herself in matters of war. Phillips had served under Ellroy in his final years with the army. Ellroy had been in command of the forces in and around Central City for the last few years. Standing behind the Field Marshall, partially hidden by his shoulder, and looking uncomfortable in the public glare was a smaller man in a civilian suit. His pale skin was covered in a glistening sheen of sweat, he was unshaven and his hair was ruffled. It was Edward 'Teddy' Davies, the Head of State Security Forces, the man who led the powerful intelligence and black-ops of the State. Phillips had worked for Davies when he was an agent with the Security Forces, but he had never met him. His presence had pervaded the civil war in Central City since the start. Agents of the Security Forces had infiltrated the Independents early on, spreading paranoia and betrayal. The volunteer rebel army was ill-equipped to deal with the sophisticated games and dark arts of the intelligence world. They had no spy network of their own, no counter-intelligence department and no vetting system for volunteers. It had been a steep learning curve. They had gradually come to understand the rules of the game that Davies played. Information was compartmentalised, newcomers were kept at a distance from command and only a few trusted individuals were given access to plans and operations. Phillips developed a circle of a few people around him with whom he would share information. They had established their own internal security force to hunt down the State informers, but they had never been able to compete with the resources that Davies had at his disposal. This disparity was one of the main reasons they had lost their grip on Central City.

The clip unfroze and Lucinda Románes addressed the camera directly, her steel-grey eyes staring straight down the lens and into millions of homes across the State. Now in her mid-seventies, she still possessed lustrous dark hair, smooth skin and a healthy complexion. Her voice was strong. There was no sign of age withering her health or sharpness. As the moving image stuttered along, Phillips listened to the address.

'My fellow citizens, today is a momentous day, not just for the State or the Party, but for the world. The First Strike War has dominated this planet for over half a century. Many have died, no one has been left untouched by the devastating conflict that began with the murder of millions of people in the Civil States of America. Throughout the conflict that began on that fateful day, we have done our duty as a faithful partner of our allies. We have fought bravely. There have been many victories and some unavoidable losses. We have never buckled under the strain, nor shirked our responsibility. Together with our allies, we have protected our beliefs and values, as well as our beloved country. Our borders have remained secure. You, the citizens of this State, have been able to continue to live in safety thanks to the efforts of our military. The First Strike War, as hard fought as it has been, can only be regarded as an overwhelming success, a validation of decisions taken by your leaders, by the Party and the Senate over a number of decades, that has saved the State from defeat and collapse.'

Phillips bristled. He knew the truth behind the repeated lies. The war was about money, economics, industry and power. It began with a nuclear accident. No one had attacked the Civil States. The war had kept the population of the world living in patriotic fervour and fear, lining the pockets of those in charge and propping up corrupt governments across the planet.

Románes carried on, 'In recent years we have suffered the torture of civil war, brought on by the evil and mindless actions of the degenerate traitors who call themselves the Independents. It would be untrue to deny this internal conflict has not placed our military and attendant capabilities under great strain. While we are winning this war, defeating the cancer that exists within our very own walls, it has depleted resources and forced the Senate to reassess our priorities.'

Phillips listened with renewed interest, noting the change in tone of the address. An admission that the State Forces were strained was an unexpected earthquake in political terms. Phillips could not recall any State official admitting to weakness on any level in the past, now the Chancellor herself was admitting that the State Forces had been weakened.

'In acknowledging this stress on our resources,' the speech continued, 'your Chancellor and her government, as always, have been taking the appropriate steps to ensure the safety of the State and her citizens. Thanks to diplomatic and political undertakings behind closed doors with our allies and partners, I am today announcing that the State will withdraw from the battlefields of the First Strike War across the globe. The leaders of the Civil American States and those of our former enemies in the

Zhonghua Republic and the Soviet Socialist Republics have agreed to a unilateral ceasefire of all hostilities. A new body comprised of representatives from all the major countries and unions in the world will convene in order to begin discussions about the way forward. There will be many difficult days ahead, but I stand before you today and say confidently that the hostilities of the First Strike War will officially end within the next month.'

Phillips felt dizzy. He could not remember a time without the First Strike War. He had been a boy when the war had broken out. The United Nations had been disbanded as the major players withdrew from it one after another. Now they were talking about creating a new body. The war had defined his entire adult life, as it had for all the citizens of the State. Phillips had fought and killed in the war, it had made him the person he was, for better or worse. And just like that, in the blink of an eye, it was over.

There were muted gasps from those in the press room in the Palace. The announcement was clearly unexpected.

The grey eyes narrowed into a harsh, piercing stare. 'For many countries and citizens around the world this news signals an end to all fighting, to threat, to danger, to destruction. However, in this State, we have our own evil that we must face. I make this vow to the good, loyal citizens of our beloved State: we will not rest until every last one of the rebels has been captured and destroyed. Our entire military force will now be concentrated on crushing the rebellion that has gone on for far too long already. As the rest of the world celebrates peace, we will no longer tolerate the insurrection that has infested the northern cities of our great country. There will be no compromise, no forgiveness and no pardon. We will end our own war now. I urge all the good citizens of the State: join us in this fight, together we can defeat this enemy. Take up arms against the rebels, do not shelter them. Help the military, the heroes who have protected you for so long. Rise up against the traitors. United, this State can defeat anyone. We have shown that around the world for fifty years, now we must show it to those who would seek to destroy us from within.'

Figures stood in the press briefing room, erupting into enthusiastic applause and cheers. There would not be any dissenting voice among the gathered journalists, questioning the narrative that the Chancellor had just presented. They were all employed by media organisations owned by the State. None of them wavered from the Party line.

Phillips thought of Maxine Aubert and the Star Tribune. The Tribune had been the last independent media outlet allowed by the State. Maxine had been a reporter there, until she was suspended for questioning the Chancellor. Phillips had met her and used her, exploiting her sympathies against the regime to help start the civil war.

Shortly after the war had begun, the Star Tribune was closed down. Its veteran editor, Byron Mayfield, had mysteriously disappeared. Official sources suggested he had left the country, retiring overseas to live out his remaining years in peace. Not many people believed this was the truth.

Mayfield had sent another veteran journalist, John Curran, to Central City as a war correspondent for the Tribune. The Party were not happy with the tone of Curran's reports. He was deemed to be too negative in his portrayal of the State Military's violent and excessive tactics, and too sympathetic to the rebels and the citizens.

When one of Curran's reports mentioned the conspiracy theory that drove the rebel leader Phillips, his belief that the First Strike War was a fraud, the Tribune was threatened with closure by the State. The following week Curran was killed by a stray bullet in a skirmish between State soldiers and rebels. Byron Mayfield suggested the death of his reporter may not have been an accident. In response, the Party withdrew the Star Tribune's license and the last independent media organisation was closed down. The remaining outlets continued to publish and broadcast the State's propaganda and the Independents faced an unanswered media onslaught that painted them as evil, the enemy of the State. There were no crusading journalists like Maxine Aubert left to question the information presented by the Central Alliance Party. Phillips regretted killing her for that reason alone.

The officials lined up behind the Chancellor joined in the fervent applause. Romànes shook hands with each of them, smiling and waving. She saved a lengthy handshake for Field Marshall Ellroy. Teddy Davies had already vacated the stage.

The clip froze as it came to an end. Phillips tried to take in everything he had just heard and mull it over. There was another way to look at it, if any of the citizens had the inclination to think for themselves. This was a surrender. This was the State admitting it was too weak to continue the fight in the First Strike War. In the great war of attrition, the State had finally been brought to its knees. Others may have agreed to a ceasefire, but only the State had admitted that it had needed one.

It was small consolation to Phillips. Without the First Strike War to preoccupy the State Forces, limitless resources would be at their disposal to take on the rebels in the north. The situation in Central City was untenable already. They were in no fit state to deal with an influx of fresh enemy troops, technology and artillery.

Phillips coughed, his head ached. They should have retreated from the city weeks ago, he told himself. Now they had only a matter of days. How long had the State known about this global ceasefire? They could have been withdrawing troops and equipment from around the world for weeks already, repatriating them for a full scale assault in Central City.

'Has everyone seen this?' Phillips asked Harley, who had obediently waited at a discreet distance while the commander had viewed the clip.

'Word has spread pretty quickly.'

'What is the mood like?'

'Worried.'

Phillips nodded. 'Start leaking it quietly to small groups. We will begin heading north at nightfall. No one is to panic, this is a strategic decision. Our base is strongest in the HighLands. We will gather there and draw the State Forces into our territory.'

Harley said nothing. He saluted and turned to leave.

Phillips called after him. 'Call the council. We will meet here at sundown.'

The council was the name they used for the circle of trusted senior officers that surrounded Phillips. They would be the only ones that Phillips would discuss his idea with, the idea that had stirred in his mind when he had seen the arms factory in ruins. It would be only them who would mount his final act of war in Central City.

6

Rain dripped from Gabriella's forehead onto the rifle sight. She tracked the sentry as he walked round the front of the building, a large dog on a lead by his side, rifle over his shoulder. She picked out guard positions on the corners of the third floor. Bollards and concrete blocks formed a fortified ring around the entrance, restricting road access. Security cameras were trained on the main doors and each time someone entered, she caught a glimpse of armed guards positioned inside the doorway.

'That place is a fortress, not a hospital.'

Danny lay beside her and scanned the cityscape through binoculars. The hospital was two kilometres away, standing eight storeys high, rising above the sea of flattened rubble surrounding it.

'It's a lot of protection for a building full of invalids.'

'There's no way they're just keeping some patients and orphaned kids behind that much security.' Gabriella shifted on the uncomfortable concrete.

'So how do we get in?' he asked.

'Easiest way would be from the roof, if the orphanage is near the top. If we had a spare helicopter we could land it on the helipad and be out in two minutes.'

'Cover of darkness?' Danny suggested.

'Their night vision capabilities will be a hell of a lot better than ours. They would see us coming from a kilometre away.'

'Anything positive to add?'

'People are going in without eye or palm scans. Either the scanners are broken or they don't have a connection to the database.'

'The security cameras could still be running facial recognition.'

'By the time they got a match on any of us, we would be long gone.'

'You want to go in the front door?'

'Getting inside will be the easy bit, it's getting away clean with the boy in tow that will be difficult.' She looked over at him. 'You're sure the boy will want to leave with his mother?'

'My guess is he will. He was very close to her when they lived together.'

'Maybe he loves staying in the orphanage. He's safe, he could have friends there.'

Danny had no reply. He knew she could be right. 'We could always try walking up to the front door and asking if we could take him away with us.'

'I'm pretty sure they wouldn't let that happen, and if Eilidh wanted to pursue it through the legal courts it would take her years to win back custody. More than likely it would end up with her, and us, in prison. We're all undesirables here.'

'You got a plan?'

'I have an idea.'

'What odds do you give us?'

'No better than fifty-fifty.'

'I don't like the sound of that.'

Gabriella smiled, the scarred side of her face curling upwards to give the appearance of a devilish smirk, 'I've faced worse.'

***

Kyle looked at his old analogue wristwatch. The others should have been in position by now.

'Okay, let's hope this old heap still runs.'

Zeb raised his rifle and waved Kyle on, keeping a roving eye on their surroundings while Kyle approached the car, which he had spotted on a previous scouting mission in the city. He got to the driver side door and crouched beside it, reached up and pulled the handle. It didn't budge. He yanked it harder. It wasn't locked, it was just rusted shut. He put both hands on the handle and heaved. The wing-door jerked upwards with a complaining screech. Kyle jumped into the dusty driver's seat and located the starter. Memories of the car he had once owned and driven came back to him. He jabbed at the ignition button and heard the sound of a faint spark. There was some juice left in the engine. 'Come on,' he pleaded with the vehicle. He punched the starter twice more. There was a stuttering whirr which finally caught. He nursed the accelerator pedal, slowly increasing the power until he was confident it would run.

That morning Gabriella and Danny had called them all together. They had been to scope out the hospital and told them their plan. It was dangerous and unlike any other mission they had so far undertaken. They were taking a huge risk to rescue one child. It would involve them attacking and infiltrating a State Forces stronghold, and there was a good chance they would be identified. Each of them would become a high priority State target. They had all agreed to the plan without hesitation.

They spent an hour stowing everything away they would not be taking with them, leaving it hidden in a shallow grave, covered with concrete bricks and rubble. It was unlikely they would be able to come back and reclaim the supplies in the near future.

'Everyone clear?' Gabriella asked as they set out. All nodded affirmation.

Kyle tapped the windscreen as Zeb rounded the front of the car. The big man moved to the passenger side door and, after a couple of attempts, pulled the resisting door open. His huge bulk settled into the seat. He pressed the switch on his door to open the window, but nothing happened, the electrics were shot. He turned his rifle round and used the butt of the gun to pound the glass. After three powerful blows the window shattered. Zeb cleared the remaining shards from around the edges, then mounted his gun on the ledge, aiming out into the street.

'Let's go.'

Kyle released the brake. With a final resisting screech the rusted wheels began to revolve. Kyle drove slowly down the road, weaving around the debris that littered their way. Zeb sat with his finger on the trigger of his gun, ready to react. A moving vehicle would attract attention if anyone was around to see it. They needed to remain undiscovered until they were in position. The abandoned car was badly dented and rusted, but it still worked. They only needed it to drive a few blocks.

This part of Central City was a tightly packed section of grids, which remained intact despite the damage done to the buildings. They had to take a diversion to avoid a road that was unpassable.

'The old police headquarters,' Kyle said, pointing to the huge pile of rubble that blocked the road. They travelled a further block south to manoeuvre around the obstruction and then doubled back in the right direction.

Gabriella saw them approach through her rifle scope. The rusted contraption crawled forwards, camouflaged by the surrounding decay of the war-torn city. She followed it through her lens, then swept away to the hospital building. A few metres more and the car would be in position. So far there was no sign that it had been spotted.

'Time to move,' she said. Behind her, crouched out of sight, Hassan, Eilidh and Danny stood, and followed her in single file towards the hospital, using the rubble as cover.

Kyle tensed as they approached the position they had agreed upon. He scanned the roadside, but there was no sign of the others. He had to trust they were there. By now, their approach must have been spotted, if not by the lookouts then by a movement sensor that would have triggered an alarm. Zeb trained his rifle on the hospital building ahead.

A deafening siren split the air.

'I think they've seen us,' said Zeb.

An automated warning boomed from unseen speakers, 'Unidentified vehicle, you are entering State territory. Stop immediately.' The siren continued to wail. Kyle gripped the wheel and braked, easing the car to a standstill.

'Movement,' said Zeb, pointing to the hospital entrance. The doors opened and soldiers filed out, taking up position behind the concrete barriers that guarded the entrance. Others fanned out in an attack formation and headed towards them.

'Time to go,' Kyle said. They both prised their wing doors open. Kyle stamped the accelerator and they jumped out of the car, rolling onto the ground. The car crawled forward another twenty metres. Kyle joined Zeb and they ducked behind the remains of a building wall. Over the din of the siren they could hear the shouts of the approaching State troops.

'Anytime you're ready, Verona,' Kyle muttered.

On cue a short-range missile cut through the air with a rushing whistle. Kyle felt the breeze it created on his face before the projectile impacted with the car they had just vacated. The vehicle flipped upwards as the explosion ripped through it, spinning in mid-air and landing on its roof in a fireball that sent flames leaping into the sky. The State soldiers took cover and crouched down, unsure where to direct their fire. Before the flaming car had settled a volley of gunshots began. From surrounding buildings, bullets sprayed across the area. The State troops began retaliating, firing aimlessly, searching for tell-tale signs of muzzle flash and smoke to try and pinpoint their attackers' positions.

Kyle and Zeb fell back and joined in the firing. Confusion engulfed the area. Somewhere to their right, Verona and Lachlan held an elevated position on the first floor of a bombed out residential block. To their left, Rodrigo and the newcomer Tyrell were situated in the remains of a hotel. Kyle maintained his location on the ground while Zeb ducked into a doorway and searched for an elevated position. It was vital that they occupied the State troops for long enough. They had no intention of mounting a serious attack. Their only task was to create a realistic diversion before retreating.

Above his head, Kyle heard the report of Zeb's rifle as he fired off single shots. Kyle switched his weapon to rapid fire and stepped round the side of the wall. He pulled the trigger and held it down, sweeping the gun back and forth.

The explosion of the car had been perfect. The missile had struck when it had been within a hundred metres of the hospital entrance. The distraction had worked. Gunfire followed the first explosion.

'Ready?' she asked Hassan, crouched at her shoulder.

'Ready,' he replied.

'Wait here,' Gabriella told Danny and Eilidh. They disappeared around the corner.

As expected, the State troops were focused on the battle being waged on the opposite side of the hospital building. Gabriella crept up behind the young soldier who was too busy staring at the excitement. She had her arm around his neck and her sidearm pressed against his head before he had the chance to do anything. Ten metres away, Hassan took a more direct approach. He flattened a guard with one blow, rendering her unconscious.

'Come with me and I promise you will live,' Gabriella said into the young soldier's ear. He nodded his agreement. She dragged him backwards, keeping an eye on the hospital in front of them. Hassan grabbed his fallen soldier under her arms and dragged her along the ground.

They returned to Danny and Eilidh. Hassan began stripping the soldier of her uniform. Gabriella pointed the gun at her captured man. 'Strip,' she commanded him. He started to undress instantly, a puzzled look on his face. The gun pointing at him stopped him from asking any questions. When shirts and combat trousers had been removed Gabriella tossed the female's garments to Eilidh, who started putting them on over her own clothes. She picked up the male's uniform and handed it to Hassan. 'They should just about fit you.'

In two minutes Eilidh and Hassan were dressed in their newly-acquired State uniforms.

'They'll do,' said Gabriella, inspecting them. The gunfire continued in the distance, accompanied now by grenades exploding.

Gabriella took the serrated knife from her belt. Danny stared at the evil-looking blade.

'Ready?' she asked, handing the blade to him.

She removed the eyepatch from her head. Danny looked into the dark slit that had replaced the emerald green eye. The socket was scarred like the surrounding side of Gabriella's face.

'Make it look good.'

Danny took the blade and held it a centimetre from Gabriella's forehead. He took a breath, then slashed the blade across the scarred skin. Blood poured from the wound, over the eye socket and spreading over her scars, following the pattern of the cracked and fractured skin like a river network sprawling across a delta.

'Sonovabitch,' Gabriella swore, then held her hand out. Danny returned the knife. 'Your turn.'

Danny closed his eyes as Gabriella raised the knife. She didn't give him any warning. He felt the cold metal cut through his clothes and skin. At first he felt nothing, then the sharp pain developed. He opened his eyes and looked down at the wound on his upper arm. A line of blood began to seep through his shirt. He touched it with his hand, feeling the split in his skin under the cloth.

'Spread it about a bit,' suggested Gabriella, one side of her face now covered in dripping blood. 'We have to move.'

Infantry soldier Peter Fielding had never seen any real action. He had signed up in the weeks after the outbreak of the civil war and had been sent to Central City after only two weeks of basic training. The State flooded the city with troops in the hope of bringing the conflict to a swift end. He had been assigned to a detail at the hospital and had been there ever since. Fielding had fulfilled his duty, never missed a shift, and never even been late. By virtue of others leaving and moving on, he had risen to a supervisory role. The main entrance of the hospital was his domain. Although not holding an officer rank, it was understood by all that he was the man in charge of the gateway to the hospital. He had learned a few things in his position of responsibility, things that the State would prefer to keep quiet, like the rebel prisoners held in the basement, the torture rooms, and the use of the second and third floors as barracks for the State army. He had watched air strikes and tanks destroy the buildings around the hospital and had been on duty when street fighting had threatened to stray into the boundaries of the hospital grounds, but that was the closest he had got to the actual fighting. By and large he was sitting out the war in relative comfort, and he was quite happy to be in that position. The gusto he had felt when he had signed up for the fight had vanished. He had no desire to join his comrades in the hospital beds with missing limbs, burn wounds and worse.

All of which meant infantry soldier Fielding was unprepared for the gun battle that had just erupted on the doorstep of the hospital entrance. He watched the rapid response troops flood out of the door and shouted orders to the men on guard duty to maintain their posts and remain vigilant. He prayed the gunfire would recede into the distance. Standing at the edge of his territory, sheltered behind the concrete blocks that had kept him safe throughout the war, he stared in the direction of the fighting and forgot to follow his own advice. He was caught off-guard by two soldiers calling out to him. They were within fifty metres of him, each supporting an injured person as they made their way towards the hospital. A woman had a serious head wound with blood pouring down her face, he saw that she was missing an eye and had suffered burns to her skin. The other invalid was less serious, a middle-aged man with blood dripping from a wound on his upper arm.

The male soldier, a tall, dark, muscular man that Fielding did not recognise, called out to him. 'Let us in,' he shouted with authority, 'we've got wounded citizens here, caught up in the fighting.'

In the ongoing cacophony of sound and confusion, Fielding stuck to official procedure. 'I need identification.'

'Can't you see what's happening? We're under attack, we don't have time for your bloody regulations just now. I've got injured men out there.' The man was in Fielding's face now. He was a good head taller than him. Fielding knew the path of least resistance was always the best option. The injuries were clearly genuine, it was better to obey than have the consequence of denying them entry on his conscience. He let them pass and activated the bomb-proof door for them. When they were inside he closed it behind them. The firing was continuing and Fielding stared past the bunker walls to see what was happening. He quickly forgot about the group he had just let pass.

A doctor in green scrubs rushed towards them as they entered the hospital foyer. A makeshift triage area was being hastily assembled: gurneys, wheelchairs, IV drip stands and trolleys of bandages, scissors and medical implements were being wheeled in and lined up ready for use. Orderlies and nurses rushed backwards and forwards. The confusion and hustle worked in their favour. No one had any time to worry about a couple of injured citizens. The doctor assessed the wounds and saw that neither was fatal. He paused looking at the scar tissue on Gabriella's face, pondering the old wounds, but the blood and the cut were definitely fresh.

'Citizens to the fourth floor. This space is for wounded soldiers.' He pushed them towards the elevators at the side of the foyer and disappeared, shouting at a porter who was blocking a passageway with a stretcher. Hassan pushed the button to call the elevator. While they waited, Eilidh pulled open a drawer on a trolley and collected some gauze bandage, large plasters, scissors and tape. The elevator arrived and a horde of doctors and nurses rushed out as the doors opened. They got inside. Just as the door was sliding shut a hand stopped it. A burly man in State military uniform pushed his way in, nodding to Hassan and Eilidh before turning to face the door.

'Third floor,' the new arrival instructed the elevator. They started moving upwards, leaving the chaos of the foyer behind. Danny found he was holding his breath. He threw Gabriella a worried look, gesturing at the back of the soldier. She returned it with a stare that said keep calm.

The lift stopped, the man stood to the side to let them out first, his hand across the edge of the door to make sure it didn't close on them. There was an awkward pause when they made no move to leave the elevator. Hassan stepped forward, 'Not our floor, sorry.' He gave the soldier's hand a nudge and the door slid closed as he exited.

'Floor seven,' Hassan said. The elevator resumed sliding upwards.

Now that they were alone, Hassan and Eilidh let go of Danny and Gabriella. They arrived at the seventh floor and the doors slid open. Gabriella peered out into an empty corridor. There was no noise here, no hint of the manic action that was happening on the floors below. They stepped out of the elevator. Eilidh rolled up Danny's shirt sleeve, dabbed away some of the blood and dressed the knife wound with a bandage. Hassan cleared the blood from Gabriella's face and smeared some petroleum jelly across the cut on her head to stem the blood flow. Gabriella slipped her eye-patch back on. It took them less than thirty seconds and then they moved down the corridor, weapons drawn. Along the corridor were several doors which they checked as they passed, but there was no sign of anyone in the empty rooms. At the end of the corridor it widened out into an open plan floor space. The walls were bright yellow, and covered in colourful cartoon characters. Pictures and paintings done by children were pinned to boards, toys lay around the floor, some old-fashioned things like balls and scooters. Small tables and chairs sat tidily along the walls with TouchScreens on them, some were still turned on, their screens illuminated. There were plates and bowls with half-finished meals in them, and cups half-full with water. Gabriella called them to a halt with a raised fist. They could make out the faint noise of childish chatter coming from further up ahead. They moved forward at a faster pace, time was crucial.

They found the children gathered in the front corner of the room where a large window of reinforced glass looked out onto the city below. They were engrossed watching the gun battle taking place outside. There were excited shouts mixed in with cries and tears. Three nurses were with them, equally absorbed. At this height and through the thick glass, the sound of artillery fire was dull and less threatening. A heavy blast shook the building and the lights flickered, eliciting a mix of exhilarated squeals and nervous laughter from the group. Danny figured the State troops had fired a tank missile. Gabriella got to within five metres of their backs, treading without making a sound on the carpeted floor, before she stopped and signalled for the others to lower their weapons. A small boy turned and saw them. He didn't say anything, he just stared at them, his eyes wide. Then one of the nurses noticed and turned to see what he was staring at. She instinctively grabbed the small boy, pulling him close to her. Others now turned to see what the disturbance was.

Gabriella stepped forward, arms outstretched, palms forward, in a gesture of placation. Everyone stood still, the children stared. Danny looked across at Eilidh. She was anxiously scanning the faces of the children, searching for her son. He would be eight or nine now. Would he have changed that much since she had last seen him? Danny was sure he would be able to recognise him straightaway, but none of the boys he saw in front of them resembled the short, fair-skinned boy with sandy-brown hair he remembered from the wilderness.

'Relax,' Gabriella said. 'We're not here to hurt you. We're looking for Lucas.' No one said anything. One girl, a little older than the others, glanced to the side. She was pretty, perhaps seventeen or eighteen, on the cusp of womanhood with long, dark tangled hair. One sleeve of her top hung limply by her side, the lower arm and hand were missing. She had looked at a door to the side of them.

Gabriella tried again to encourage an answer, 'Lucas, a boy, about eight years old.'

Danny caught the older girl's eye and they stared at each other. Again she had glanced towards the door. Danny moved towards it and brought his gun up. With his foot he nudged the bottom of the door. It started to creep open. Danny leaned against it, gun leading, opening it wider. He saw beds lined up along one side of the room. It was a dormitory where the children must have slept. At the far end was a boy sitting on one of the beds with his back to the door. Danny knew as soon as he saw the flop of sandy hair. Before he could move into the room, Eilidh rushed past him.

'Lucas.'

The boy turned. His face changed from a detached frown to bewildered confusion as a woman in an ill-fitting State military uniform rushed towards him. Eilidh gathered him up in her arms, engulfing him in a wide embrace. He didn't respond at first. Perhaps it was the smell, or the feeling of that once familiar embrace that eventually triggered his memory. Hesitantly, he looked into Eilidh's face and brought his arms up to reciprocate the hug.

'Mum?'

7

'We have to go,' Gabriella urged them from the door.

The battle in the street below was de-escalating as the State soldiers pushed the attackers away from the hospital and pursued them through the city. Before long they would kill or capture them, or the soldiers would be satisfied that the threat had been repelled and would return to base. They had to get out of the hospital before they were discovered.

'Go where?' Lucas asked, looking at Eilidh.

'We've come to take you away from here.'

The boy looked unsure, staring at the woman he recognised but hardly knew.

'And go where?' He looked wary and scared. Danny could tell he was torn, unsure of what to do.

'Out of the State, away from the war, to somewhere better.'

'All of us?'

'Just you,' Eilidh explained.

Lucas's face fell 'What about the others?'

'We can't take everyone.'

Gabriella interrupted them urgently, 'Come on.'

Lucas was confused. He had no idea what to do. Danny made his decision for him. They didn't have time to gently persuade him that this was for the best. There was no time for a debate on the matter, no time to explain about a cure for his disease and a new life in another country. They had to go now, whether the boy wanted to or not. Danny took his arm, prising him away from his mother and walking him down the dormitory in a hurry. Eilidh followed. Lucas did not resist, he allowed himself to be pulled along. In the main room, Hassan was standing in front of the group at the window.

'Get what you need,' Danny told Eilidh.

Eilidh walked up to one of the nurses. 'Where do you keep his insulin supply?' The woman stood motionless and didn't reply.

'It's over here.' The girl with the missing arm walked towards a cupboard on the wall and opened it. 'All his stuff is kept in here.' Danny picked up an empty child's backpack from the floor and threw it to Eilidh. She swept everything from the cupboard into the bag.

'Fresh vials of insulin?'

'The refrigerator in the kitchen, I'll show you.'

'Be quick,' called Gabriella as the girl led Eilidh to a door on the other side of the room.

Danny felt a tug at his sleeve and looked down at Lucas, who stared at him. 'It's you, isn't it?' He had recognised the man who had lived in the village in the wilderness with them for a few months, who had helped his mother, and who had taken him away from his life there and brought him to the city and the hospital.

'It's me.'

'You cannot take anyone else?'

Danny bent down so their eyes were at the same level. 'It's not easy. People aren't allowed to leave the State. We have to sneak you out. The more people we try and sneak out, the more dangerous it is.'

'What about one more person?'

'Who?'

Lucas pointed as Eilidh reappeared with the one-armed girl.

'Okay, we can go.' Eilidh stuffed a thermal cool bag inside the backpack and zipped it shut. It would keep the vials of insulin cool enough until they were needed.

Danny looked at Gabriella. She had heard the conversation between them and she knew what Danny was going to ask her. She knew it was pointless to resist and they had no time to debate the issue.

'Only if she wants to go.'

All eyes turned to the girl. 'Go where?' she asked.

'Away from here, Jenny,' Lucas answered.

'We have to go,' urged Gabriella.

Danny started to move, pulling Lucas along with him. Eilidh looked at Jenny. 'You have to decide now.'

Jenny hesitated for a moment, torn between leaving and staying with the others in the orphanage. She was eighteen, no longer officially a ward of the State. If it hadn't been for the war in the city she would have left the orphanage two years ago and been sent out into the world with a State income and a home of her own. When the war ended that would be her fate, but there were no homes left in the city and the State had stopped paying citizens in Central City any income. The orphanage was the only home she had known. The other children were her family, the nurses the closest thing she had to parents.

'Decide,' Danny insisted.

Jenny thought back to the sick, underweight boy who had sat quietly on his bed when he had first arrived. She had taken on his insulin treatment, she had checked his blood sugar levels, measured the carbohydrates in his meals and administered the correct insulin dosages. She had woken in the middle of the night to ensure he was not slipping into hypoglycaemia, waking him to feed him a sweet or a biscuit if he needed a sugar hit. While he sleepily ate his snack, she would sit and read stories to him, or they would look at the stars in the night sky and the tracer fire arching over the city rooftops.

'A new life, Jenny,' said Lucas. They had talked of a new life during those night time moments, dreaming of a place without bombs or bloodshed, a normal life where people walked down the street or played in the park without fear.

She made her decision. She took Lucas's hand in hers and they followed Eilidh and Gabriella along the corridor. They took nothing with them.

Danny and Hassan followed them, leaving the nurses and the other children behind. They could only hope they would continue to be safe within the hospital until the end of the war, whenever that might be.

'Will we make it?' Eilidh asked as they took the elevator down.

Gabriella shrugged, 'They should have figured out there is no real attack on the hospital by now. The soldiers will be returning. If there is enough confusion, a few injuries, maybe we will have enough time to make it out.'

The elevator slid down through the floors, passing the ground level and continuing to descend below street level, into the basement. Hassan and Gabriella raised their weapons as the doors slid open. Down here the bright, diode-lit corridors of the upper floors were replaced by a low, orange glow which dimly lit plain, grey concrete walls and cast menacing shadows into corners. Gabriella led them out, sweeping her gun across the space, ensuring they were alone. They filed out after her: Danny, Jenny and Lucas, Eilidh, and Hassan brought up the rear.

'Left,' Danny whispered when they reached the end of a corridor. The exit strategy had been his part of the plan. He knew about the basement from his days as a police officer visiting the hospital mortuary. There was a steel double-door in front of them which opened when Gabriella pushed it. They filed through. The same ominous lighting filled the room beyond. There were sounds: low murmurs, breathing, shuffling feet on the hard, cold floor. The room consisted of a central corridor that ran between rows of metal bars. Danny realised they were prison cells as they moved along them. He peered to the side, trying to make out what was inside each cell.

'Please,' a husky voice called from the shadows.

Danny took a step towards the voice. From the murky darkness, two hands grasped the metal bars. A face emerged, gaunt, dirty and bloodied. The hair was overgrown, tangled and greasy. The smell of excrement and foul body odour pervaded the room.

'Help us,' the apparition said. His eyes were deep hollows, sunken into a malnourished face, and tattered rags failed to cover his emaciated skeleton. Stick-like arms sprang through the gaps between the cell bars, grasping at Danny's clothes. He got a hold of Danny and pulled him towards the bars. The grip was strong in spite of the weak appearance of the man. 'You have to save us,' his hoarse voice whispered.

Danny hit out at the hands that held him and broke free, stumbling backwards. Now he noticed more movement in the room. From each cell came a mix of pleading male and female voices. Hassan pulled a torch from his utility belt and switched it on. He passed it along the row of cells, up one side and down the other. Faces blinked and hands covered eyes as the light traced across the collection of ghostly prisoners. There was more than one prisoner in each cell. Lucas held onto Jenny while the others looked around them, guns raised.

'Quiet,' hissed Gabriella. 'They will hear you.' The pleading became a muted murmur.

Danny stepped towards the first prisoner who had grabbed him. 'Who are you?'

'We are Independents. Captured rebels. They brought us here. They torture us, ask us questions. Try to get us to betray our comrades.'

'The guards? Where are the guards?'

'They ran out. We heard the gunfire and explosions. Have our comrades finally come to rescue us?'

Danny shook his head, 'I'm sorry.'

'Then you have to help us. Set us free. They will kill us soon. Some of us have already died. We have to shit in the corner of our cells, we sleep on the floor. They give us only water and bread once a day.'

Another voice shouted out, a female one, 'They hook us up to electrodes.'

'They pour scalding water down our throats.'

'They stretch us on racks.'

The clamour of voices swelled again until Gabriella raised her hands. 'You must be quiet,' she pleaded with them, 'or the guards will return. Danny, we have to stick to the exit plan.'

Danny hustled past her and kept going, passing more cells and feeling the eyes boring into him. At the far end he found the concrete wall he had expected. He quickly unpacked the packet of Semtex. He moulded the clay into a ball and pressed it onto the wall, then pushed in the metal detonators. There was no need for a timer on this crude bomb, instead he connected wires to the detonators and began unravelling them as he backed away.

Faces watched him. 'Get back as far as you can,' he warned them. The figures withdrew into the shadows of their cells. He reached the others. Gabriella handed him the trigger. He carefully screwed each of the wires into place.

'Set,' he said.

'Everyone down,' Gabriella crouched beside him. 'You better be right about this,' she said to Danny.

'Only one way to find out,' he replied, and covered his head with his arms as he pressed the trigger.

There was coughing all around. Danny's ears were ringing as he struggled to his feet. The dust settled. There was a jagged hole in the wall. Hassan and Gabriella clawed and pulled at loose bricks until it was wide enough for a person to squeeze through. Gabriella shone a torch through to the other side and saw a sewage tunnel, as Danny had said there would be. The explosion had shaken the foundations of the building, soldiers would be on their way down to the basement.

'Move,' Gabriella ordered.

'Please,' the man who had grabbed Danny called to him again, his outstretched arms straining through the bars of his cell. 'They will kill us for sure. The keys,' he pleaded.

Hassan shone his torch where the man pointed at the wall. Beside the steel door through which they had entered the room, old-fashioned metal keys hung on a hook. The basic cells were not fitted with modern electronic release mechanisms, but had primitive mortise locks.

Danny ran back to the door and grabbed the keys.

'Come on,' shouted Gabriella.

'Go,' Danny shouted to Hassan.

The tall man moved quickly, pushing Eilidh, Lucas and Jenny along with him and sprinting to the opening in the wall where Gabriella stood waiting for them. Danny brought up the rear. He stopped at the cell with the man who had spoken to him in it, and tried the first key in the lock. It didn't turn. He fumbled the keys and tried the next one.

'We're not waiting for you,' Gabriella shouted. Danny saw her duck through the hole in the wall.

Danny swore as he tried one key after another. Finally, the lock turned and clicked. He wrenched the cell door open and the man stumbled out. Danny pressed the keys into his hand.

'You have to do it yourself, you understand? You cannot follow us.'

The man nodded gratefully, 'Thank you.'

Four others emerged from the same cell. The man passed the keys to one of them who went to the next cell and began trying keys in the lock. Danny wished he could do more to help them, but there was no time. From behind the steel door the distant sound of running boots and shouted commands emerged. He took his sidearm and two flash bombs from his belt and handed them to the man.

'Here. Good luck.' Danny tore himself away and sprinted for the tunnel.

'Good luck to you, comrade,' the prisoner shouted after him.

Danny splashed through the rancid sewers and caught up with the others at a crossroads where four tunnels met.

'Which way?' asked Gabriella, handing a torch to Danny. He knew the city best, especially the warren of underground tunnels below the streets. He had some knowledge from his previous life as a police officer and since the beginning of the war had made it his mission to fully explore the underworld. With the war being fought in the streets, underground had become the safest way to move around the city.

There was a bright flash behind them, accompanied by a bang and then gunfire and shouting. State soldiers had arrived at the basement cells. The sound of fighting grew nearer. Danny turned to the right and started running. The others followed, sloshing through the dirty water and waste, moving as fast as they could in the dimly-lit tunnel. As one would lose their footing and stumble, another would help them up and push them forward. Hassan picked up Lucas and carried him. They had no idea if they were being pursued. The fighting faded away behind them. The prisoners had kept their word, they had not followed the tunnel taken by Danny. They would never know what became of them. Danny hoped at least some of them had made it out.

After ten minutes, they arrived at a metal door in the sewer wall. Danny tried to open it, but it didn't budge. Hassan came forward and together he and Danny forced the heavy steel ajar. Gabriella was first through the gap, Danny helped Jenny and Eilidh through while Hassan picked up Lucas again, the boy's arms clinging round his thick neck. On the other side of the door was another tunnel, this one was rounded and along the ground ran old railway sleepers. They were in a city subway tunnel, part of the old network that had been out of use for decades.

'Recognise where we are?' Danny asked Gabriella.

'All these dark tunnels look the same to me,' she lied. She remembered the underground nightclub where the rich and privileged of the State had gathered to drink and gamble, flouting the State laws that the majority of citizens were forced to obey. She had seduced the City Consul there, before killing him. 'Get us out of here.'

They travelled underground for another four kilometres, passing through three eerie abandoned stations where the tunnel widened out and haunted platforms stood empty, waiting for commuters who had disappeared long ago. At the fourth station Danny found stairs at the side of the tracks that allowed them to climb up onto the dust-covered platform. At the end of the station the tracks curved away north. This was as far east as the tunnels went.

Danny pulled Jenny and Eilidh up onto the platform. Hassan climbed the stairs with Lucas still on his back.

Gabriella came up last and checked her watch. 'The sun will be setting, we should keep going for a couple of hours before we stop.'

They hurried along the platform to stairs that led up to the world above. Weak grey light crept downwards, struggling to penetrate the gloom of the underworld. Ducking under disused barriers, they emerged onto a street relatively undamaged by the war, with a few buildings that were still intact. Here, further away from the centre of the city, the fighting had been less concentrated. Citizens lived in the buildings that still stood, surviving as best they could. Jenny and Lucas breathed in fresh air and stared at their new surroundings. It was the first time they had been outside the hospital since the start of the war. The air tasted different, unfiltered by air conditioning. They felt unfamiliar moisture in the atmosphere.

Gabriella led them on in single file. Danny took a turn carrying Lucas while Hassan covered the rear of their small column. They kept their weapons drawn and ready, but the streets remained quiet. In her peripheral vision, Gabriella saw movement in the shadows and doorways, furtive eyes watching them pass. Framed in small windows that looked onto the road, she saw makeshift curtains flicker. The citizens stayed hidden inside, it was best not to get involved with any armed soldiers on the streets, no matter which side they belonged to.

They pushed on for another hour and found the main highway, the artery that joined the west and east sides of Central City. They followed the straight road, keeping to the smaller residential streets that ran alongside it. Gabriella would have preferred to have gone further east before they stopped for the night, but the others were tiring. When they came upon an abandoned multi-storey parking garage she led them inside. It had gaping craters in the walls and floors and water dripped through the structure, puddling in various places. Broken electricity wires dangled down and rubble littered the ground. They walked up a winding ramp to the second level and found a space that was relatively dry before bedding down for the night on the uncomfortable, cold floor. Jenny checked Lucas and fed him a glucose supplement to raise his blood sugar. Within minutes they were asleep, cuddled into each other while Eilidh lay next to her son, stroking his hair. Hassan, Danny and Gabriella agreed to take turns keeping watch. Gabriella took the first shift, sitting off to the side, using a gap in the wall to see the street outside and monitor the entrance to the garage. An uneasy quiet settled over them, broken only by the sound of the rain beginning to fall hard again.

Jenny stirred when Gabriella woke Danny for his spell of guard duty. The girl took out the monitoring device Danny had seen her using earlier and checked Lucas's blood glucose levels without waking him. They had dipped too low again and she was forced to wake him. She gave him a small cup of glucose juice from the supplies she had taken from the hospital, and a biscuit to follow.

Danny watched her caring for him. 'You get back to sleep, I'll sit up with him,' he offered.

Jenny eyed him suspiciously, she was used to being Lucas's carer and was reluctant to trust that duty to anyone else.

'You're tired, you need to rest, we will have a long day tomorrow,' Danny said.

With reluctance, she acquiesced, huddling back down. Danny sat next to Lucas on a raised kerb. The boy leaned into him, nibbling on the biscuit.

'Thank you,' Lucas said.

'Thank you?'

'For saving me. Not now, I mean, back then. I never got the chance to say thank you.'

'You don't need to thank me. It was the doctors that saved you.'

'I would have died without you getting me there.'

Danny didn't say anything. He had only done what anyone who cared for a child would have done in the same situation. He looked at Eilidh, who was having a disturbed sleep near to them.

'You should thank your mother too, you know. It wasn't easy for her to let you go.'

'I guess.'

Danny sensed the boy's insecurity. He imagined what it must have felt like when Lucas's mother had let him be taken away. 'She did it to save you. The last thing she wanted was to let you go, but she had no choice.'

'Because of my stupid diabetes.'

'Exactly, and now she has come back for you. She's risked a lot.'

'She says they've found a cure. Do you believe it?'

'Your mother does.'

'I hope so.'

They lapsed into silence, with just the sound of the rain falling and the small crunching noise of Lucas eating more of the biscuit breaking the peace of the night.

'Feeling okay?' Danny asked.

'Fine, this happens most nights.' Lucas paused. 'Do you think you will come with us?'

'To the European Union?'

Lucas nodded.

'Would you want me to come with you and your mother?'

'I think she would like it if you did.'

'Would you like it?'

'I guess so,' Lucas shrugged.

'I hadn't really thought about it,' Danny answered. At the moment he was only concerned with getting them to the coast and out of the State.

'It would be good,' said Lucas as he swallowed the last piece of biscuit. He picked himself up and shuffled back to the blanket he shared with Jenny. Danny watched him lie down and fall asleep straight away.

It would be good, Danny thought to himself, if Eilidh wanted it too. He would have a reason to leave this city behind, something more to live for than scavenging around the edges of the civil war, waiting for it to end. How much more could he take? He had seen and done enough.

For the rest of his watch Danny contemplated a future worth living for, and he found that he liked the idea. Hassan took over from him in the early hours of the morning and when Danny closed his eyes he saw himself with Eilidh and Lucas, living a new life in a far off place, away from the bombs and the rain and the destruction.

THE WANDERER

The rain drummed down. It was hard to find peace in the city. That's why he had come out here to the city walls. They used to mark the boundary between the city and the wilderness, now wilderness existed on both sides. As the city crumbled, nature crept back in creating urban meadows of grass and wild flowers. The walls still kept the citizens enclosed, but animals had found ways through the unguarded border. Not just wild dogs and wolves, but there, standing in the middle of a street, a stag. It looked at him, sensing he was there. He kept still and stared back, watching the full, dark eyes, the sleek brown coat and the huge antlers that were shedding their furry coat. He felt a calmness between them in the silence, an imaginary bond with nature.

A distant explosion broke the spell. The stag bolted, hooves rattling over concrete until he was out of sight. The explosion was followed by gunshots. A battle had erupted. It was unusual on this side of the city. The fighting had moved to the east as the rebels had retreated. He had come west to avoid the fighting, but the violence followed him now. There was no escape.

He walked on. His stomach growled. He needed food. He was a scavenger rather than a hunter. He kept his eyes open for a fallen bird or a starving dog. There were few animals he had not eaten in order to survive. Nothing presented itself as he carried on, following the wall. He heard the river. It grew louder as he neared the huge dam.

Eventually the wall began to slope upwards, getting higher as it merged into the dam that spanned the wide mouth of the river. The climate emergency had necessitated the building of the dam in order to protect the city. They built it where an existing bridge had spanned the tidal river mouth. A road still ran along the top of it.

A steep ramp led him onto the top of the dam wall. As he walked upwards he could see the city on one side, broken and ruined. The river ran through it, curving towards the dam which brought it to an abrupt halt. On this side of the dam the water was calm and tranquil. Giant fans, built into the huge concrete face, no longer turned. They had been used to clean the air, removing carbon dioxide, nitrogen oxides and other harmful gases, and storing them for reuse. They were not needed any longer. With the start of the war in the city came the end of excessive gas emissions. The war was a reset, nature the beneficiary. Under the giant fans were the sluice gates which no longer opened. A covering layer of debris – timber, litter and white scum – which the river had collected as it wound through the city, gathered on the surface of the water with nowhere to escape to. Like him, the river was trapped inside the city, unable to take that final exit.

He crossed the highway to the other side of the dam, jumping over a metal barrier that divided the empty traffic lanes. On this side the river was transformed into a vast sea that swirled and swelled. Waves rolled in and crashed into the concrete wall. The water spread wide, flooding fields on either side. The original river banks had long since been sacrificed and the agricultural farmland abandoned to the rising tides. It was nature knocking at the door of the city, demanding to reclaim the valley basin beyond, a flood waiting to be unleashed that could wash away the sins of the city.

The dam had been built and then extended, getting wider and wider as it strained to hold back the sea. He reached the middle of the dam where the highway was at its highest point and looked left and right. The sea stretched away to the horizon. It was in constant uproar. On calm summer days he had been here and still the sea churned as though moved by an eternal storm. Spray lashed his face, invigorating him.

Without the dam there would be no city, it was essential to protect it. Like the hospital, the bombs had not fallen here, but maintenance of the vital structure had ceased since the start of the war. Now paintwork flaked, metal rusted and concrete crumbled. Eventually nature would triumph, as it always does. Humankind can only keep it at bay for so long. One crack, one fissure and a tiny waterfall would signal the beginning of the end.

An object cut across the chopping waves as he stood in contemplation. It was grey, with dashes of orange, bouncing up into the air like it was flying, then crashing down into the waves, lost from view. It travelled towards him, becoming larger. It was a boat, a dinghy with an outboard motor that pushed it through the swell. As it neared he could see people on board. He crouched below the parapet as it approached the dam. It swooped left, then turned right, tracing a path along the length of the wall.

In the days before the fighting, it would not have been allowed. No vessels were allowed within two miles of the dam on the seaward side. The police boats patrolled downstream to make sure no one approached. Barriers had been in place. He had visited them as part of his job protecting the borders of his city.

The small boat was taking a huge risk. One unexpected wave, one large swell and they would be dashed against the concrete. The pilot was skilful though, ensuring they kept a safe distance away. One man on board the boat had binoculars and was scanning the dam wall back and forth. What was he looking for? Were they from the State? Were they checking for damage, a crack that could spell doom? Had there been reports of the dam weakening? The man pointed and there was a shouted conversation, but he could not make out what was said.

Finally the man with the binoculars gave a signal to the pilot. They had seen all they wanted and the grey dinghy turned and headed away, pushing against the tide. He watched them retreat towards the northern bank. They reached the shore at the very limit of his view.

The rain grew heavier, closing round him like a curtain. He lost the point on the shore where the boat had made landfall. He continued across the bridge, down the far side of the dam to the southern bank. Once more he sought shelter.

The vision of the drowning city resurfaced as the rain engulfed everything, drilling violently into the broken world.

8

Phillips was sick of the rain. He was sick of this pitiful city and the citizens who cowered within it. He wondered if there was a link between the constant miserable weather and the downtrodden population. He had once thought the seeds of revolution could be found in the meek people of this place. He had been wrong. The city was lost, so were the people who inhabited it. Perhaps he would find braver souls in the north.

They had abandoned the jeep an hour ago once they had ventured beyond the limits of the rebel enclave. It was too conspicuous to be seen driving in, and the roads that lay ahead were in a poor state. Now they trudged along in single file. Casper was in front of him leading the way. Kruger and Mitchell followed behind him. They were capable lieutenants who would not shirk from the task that lay ahead of them. Many of his supporters, even the most loyal who had fought alongside him since the beginning of the uprising, would hesitate to go along with the course of action he was planning.

There were few options left when it came to Central City. He could not summon the forces required to repel the State military any longer, especially if their numbers were about to be swelled by the ceasefire in the First Strike War. Any battle with them would result in a crushing defeat and massive losses. It would be the end of the rebellion.

While Phillips and his small team headed west, Harley was leading the rest of the Independents north through the wilderness. It would not take the State Forces long to realise that the Independents had abandoned Central City. Hopefully, they would have enough time to reach their forces in the north and the relative safety of the HighLand City. Phillips would join them there once his final mission in Central City was complete. Then they could regroup and decide on a strategy to turn the tide of the war in their favour.

Kruger approached him. Her dark hair hung around her face in wet strands, raindrops running down it and onto her shoulders. Her poncho was soaked through. Each of them carried a backpack loaded with equipment. Phillips admired how the small, slight Kruger carried her pack with ease. She was a soldier he would have been proud to have commanded during the First Strike War.

'Giesler has been on the radio,' she announced, with the distinctive hint of Germanic in her accent. 'They have completed their recce.'

'Good,' replied Phillips. 'Tell him we will hear his full report when we meet them.'

'They have started setting up camp at the meeting place.'

'How far away are we?'

'Another fifty kilometres, it will be nightfall before we get there.'

'Very well. It is safer to keep moving until we join them. Let them know to expect us after dark.'

Kruger left him to relay his message, dropping back to join Mitchell, who carried the old radio equipment.

Phillips tramped on, following the footsteps Casper made fifteen metres in front of him. The younger man made light work of the wet, slippery ground.

They had not encountered any enemy forces since they had left the base. With the poor visibility and treacherous conditions, it was unlikely anyone would be out patrolling. It was the safest time to travel: the drones would not be risked in the heavy rain, and satellites would struggle to penetrate the clouds. Their small unit of four people would barely register but the main protection they had from State surveillance was their position and their direction of travel. They were walking along the edge of the city perimeter where there had been little fighting and which held little strategic value. It would have been quicker to travel the more direct route through the city, covering a shorter distance and using the streets. Following the city boundary as it curved round added kilometres onto their hike, but it was worth it to avoid any skirmishes. The success of the mission depended on their remaining undetected.

He had only revealed his plan to his close council, comprising of Kruger, Mitchell, Harley and Casper, the previous evening. He explained the sequence of events that had led him to draw up this drastic action: the city almost lost; the arms factory destroyed; more State Forces en route. The Chancellor's statement earlier in the day ending the First Strike War had been the final straw. There was only one option left to them in Central City.

After a moment of disbelief, Casper had been the first to speak. 'You will destroy the city,' he said.

'That is the idea.'

'Then we are conceding defeat?' Kruger asked.

'The city is lost, we do not have the resources to win it back.'

'Not now, but in the future, we could return. We could win it back.'

Phillips shook his head. The orange glow of the candle cast his shadow against the side of the tent, his grey head moving from side to side against the canvas. 'We cannot leave the city to the State.'

'Scorched earth,' said Mitchell.

'Exactly, we leave them nothing. No resources, buildings, land, materials. We bury it all.'

'You'll kill thousands of citizens. Millions.' Kruger's eyes were wide. Phillips had anticipated her being the hardest to convince. She was not ex-military, she had not been exposed to the harsh realities of war before it had arrived on her own doorstep. He knew she had once worked for the State, part of the bureaucracy that had kept the citizens in place. She had joined their cause out of necessity, when she had nowhere else to turn after the Party had let her down completely. She had questioned him about the First Strike War. How did he know the truth? Who was his source? Did he have any proof? How did he find out about the Montana accident? She looked in vain for a flaw in his argument, only to be convinced that what he had learned was the truth.

'And what of them?' Phillips countered. 'The citizens have proved useless to us. They sat back and let their city be destroyed by the State. They were idle for years, letting a corrupt party rule them without protest. When the corruption was exposed and the opportunity to fight back presented itself, they did nothing. They could have joined us in the struggle. If they had, we would have been victorious before now. It would be over. Instead they have idly refused to help us. They would sooner the State won so they could return to their comfortable existence, letting murderers rule them, unpunished for their crimes and free to continue as they wish.' Phillips paused, collecting himself and continuing in a calmer vein. 'They are collateral damage. Our retreat can still deliver a fatal blow to the rule of the Party. Think what those in Capital City will think if they see an entire city destroyed by the rebels. It will galvanise our sympathisers in the other cities.'

'Can it be done?' Mitchell asked, practical as ever.

'We think so.' Phillips pointed at the schema and map on the table in front of them. By the dim candlelight they were just able to make out the print on the paper. 'Giesler has been sent ahead. I have discussed it with him and based on these plans we have enough ordnance. It just needs to be rigged correctly.'

He pointed to the map, showing the western half of Central City.

'The original dam spanned a kilometre, covering the centre of the valley. As the seas rose, they expanded it on either side, adding sections as needed until the sea levels stabilised.'

He picked up the schema of the dam. 'It is these additional sections that provide us with our opportunity. Each is solid in its own right, but where the new sections meet the original dam there is a potential fault line. Giesler is sure that enough explosive along these fault lines will be enough to breach the dam. Once the water seizes an opportunity to break through, it will rush forward. We rig explosives on either side of the original section and the gaps created will be enough to bring the whole thing crumbling down.'

'Makes sense,' Mitchell nodded.

Phillips turned back to the map. 'Within an hour, half the city will be under water.' He traced a line along the river. 'The arms factory, the main square and the remains of the parliament building, the State military bases, the hospital, the main airport. All of them will be gone.'

'You're sure this is what you want to do?' Casper asked.

'It is the right move, nothing more.'

'I agree,' Casper said. Phillips knew he could rely on the loyal soldier to follow him.

'The sacrifice is worth it for the greater triumph,' said Mitchell.

The three men turned to look at Kruger.

'Very well,' she said. Phillips caught a hint of reluctance in her attitude. 'If you really believe it must be done then I am with you. If there is no other way in which to hurt the State, then we must do it.'

Phillips smiled. 'Giesler has Jonas and Jarrod with him. Together with the four of us that should be enough. Harley will lead the retreat of our main force, they will begin to fall back at first light. Our plans must remain secret, not even our own people must know what we intend to do. There will be those within our ranks who will not agree with it, they may even try to stop us. We can give no one any warning.'

'Should we warn the citizens?' Kruger asked. 'They could evacuate. We could still achieve our goal of destroying the city but save some lives.'

'No,' Phillips raised his voice. 'There will be no warning. We cannot risk our plan being compromised.'

The rain had eased, bringing some relief. Kruger and Mitchell were still at the rear. Casper fell back to walk alongside his commander. He had been a naïve child when he had arrived in the city on the cusp of war. Phillips had seen the potential in him, especially when he saw how he could handle a rifle: Gabriella was the only sniper Phillips had seen who could better Casper. He was also trained in a rare form of martial art that had been largely forgotten by the modern State. Phillips had seen Casper take down State troops with a single blow.

'How does this play out?' Casper asked him now. 'What's the end goal? We destroy the city and regroup in the north. Then what?'

'The city will be gone, but more than that, the sea will cut the northern half of the country off. There will be a physical barrier, which creates an opportunity. Any land border that remained would be narrow enough for us to control.'

'How would we control it? A wall? Border checks?'

'By whatever means is necessary. We could keep the State out of the HighLands. We could create our own country, a new start. There are only a few resources in the north that the State cares about. They may even decide that losing the HighLands is an acceptable loss and leave us be.'

Casper had learned enough about the State to know this was not as crazy as it seemed. With Central City gone and the HighLand City cut off, the State would see a sizeable reduction in the amount of electricity it was able to produce. There were vast wind power plants off the northern coast and on the high peaks of the HighLand mountain ranges, there were the hydro and wave power plants off the stormy west coast. Perhaps the exchange of energy could be the start of a trade negotiation once the hostilities had ended.

'You would lead us?'

Phillips laughed, 'Not me. I carry too much baggage, and that's before we destroy an entire State city.' Phillips was not a politician, he did not possess the necessary skills to rule a country or create a constitution. He was a soldier and he could see the way forward in terms of winning against an enemy.

'Our people would follow you.'

'They might,' Phillips agreed, 'but many would not be able to understand the sacrifice we are making. They would see me as a murderer of their fellow citizens, which is true. I would never be able to bring the people together, and a new country needs harmony if it is to succeed.'

'Then who would be able to lead this new country?'

'The wilderness is full of noble people who have lived outside of the State, defying the rules and laws of the Party. Perhaps there is a leader among them who would rise to the challenge.'

Casper was quiet for a moment, contemplating what Phillips had said. 'What would become of you in this new country?'

'There would be no place for me. I represent the past. I have done what I thought was right to lead the citizens of the State out of their misery.'

'You would leave?'

'There are still those who must be made to pay for what has happened in this world for the last fifty years. The leaders in the Civil American States, the leaders of the Axis Powers, they all carry the same guilt that the Central Alliance Party does. The citizens of the State are not the only ones who need to be woken from a blind and unknowing servitude.'

They walked on, shoulder-to-shoulder. 'It will never end, will it?' Casper asked.

Phillips looked into the eyes of the young man. He was too tired to go into the politics of power and corruption, of economics and trade and the whole system of rule that oppressed so many and protected the privileged few. 'No,' he replied simply, 'it will never end.'

'Then why…?'

Phillips pre-empted the question. 'Because the struggle must continue. There must be hope. There must be faith that this world could yet be a better place for all.' Phillips quickened his pace and moved ahead, pushing the overgrown foliage out of his path as they followed the city walls.

'Come on,' he called back, 'we can still make the rendezvous before midnight.'

9

The sun broke over a fresh morning. Danny and Gabriella woke the others and ate a small breakfast of nutrition tablets, water and the last of the berries they had brought with them from the camp. Eilidh sat with Lucas and Jenny, asking what life had been like in the hospital orphanage. She kept brushing her son's hair around the back of his ears, a tentative attempt at re-establishing a familial bond.

'They treated us well,' Jenny explained, 'we were like one big family.'

'I will miss them,' Lucas added.

Jenny squeezed his hand. 'Before the war we went out, but after the fighting started they kept us inside for our own safety.'

'They kept you locked inside all this time?' Eilidh asked.

'For our own good,' Lucas answered defensively.

'Sometimes safety has to be weighed up against quality of life and a person's rights.'

'We didn't complain,' Jenny said, 'we were comfortable and compared to what others had to sacrifice and go through, we thought of ourselves as the lucky ones.'

Eilidh decided against arguing with them further.

Gabriella dug her elbow into Danny's ribs. He had been staring at Eilidh. 'Time to get moving,' she said, and stood up to begin packing away their gear.

They set off at ten. The hard work of the previous day was behind them, today was an easier walk through deserted streets. They had to cover about twenty kilometres to reach the castle in the old part of the city, where the others would meet them, provided they had escaped safely from their skirmish with the State outside the hospital. They had specified nightfall as the time to meet. Until then they had no idea what had happened to their comrades.

The atmosphere was relaxed, though Hassan and Gabriella kept their weapons drawn and constantly scanned the streets through which they walked. Danny joined Eilidh, Lucas and Jenny in their conversation. Eilidh told them about the life in the village now that it had become a refugee camp. She described the squalor and deprivation of the people there. There was not enough water or food, different factions within the camp led to in-fighting and disease spread through the tents like wildfire. It had become like any other refugee camp on the planet.

'You will never return?' Danny asked.

Eilidh shook her head, 'There is nothing to return to.'

Danny felt a sadness. He pictured the shack he had lived in with his small patch of land. It had not been much, but he had found peace for the first time since Rosa and his children had died. He would have welcomed the chance to go back to that life. Now it was gone, another victim of the war.

Eilidh saw Danny's face cloud over. 'You could come with us,' she suggested.

He looked at her.

She smiled at him with a look of encouragement. 'You could leave the State too. Lucas would love to have you with us and I could use the help in a new country.'

'I can't leave.' Even as he uttered the words Danny's mind questioned them. He could leave if he wanted to. It was no longer the city he had grown up in, that life had disappeared. He knew Gabriella and the others could survive without him. They would not mourn his loss if he decided his future lay elsewhere, and Gabriella would not stand in his way.

What was holding him to this failed State which he had come to hate? Why did he care about the people who sheltered behind the ruins of the city? He owed them nothing. He could leave knowing he had done all he could to help and protect them. Once, he had fled from the city and abandoned his fellow citizens to their fate, knowing that the leaders of the State would sacrifice their own people in order to hold onto power, but he had made amends for that in the years since his return.

'Think about it,' Eilidh interrupted his thoughts. 'For Lucas's sake.'

They made good progress and the further they travelled into the old town, the more citizens they encountered on the streets. Here, compared to the quiet avenues in the west, where citizens cowered in bombed out buildings, there was a sense of a society insisting on living a normal life amongst the chaos of war. The autumnal sunshine added to the feeling of optimism. As they passed there were some looks of concern, but though armed and in combat fatigues, they were clearly not State troops, and the appearance of Lucas seemed to reassure people that they were not a military hit squad.

As the sun reached its zenith, the castle came into view in the distance, sitting on its eyrie. Below it the streets of the old town widened and became free of rubble and debris. This area of the city had been saved from modern regeneration thanks to the heritage of its buildings, although without the war it would have soon been redeveloped. In these streets they would be able to barter for food and thoughts turned towards a meal. They headed towards a wide thoroughfare that bordered an area of green parkland beneath the large cliff on which the castle sat. The amount of people around them grew, until they were walking through a street that was bustling with citizens. Danny glanced at Gabriella and saw tension in her face. This was not normal, and their natural thought was to fear that something was wrong.

But the faces that passed were happy. They were smiling and there was laughter. There were children and families out enjoying a walk through the street. Along one side of the wide road makeshift stalls appeared, made of old tables, chairs, crates and rocks. Some vendors had simply laid their wares on top of a sheet on the ground. The stall owners were selling anything they could find that had any value.

'A market,' Hassan commented.

'Seems that way,' Danny answered. The war had given rise to a black market in all sorts of goods – medicine, food, technology. The buying and selling was mostly conducted in dark alleys and small rooms away from the prying eyes of the State Forces. It was unusual to find such a public gathering and display of community.

Lucas and Jenny ran ahead, going from stall to stall, greeting people and investigating what was on offer. Most of the food looked far from nourishing, much of it was nothing more than scraps. One man sat on an old overturned bucket with the carcases of a number of dead dogs lying on the pavement in front of him. He was doing a decent trade, carving off sections of raw red meat to a steady string of customers. Others sold small, home-grown fruit or vegetables, some passed off weeds and wild flowers as exotic salad. A particularly busy stall had flasks of a homemade brew lined up, and full cups were handed out in exchange for anything the consumer had to offer. If they had nothing to give, the brewer seemed happy to give a mug of his drink away for free. No money exchanged hands, the electronic currency system that the State economy ran on had broken down in the city when the war had started. Goods were exchanged for other goods – clothes and food held the most value, but they saw pieces of wood and metal traded, plates, bowls, spoons, knives, bottles of glass and plastic, jewellery and even antique items like books, paper and writing pencils. Nothing was valueless when it came to bartering. There was a stall that seemed to specialise in broken items, glass and china knick-knacks that had survived a bombing moderately intact. One woman enthusiastically shouted and waved prospective customers towards her table heaped with redundant SmartLenses and TouchScreens. They had once been omnipresent, part of every citizen's life and as ubiquitous as the clothes that everyone wore. The civil war had reduced them to useless rubble, like the buildings that surrounded them.

'All in perfect working order,' the woman beamed. Without any power or the State internet to connect to, the technology was nothing but junk, yet even she too seemed to be doing brisk business. With enough know-how, perhaps some could make use of the devices, or they could strip them down and make use of the raw materials.

They began to relax as they moved along the stalls, exchanging pleasant greetings with fellow citizens. In the city before the war a scene like this was unthinkable. Gatherings of this size were not permitted and no one needed to leave the house in order to shop. Despite the over-crowding of the mega-cities, the streets had never been this crammed with people. In adversity the citizens had discovered a new social spirit, built on personal contact with fellow people. Individual struggles were shared, citizens were not alone and they could face their hardships together. Danny took Eilidh's hand, pulling her through the crowd as they tried to keep up with Lucas and Jenny.

Gabriella and Hassan found a stall selling fruit – apples that were over ripe and grapes that had begun to shrivel on the vine. They exchanged some fresh water, a length of rope and a hunting knife to secure enough for a passable meal for everyone. The sight of their weapons helped the vendor make a quick decision to trade.

'I've never seen a market so busy. Special day?' Gabriella asked the seller as he inspected his newly acquired goods.

'A wedding,' he smiled. He pointed further down the road, beyond the main throng of people, to a large monument, scarred with blast marks but still standing. It commemorated some long forgotten writer and had been preserved by the State for aesthetic and tourist value, long after his books had been added to the restricted lists. Gabriella could make out a figure in a white dress on the dais of the monument, the skirt of her outfit billowing around her, along with a veil around her head. She held a bouquet of bright red flowers and was posing for a photograph. A man dressed in a smart suit, joined her and they kissed. It was a scene from history. Traditional weddings like this had died out decades ago, replaced by purely legal formalities. The war had seen a rise in nostalgia for times past.

'Our chance to show the war two fingers,' the seller added. Gabriella smiled, noting that he refused to curse, despite there being no chance any State authority could be listening to their conversation. Old habits die hard, even in a war zone. 'Plus,' he continued, smiling back, 'the sun is out, life goes on.'

Somewhere near the monument, music began to play, an uplifting rhythm beaten out on an old metal oil drum accompanied by a fiddle of some kind. The vendor handed Gabriella their apples and grapes. 'Enjoy it,' he advised, 'who knows what tomorrow will bring.'

Gabriella thanked him and moved on, until she caught up with Eilidh and Danny. They stood watching Lucas and Jenny who had joined some other children dancing to the distant music. It felt good to see people enjoying life for a moment. The scene was unreal. The laughter, the golden leaves and the green grass, the faces whirling around. The perpetual grey pall that covered Central City was cast away. This was what citizens wished for: a simple, happy life without worry and oppression. Later they would return to their broken homes, with cold, damp beds and their hungry stomachs would remind them of the real world. For this moment, everyone was able to forget.

The gunshot ripped through the sky like a crack of thunder. Gabriella was the first to react, throwing herself to the ground. Another shot rang out. The music stopped, replaced by screaming close to them. Another shot. Panic raced through the crowded market and the wedding party. People began running in every direction.

Hassan was crouched next to Gabriella.

'A sniper,' he said, pointing towards the opposite side of the road, where a row of tall buildings stood. 'Somewhere over there.' As he spoke more gunfire came from the rooftop. Gabriella saw Danny dashing through the crowd. He made it to Lucas and Jenny and threw them to the ground, covering them with his body.

'It's random,' Gabriella shouted. The shooter was not targeting anyone in particular. The shots were sporadic and wild, each one picking a different area of the crowd. Gabriella counted a gap of ten seconds between each shot. 'Come on,' she shouted at Hassan. They stood and ran towards Danny, throwing themselves down just as the next shot exploded in the air.

'Where's Eilidh?' Gabriella shouted into Danny's ear.

'I lost her somewhere when the shooting started,' he called back.

'We have to get out of here.'

The shooter had the high ground. They didn't know if there were more than one. It could be a lone gunman with one rifle, or there could be a group with missile launchers ready to go. It may have been a rogue State group, a rebel faction or terrorists. It was because of the threat of terror attacks like this that the State had banned gatherings of so many people. Gabriella had been through enough war zones to know that looking for a rational answer would drive you insane. Lying on her front she scanned the area around them and saw Eilidh standing ten metres from them, wildly looking around for them.

'Over there,' she tapped Hassan's shoulder and he leapt up and went towards Eilidh. Before another shot could be fired he returned pulling her with him. They needed to find somewhere with more cover. People cowered behind upturned stalls, others dashed across the

road, seeking shelter in the shadows of the buildings.
'The monument,' Gabriella called to Danny and Hassan.

They waited for the next shot to be fired. That was their cue to sprint across the open area of parkland.

'Fast as you can,' Gabriella shouted. Lucas began to fall behind, Gabriella scooped his slight frame up and carried him. People were running in every direction, colliding with each other, sending bodies flying in the confusion. Danny dodged past a woman fleeing straight out into the open. As he watched, another shot boomed out. The woman collapsed in a heap.

The monument seemed to move further away, but finally they made it and crowded together against the solid brick shield. Lucas covered his ears with his hands, Eilidh drew him close to her. Gabriella ducked her head out from behind the monument to see what was going on. She saw him. He was on top of one of the ornate buildings, an old department store that had been converted into housing. He paced from side to side and threw something off the building. She couldn't be sure but it looked like a rifle. Then he continued pacing

'What's happening?' asked Danny urgently. 'Why isn't he firing?'

Gabriella kept watching. 'I see him. He's thinking about his next move. Keep back.' She motioned them to stay tight against the wall. The screaming had subsided. The area around the monument and the makeshift market had emptied apart from a few remaining huddles of people who had taken cover behind assorted shelters. An eerie quiet fell, an intake of breath as they waited for the gunman's next move. Muffled sobbing and cries of pain broke the silence. Gabriella saw the shooter pull an object from his belt. He moved a pace forward and stood on the edge of the rooftop, standing to attention. He pointed the object at his head.

'You could take him out from here,' Danny urged her. He was right, it was a relatively simple shot despite the upward trajectory, but there was no need.

'Too late.'

The gunman's head jolted and his body crumpled as it fell from the roof before the sound of the pistol shot reached them. There was a faint thud as the body hit the concrete pavement below.

'It's over.' Gabriella turned back to the others. 'He's gone.' They would never find out who the shooter was, or what had motivated him. He could have been a State Forces infantryman or a decorated general with a distinguished career. He could have been an Independent who feared the war was lost. He could have been a family man who had lost everything. He could have found out his partner had betrayed him with someone else. There was no point in trying to make sense out of it, there were always plenty of reasons why someone would take their own life in a war zone.

'Come on, we should head for the castle. We can eat on the way.'

The group left the sanctuary of the monument. As they walked round the side of it and back towards the street, Eilidh kept Lucas close to her, averting his eyes from the bloodshed around them.

On the steps of the monument, contrasted against the black-brown bricks, lay the bride. Her wedding dress and veil still billowed gently in the breeze, the red flowers lay across her chest, held in a loose grip by her limp hand. Beneath them a blotch of dark red blood spread across her chest, staining the pure white material. Her eyes were open, looking up to the blue sky, where the sun still shone. Her mouth was set in a frozen smile, a ghostly reminder of the brief moment of joy hidden among the brutal wasteland.

10

The Independents had occupied the castle early in the war. It was a symbolic victory, a claim of heritage and history, rather than holding any strategic value. Modern technology had long ago rendered the geography of a fortified cliff top redundant. The ramparts had been decorated with graffiti, Maxine Aubert's face appeared in various guises among different slogans proclaiming freedom, justice, liberty and revenge. Apart from the added artwork, the walls were relatively untouched by the war that had been fought in the streets below. The State Forces made little effort to reclaim the castle, they could have destroyed it at any moment with the aid of a drone strike. As the rebels had been pushed further east they had abandoned it, leaving the old fortress empty. Soon the walls that had survived for thousands of years found a new purpose providing shelter for citizens who had lost their homes. A community began to gather inside the ancient hallways, the rooms were filled with families and individuals seeking a place to stay. Once every room, cupboard and cell was occupied, a bustling campsite sprawled across the courtyard and spilled out onto the approaching esplanade and surrounding streets. The castle became a central focal point for the displaced community. For the first time since it had been built at the end of the Middle Ages, it reclaimed its place as a focal point for the people of the city.

The steep streets leading up to the castle were paved with original cobblestones. A fresh downfall had made them damp and slippery. Gabriella led them up the hill, picking their way through the various temporary shelters that lined the route and searching for a space they could settle into for the night. Not far from the drawbridge, they found a small corner that would allow them to put up one of their bivouacs. Neighbours viewed them with suspicion, but left them alone. New arrivals had to earn their place before being accepted into the community, but they were only planning to stay for one night. Hassan and Danny put the shelter up, while Gabriella set about building a small fire. As the light began to fade and the temperature dropped, similar orange flames began to appear dotted around the encampment. Jenny and Lucas collected donations of sticks from generous citizens, a child and a young woman with a missing limb elicited a charitable nature from some people.

Once they had set up their small camp, Lucas and Jenny lay down under the awning and were soon dozing, wrapped under a blanket. The others sat around the fire, keeping a watch on their surroundings while resting their tired limbs. The animated chatter of the campsite began to fade as another night under the stars began. Occasionally, a loud shout, a drunken call or an eruption of laughter broke the stillness. They had eaten the fruit on the walk to the castle, but they had nothing for an evening meal. They did have the last of their fresh water though, and some leaves to infuse it with some flavour. They boiled the mixture and then sat sipping from metal cups that warmed their cold fingers.

'They should be here by now,' Hassan said, as they pondered what had happened to the others.

'They'll be here,' Gabriella assured him. 'We'll take it in turns to keep watch through the night. Hassan and I will take the first shift.'

Eilidh and Danny shared a sheet, lying down next to each other, their bodies pressed together, the contact allowing them to share body warmth. Danny wrapped his arm over Eilidh as they lay on their sides. His face lay against her hair and he breathed in her scent. They had spent nights like this before in the small lean-to that had been Eilidh's home in the village. Their legs entwined, Eilidh took Danny's arm and drew it tighter around her. They drifted off into a light sleep in the comfort of each other's arms.

It was an hour later that Gabriella stood up. Hassan and she had been talking about their different experiences during the First Strike War. She had seen already that he was a capable and reliable soldier.

'I'm going to take a walk round the perimeter,' Gabriella announced.

'Sure,' Hassan replied. He watched her shadow disappear along the edge of the encampment. He stoked the fire and added the last few remaining pieces of scavenged wood. It would just about keep burning until daybreak, he thought. He could feel his eyes getting heavy. He had been travelling for weeks, first with Eilidh to the city, then with this group. The long nights of staying alert were catching up with him. His mind wandered again to the problem that lay ahead of him, as it had done during the last few days and nights. Once he had helped Eilidh and Lucas to safety, what was his next move? He could go back to the refugee camp, but there was nothing waiting for him there. He had no desire to be caught up in the war in the city. Though his sympathies lay with the Independents, he disagreed with the way they had gone about trying to achieve their aims. The last few days travelling through the wreckage of the landscape had only hardened his anti-war stance. He wondered if Gabriella and Danny would allow him to become part of their band. It would be another mouth to feed but he was sure they would see value in having another able-bodied, trained soldier on their team.

The cold steel on his neck woke him from his daydream in an instant. He froze. A familiar laugh eased the tension.

'You really should be more alert if you're on watch,' Kyle whispered.

Hassan felt the gun pull away and relaxed, raising his arms in mock surrender. 'You got me,' he smiled. Tyrell stood next to Kyle, smiling at his old friend.

Hassan saw the movement behind them.

Gabriella stepped from the shadows, her gun pointed at Kyle's head. 'And you should know better than to try and get one over on me.'

Kyle slumped and lowered his weapon. 'Has anyone ever managed to catch you out?' They holstered their weapons and embraced.

'One or two,' Gabriella answered him, 'but they didn't last long enough to tell anyone about it. Where are the others?'

'Lachlan and Verona will be here in a minute, we separated to try and find you. This place has grown since we last visited. Zeb has gone ahead as agreed. He hoped to be back with word in the morning.'

'Rodrigo?'

Kyle paused. 'He didn't make it.'

Gabriella said nothing as she processed the news. It was a war, people died. She had lost fellow soldiers many times before. Nothing changed, the war goes on, but this was different. They were a family, they looked out for each other.

'How?'

'A missile hit the building he was sheltering in. Zeb pulled him out but he was already dead.'

Kyle filled in the details of their journey through the city. The State soldiers had pursued them for a few city blocks, until they gave up and returned to their base. A small team continued to harry them for a while longer, but without much enthusiasm. Once they had evaded the last State troops and had rested, they continued until they found a suitable spot to bury Rodrigo's body. With their knives they dug a shallow grave and placed him in it, covering him with soil and bricks. 'Enough so the dogs won't be able to feed on him,' Kyle added. Then they had made their way east, switching course, doubling back and varying their route to ensure they were not being followed.

'Once we reached the old town, Zeb left to track down Xavier and arrange passage on a vessel.'

Verona and Lachlan eventually found them and it was agreed they should get some rest before daylight. The new arrivals unrolled thin mats and wedged themselves into a tight space next to the bivouac. Gabriella woke Danny with a light shove. They let Eilidh sleep. Hassan took Danny's place lying next to her. Gabriella was by the fire as Danny sat down.

'Aren't you getting some rest?' he asked.

'The others need it more. I can keep going for a while yet.'

She stoked the remains of the fire, keeping the dying embers from going out. 'You could go with them,' she said, without taking her eyes from the faltering flames.

'I'm not sure,' he replied simply. Had she heard his conversation with Lucas the night before, or Eilidh's invitation that had followed? 'I wouldn't like to leave you all.'

Gabriella let out a sigh. 'I was looking after myself long before you came along. We would manage just fine without you.'

'Thanks,' Danny smiled at her with mock wounded pride.

'Not that we wouldn't miss you, but the rest of them are better soldiers than you'll ever be. I'll be honest, you put us in more danger than you're worth.'

Danny punched her lightly on the shoulder, 'Steady on.'

'You should think about it. A new start in a new place, with something to hold on to. Not many will get the chance to walk away from this war with that sort of opportunity.'

'You're right.'

Gabriella knew Danny had loved Rosa and his children, and she knew he cared deeply for Eilidh and her son. Beyond that they rarely spoke about their personal lives, but she knew Danny sought companionship in a way that she did not. She was perfectly happy to be alone, she had been for a long time now. She had the memory of her parents, which was the only love she had ever experienced and all that she required. It helped in her line of work not to become attached to people.

'What about you? What will you do?' Danny asked.

Gabriella flicked the fire with her boot, sending embers up into the dark sky. 'I'll keep doing what we have been doing. Trying to make a difference, saving a few lives, helping those that need it. This is my city too, you know, even if I'm a child of immigrants.'

Danny found it easy to forget she had been born and raised in the city in the same way he had. She had led such a varied and adventurous life compared to his own, travelling the world with the State Forces and then again while evading them.

'And when it is over?'

Gabriella scratched her scarred skin, ruffling the patchy hair that covered some of it. 'I guess I'll move on to the next war. There's always one somewhere in the world, and there will always be someone willing to pay for the services I can offer.'

'You could join us in the European Union.'

'And settle into your happy family life?' The green eye glinted at him. 'No, thanks.'

She was right, Danny knew. It was impossible to imagine her in a domestic situation. She was a soldier and a killer, it was ingrained in her. Her experiences had led her to a place where living in peace without a mission to undertake was impossible for her. She needed something to fight, something to push against. She needed that purpose. He realised the difference between them again. He wanted nothing more than for the war to end, for normality to return, for law and order to once again rule. Gabriella was a warrior, she thrived on chaos, disorder and the fight against injustice.

Tyrell emerged from the gloom, yawning and stretching, and took a seat next to Gabriella. 'Can't sleep,' he said. 'I don't mind taking a turn.'

'Maybe I'll try and get a few hours rest after all,' said Gabriella, rising from her place. There were some shuffling sounds as she made herself as comfortable as possible, and then stillness.

Fifty kilometres to the west, the long day's march was

only now coming to an end for Phillips and his small team. Overgrown vegetation along the city walls had hindered their progress. Over the final few kilometres they had hacked their way through the undergrowth with machetes that Mitchell had brought for just such an eventuality. They arrived at the camp covered in sweat and exhausted. The engineer, Giesler, greeted them with a warm meal. After eating and changing into dry clothes, they gathered in the main tent, which was big enough to allow them all to stand around a makeshift table. They were joined by Jonas and Jarrod, who had accompanied Giesler on his recce of the dam. Candles held in lanterns hung from the tent roof, sending shadows dancing across their faces. Giesler started by describing what he had learned from their recce. The structural engineer was usually neat and tidy in appearance, even through the most trying times they had experienced in the war. Now, his short sandy hair was ruffled and he had grown stubble across his smooth chin. His canvas shirt and fatigues were stained with sweat and dirt. He looked like a field archaeologist, tramping through the jungle in search of some ancient civilisation or rare artefact.

'The positioning of the explosives needs to be accurate, but not so specific as to make it impossible. As we suspected, there are two fault lines we can blow, one at either side of the dam where extensions were added.' He used a small pointing stick to tap the plans that lay on the table. 'Here and here. We will plant four explosive devices which will guarantee a total collapse. Two should be placed under the water surface, near the base of the structure, and two at the top of the fault lines. Any one of these detonations should be enough to blow a fault line on its own, so by planting four devices we give ourselves certainty of success.' The engineer finished and looked around the gathered faces.

'The dam will collapse even if the underwater explosions don't work?' Kruger asked.

'For a sudden and total collapse we would prefer the underwater devices to succeed. If only the explosions at the top of the dam are successful then there will still be some damage resulting in flooding along the river as the water flow increases and, over time, the end result would be the same.'

'How do we rig explosions at the base of the dam?' Phillips had been thinking the same question that Mitchell asked. It seemed an impossible task to get down to the depths that Giesler was suggesting.

'With the ordnance that we have, it will require volunteers to work under water. Strong swimmers, if not experienced divers. There is a good possibility that those who take on this task will not survive.'

Giesler's statement hung in the air. A gust of wind picked up outside, blowing the tent and setting the lanterns swaying back and forth.

'I'll do it.' Mitchell volunteered, looking to his leader for acceptance. Phillips nodded his assent.

'I will take the other side,' Casper said.

'No,' Phillips cut him off. 'We will need your skill with a rifle.'

Giesler stepped in before Casper could argue his case further. 'Jonas can do it. He knows the sea around here better than any of us.'

'He can be trusted?' Phillips asked, not looking at the soldier as he asked the question. He was unwilling to hand over such a vital task to someone he did not know well. Jonas was Giesler's man, not his.

'We have discussed it. He is willing to make the sacrifice.'

'Very well,' said Phillips. At least he would not be sacrificing another of his own lieutenants. 'Jonas, Casper and myself will take the north side of the dam. Giesler will take Mitchell, Kruger and Jarrod to the south side.' Phillips figured he could keep an eye on Jonas that way, and he trusted Giesler and Mitchell with the other team. 'When can we proceed?'

'I know you want to act as soon as possible, but I would suggest holding off for a day until the following morning. There will be a high tide at that time and the forecast is for a storm front to be rolling in off the sea. Together they will create the optimal conditions for a torrent of water to breach the blown dam.'

Phillips considered the advice. He would rather get on with it and blow the dam immediately. That way they could be on their way north to join up with their retreating force and be in the HighLand City by the end of the following day. But they only had explosives for one attempt. It made sense to delay until they had the best chance of success. Phillips was not a patient man, but he was an experienced soldier. He had witnessed plenty of military disasters caused by over-eagerness and haste.

He tapped the table and straightened up. 'Very well. If you think it is for the best. We wait.'

Giesler stood to attention, saluted and left the tent, followed by Jonas and Jarrod, leaving Phillips with his own council.

'Casper and Kruger, set up guard posts on either side of the camp and take the first watch. Mitchell and I will relieve you in a few hours.' They left the tent, leaving Phillips with Mitchell.

Phillips reached for his backpack and pulled out a plastic bottle.

'Drink?' he offered the bottle to Mitchell, who took it from him. Mitchell took a slug of the liquid and coughed as the strong home-brewed alcohol hit his throat. In war time the law prohibiting the intake of alcohol was still largely observed, most were so conditioned to not drink it that the slightest quantity would result in nausea and light-headedness. Phillips had acquired a taste for the finer pure malts that had been widespread in the Civil American States during his time there. This was not the same refined stuff, but it was all he had. Mitchell handed him the bottle back. Phillips tipped it towards his faithful lieutenant and took a long drink from it. He pulled a box over and sat on it, indicating Mitchell do the same. Neither man spoke, as they passed the bottle back and forth between them.

11

Edward 'Teddy' Davies was not a traditionalist, nor was he a technophile who entrusted everything to modern devices. He liked to strike a balance between signal intelligence and human intelligence gathering. The State Security Forces had changed a lot since he had joined as a young man. He had a fondness for the tales of field agents risking their lives to deliver information that was vital in changing the course of history. That childhood intrigue had steered him towards a career with the service. The technophiles began taking over the place shortly after his career began. The rush to embrace the latest and best drones, analysers, SmartTech and robotics had been done at the cost of neglecting the old established skills that had served them so well. Davies believed there was always a place for deceit and double crossing. As Head of various desks moving up through the ranks of the service, he always made sure he put in place a solid network of agents in the field to confirm or deny what the tech intel was telling them. It was human intelligence that had given him early warnings about the Axis Powers advancing through the forest in Laramidia. It was his double agent, turned and placed in the top echelons of the Union of Soviet State Republics government, who had warned about the threat of their newly-created submarine fleet. If he had to choose between robotic intelligence and human, he would back his agents every time.

When he had reached the position of Head of State Security Forces, he insisted that all departments under his control were structured in the image of his own preferences. Some of the younger generation demurred. It was hard work to train and place an agent in the field, it took time, sometimes years. The rewards from such a time-consuming venture might be limited and may not bear any fruit at all. Davies understood the temptation to take the shortcut and send in some high-tech mics and cameras or to rely on satellite and drone surveillance, but they could never give you the full picture.

Which was why Teddy Davies was feeling particularly pleased with himself this morning. His faith in human intelligence, his plan to place an agent inside the rebel army at the very beginning of the war, had finally borne fruit. He ran the agent himself without the knowledge of the Head of the Central City desk. It had been Davies alone who had taken responsibility for his agent in the field. In doing so he had broken his own rules, but it was a risk worth taking. Through all the fighting his agent had remained concealed. He had little contact with them, and up until now there had been little valuable intelligence. He worried that his agent may have been turned. Had they developed sympathies for the Independents' struggle? Months at a time went by without any word. Davies checked everything that came across his desk from the Central City department, searching for a clue that would tell him his agent was still functioning. Through disparate scraps of information he managed to trace a vague history for his agent. There was a piecemeal story of battles they had been involved in and survived, and a gradual circling of the leader, Phillips, and his inner circle. Persistence had seemingly paid off and they had finally been admitted into the core of Phillips's trusted and closest allies. Patience had been the key, now his day had arrived.

Davies was slowing down as he entered his seventh decade, but he still had plenty of life in him. The latest health procedures and pills kept his spreading waistline at bay, his head of hair had been surgically enhanced to quell the spreading bald patch and advancing grey. He had given up trying to hold back the wrinkles that now adorned his strained face. For a life built on a career where worrying was the default position, he felt he had held up well. The moment he had taken the call on the secure line in his office that morning the years had fallen away. With a spritely gait he had walked out of the white office block and jumped into the car to take him to the Palace. Now he sat waiting to be admitted to see the Chancellor, holding the TouchScreen with his hastily typed notes and congratulating himself.

The door to the Chancellor's office swung open. Alice Anderson, the Chancellor's Press Secretary for her entire forty-plus term in office, exited. Davies gave her a warm smile which she did not return. He was used to being greeted with scepticism by government officials, it came with the job.

He rose from his chair and walked into the Chancellor's office, commonly called the Dome. It was situated on the top floor of the Palace, under the domed glass ceiling that allowed natural light to flood into the airy, bright space. The modern dome had been added to the original ornamental neoclassical building. It had housed the Royal family when the State still had a monarchy. When the Central Alliance Party swept in a Republic, they commandeered the royal home as a seat of power for the newly created position of Chancellor. The leader of the State and the Party lived in the upper floors of the building, while the lower floors housed their staff and State department heads. It had been mooted at one time that the State Security Forces should also relocate inside The Palace, but those in charge had swiftly ruled that out. They liked to have their own space and they liked to keep their distance.

Davies was a regular visitor to the Dome, but he still felt intimidated by the person who sat behind the large white desk at the far end of the room. Lucinda Románes did not look up when he entered, she continued to read something on the TouchScreen in front of her. Her long, dark hair was tied back in a pony-tail that fell across her shoulder. She wore a functional black suit jacket over a familiar white blouse, the outfit she always dressed in while working. She sensed him enter the room and waved a hand at the seat opposite her. Davies crossed the carpeted floor and sat as instructed. Was the chair on this side of the desk lower than the one opposite? Once he had been made to wait for another minute in silence, the Chancellor finished reading, swiped her TouchScreen off and finally faced her Head of State Security.

'I trust everything is progressing as expected?'

She was referring to the State's strategic withdrawal from the First Strike War. While the announcement had been made in the last couple of days, they had been planning it for the last two months. The main bulk of the work had landed on Field Marshall Harris Ellroy, who was in charge of moving large numbers of military troops, technology and materiel. The planning had been painstaking and thorough. It had involved a massive amount of organisation, and detailed negotiations with their Allies. So far it appeared to be proceeding as planned. The impact on Davies and the Security Forces was subtler and required a less noticeable response. Agents in various countries around the world had been extracted. Field agents, especially those acting as doubles in foreign lands, were nervous creatures at the best of times. It had been a stressful few weeks for many of his Heads of Departments and agent runners. Some would necessarily have to be sacrificed to appease both allies and enemies. Some would be tactfully left in place should any future intelligence gathering be needed. Some who were brought back would be given a pat on the back and a comfortable pension to see out their days quietly in the Capital. Others would be redeployed once the Service had decided where it may need to concentrate its assets next.

'Oh, quite well, no problems to report,' Davies replied. With everyone else his persona was of a controlled, fearsome operator. When facing the Chancellor, he felt like a schoolboy summoned by the headmistress.

'Well?'

'This has to do with the other war,' he pulled himself together. 'Central City.'

'Can't we concentrate on getting out of one war before ending the other one?'

'Absolutely, Chancellor, of course. Only, we've had some intelligence that may help us in that regard. Good news, in fact. Positive stuff.'

'Get on with it, Teddy.' Románes was more interested now, she liked to hear good news.

'Yes, Chancellor, two bits of news actually. The first is that the rebels are abandoning Central City and taking their remaining forces north to the HighLand City.'

'So we've won then,' the Chancellor's face didn't break into a smile, the piercing eyes looked straight at him.

Teddy felt the collar of his shirt grow tighter. 'Ellroy is assembling his troops for a final push through to the east. Once the city is clear of rebels we can concentrate on taking out their northern stronghold.'

'This is confirmed intelligence?'

'Verified by two sources. Human intelligence, a source close to the inner circle of Phillips and his command.' He paused for effect, hoping the Chancellor would give some sign of appreciation that he had an agent close to the leader of the Independents. Románes's face betrayed no such emotion.

Davies continued, 'And substantiated by satellite surveillance which shows large enemy troop movement out of the city.' He tapped his TouchScreen and sent the satellite images to Románes, whose own device pinged as she received them. The Chancellor glanced at the images.

'They have abandoned the city,' she agreed and smiled. 'We will be finished with both wars a lot quicker than expected.'

Davies remained seated and cleared his throat.

Románes looked back at him. 'Something else?'

'There is one other bit of intelligence, from the same agent close to Phillips.'

'It's never simple with your department, is it?' Románes sighed. 'Spit it out, Teddy.'

'It seems Phillips is reluctant to leave the city for the State to control. They are planning to destroy a large portion of it.'

'Destroy it? They don't have the weapons capable of large scale destruction.'

Davies tapped his TouchScreen again and another message arrived on the Chancellor's screen. She opened up the files and browsed through them.

'The dam?'

'They're going to blow it and flood the city.'

'They'll kill millions.'

'Our conservative estimate is half a million. Much of the west has been abandoned by the citizens already, but many remain. It's difficult to put an exact figure on it. There are also some key tactical targets that would be affected: military bases, the hospital, airstrips. It would hinder our advance north, reducing the land border between the south and north to only a few kilometres along the eastern coast. It would effectively cut the State in two.'

'Then it must be stopped.'

'It should be fairly straightforward,' Davies nodded. 'They have sent only a small unit to carry out the attack. We know roughly where they are camped. We can send search drones and, once located, an airstrike will terminate them. There is one added bonus.'

'Which is?'

'Phillips himself is leading the attack.'

'He will be there?'

Davies nodded, 'Together with other leading officers of the Independents.'

Románes brought her hands together, interlocking her fingers and placing her chin on top of them. She thought for a moment then stood and walked over to the glass window behind her desk, with the panoramic view of the Capital beyond. She stared at the urban sprawl, the white cubes interspersed with taller glass and steel constructions. Her entire term in office, almost half a century, had been dominated by war. The First Strike

War had overshadowed everything she had wanted to achieve. Despite that, she had done much that she had pledged she would - there was no poverty, no homelessness and no illness. People lived longer and people were happier. No one worked if they didn't want to and everyone had a basic income. The war had, in part, paid for that. It was a necessary evil, that was what the citizens would never understand. She had sheltered them through the climate emergency and only recently had the energy crisis taken a grip of the country. The blackouts were no longer confined to the HighLands and Central City. The MidLands were suffering too and Capital City had started to feel the effects. Rolling blackouts and energy rationing were now the norm. They had solutions in the pipeline, but they needed time to develop the technology, time that was running out.

Davies cleared his throat, 'I have your go ahead to take out the rebel unit?'

'Uh-huh,' Románes said absent-mindedly.

'With Phillips gone the Independents would fall into disarray. It could all be over in days.'

Románes was silent for a moment longer, then turned and stared at her intelligence chief. Davies had seen this look on the Chancellor's face before. She had had an idea and he was sure he wasn't going to like it.

'Unless,' she moved back to her seat behind the table.

'Unless?'

'How long would it take to withdraw our men and materiel from the danger zone that would be flooded?'

'Only a day, perhaps a little more.'

'How much of Central City is worth saving?'

'Worth saving?' Davies began to feel uncomfortable. 'Well, a lot of the superstructure has been destroyed in the fighting. Most of the buildings have been reduced to rubble, but with effort and planning it can all be salvaged and resurrected. It will of course cost money and energy.'

'And take time,' Románes finished the assessment. The steel grey eyes stared at him, locking him into her gaze. 'What if we were to ignore this human intelligence?'

'Ignore it?'

'What if we never heard about a plan to blow the dam?'

'You mean, we do nothing?'

'Well, how could do anything if we had had no warning of what was about to occur.'

'But...' Davies stuttered, 'the citizens.'

Románes sighed and leaned over the desk towards him. 'The citizens who harboured these rebels? Most of them sympathise with the Independents, with their pictures of Maxine Aubert and their conspiracy theories about the war. Why should we show them mercy? We need to think of the wider context. We need to consider what is good for the State.'

'I'm not sure I follow.' Davies had a sinking feeling in his gut.

'We have an energy crisis and we have a civil war. We are over-populated and struggle to feed and house all our citizens. One solution, an unthinkable one for many, would be to drastically reduce the population and the energy requirements of the State.' She looked at him to make sure he was following.

'Yes,' he agreed nervously.

'Think of the benefits of having one less megalopolis to power and a million less mouths to feed. The need for extensive rebuilding which would drain our precious resources would disappear. These resources could be diverted to those who really deserve them. And all of it could be blamed on a radical rebellion that wilfully murdered millions of State citizens. And we knew nothing about it of course, because if we had done…'

'…we would have stopped it from happening.' Davies finished off the Chancellor's thought. He could see the genius in her plan.

'Exactly,' she smiled at him. 'The war will be over quickly and anyone with sympathies for the Independents would turn against them for committing such a heinous act.'

'They would still have an army, and Phillips would still be alive.'

'He would be forced to flee the country, or we would hunt him down. They may still hold the HighLands for a short time, but the MidLands and the Capital would be safe.'

Davies stared at her. It made sense, he had to admit it, but at what cost? He felt uneasy about the innocent lives that would be lost, the very lives he was sworn to protect. He was not naïve. He had lived through the First Strike War and had been involved in operations where civilian casualties had been inevitable. But they had never been their own citizens.

'That is your final decision?'

She nodded, 'Give Ellroy the order to begin evacuating our forces immediately.' Románes leaned forward and returned to her TouchScreen. Davies had been dismissed. He stood and walked back to the door. As it swung open, the Chancellor called to him, without looking up.

'Oh, and Teddy.'

'Yes?'

'Make sure the intelligence you received about this disappears. No traces.'

'Yes, Chancellor.'

12

Fires sparked into life and water was boiled for cooking, cleaning and drinking. Makeshift shelters were folded away. Permanent residents, housed in sturdier accommodation, watched on with wary eyes as the camp came to life. This morning the normal routine had an added sense of excitement.

Rumours that the Independents were retreating began circulating round the camp as the morning sun had peaked over the horizon. General chatter, spread across each huddled group around the warm fires, highlighted differing reactions to this news. How each citizen reacted depended on their view of the war. Some greeted the news with joy. The fighting was over, they could return home and the rebuilding could begin. An equal amount of people stood with arms folded and heads downcast. The rebellion was over, the battle for Central City was lost. The soldiers would return in vast numbers and State rule would once again be enforced. There was talk of severe punishment against those citizens who had backed the Independents. Curfews would be reinstated and social gatherings forbidden. How long before the Party decided to begin rebuilding? How long before the State forgave a city that had rebelled? There could be months or even years of suffering ahead.

For Danny and Gabriella the news changed nothing. Their objective was still the same. Zeb had returned in the early hours of the morning. He had made contact with Xavier's people at the coast. A boat would be arriving today and would set sail for the European Union before sundown. Business was brisk at the moment. Demand for passage out of the State was insatiable, and Xavier was cashing in while the going was good, but he would always endeavour to accommodate an old acquaintance, especially if they crossed his palm with currency. He would ask no questions – rebel or State, soldier or citizen – he did not distinguish. Zeb had informed Xavier's people that they would arrive at the coast by midday. In return he was given the co-ordinates of a harbour where the boat would land. Money would be exchanged when the passengers were safely aboard the vessel. The price was negotiable. Eilidh had a paltry figure she had brought with her, collected in old coins and trinkets from those in her village in the wilderness. Danny and Gabriella had a small sum to add to that, stored in a private electronic account. They would be relying on Xavier's generous nature to let that be enough. All arrangements were sealed with an old-fashioned handshake. Xavier's word was his reputation, he would not betray them.

A midday rendezvous meant they needed to make an early departure from the camp and travel through the morning to get to the coast in good time. Everyone was awake by seven o'clock. Eilidh and Kyle scrambled together what food they could to make a breakfast meal. Jenny tended to Lucas's medicine. He had been stable during the night, although his blood glucose levels were behaving erratically after two days of upheaval. The others packed away their camp, rolling up sleeping bags and blankets. The mood among them was upbeat as they ate. Only Zeb was not his usual talkative self. The loss of

Rodrigo had hit him the hardest. They had been together before the start of the war, joining the rebellion and fighting side-by-side against the State. When they had become disillusioned with Phillips and his leadership they had fled the Independents together. Now Rodrigo was gone. All of the group had suffered loss thanks to the war, but this was the first time that one of their unit had died. The others knew trying to make Zeb talk about it was not what he wanted. They left him to his own thoughts, he would talk to them when he was ready.

The others discussed the retreat of the Independents and what it would mean for the war. Gabriella knew Phillips well enough to know that he could not walk away without putting up some sort of resistance. If the rebels were withdrawing, it was because Phillips recognised it was the best tactical option.

'They'll head to the HighLand City,' she predicted, 'Make a new stronghold there and regroup.'

'Will the State pursue them?' Verona asked.

'Once they have secured Central City, but they will be in no rush. They will tell the citizens the war is won before the remains of the rebellion are crushed. Win the propaganda war first, the rest will follow in good time.'

'What do we do now?'

'There will still be plenty who will need help in the city. The State will want recriminations. These are still dangerous times.'

Danny looked at Eilidh, 'You still want to go?'

'War or no war, life for Lucas with a cure is worth leaving this place for.'

They set off at half past seven, picking their way through the packed refugee camp in the shadow of the castle. Once they had cleared the transitory boundary of the camp, they began to make good time.

The first hour was spent walking through city streets, between the remains of white cubes that still housed many citizens. Almost all of the houses were damaged, several had large gaps in their walls where bombs or missiles had blown holes in the structure. These gaps provided windows into the lives of those who still occupied what was left of their ruined homes. Bedrooms, living rooms and bathrooms were exposed, revealing snapshots of life in the war-strewn streets: a mother hummed a tune while brushing the hair of her daughter in front of an old-fashioned mirror; an elderly man sat staring out into the street, shouting obscenities at anyone who came within his view; another man hammered a piece of wood over the doorway of his home, creating a makeshift door; a bed was filled with a mother, father and three children huddled together under a thin sheet, oblivious to the world passing by outside.

The rain of the last couple of days had relented for now and the wind had died away to a light breeze, while patches of blue sky emerged overhead. The little warmth that the sun gave off provided pleasant conditions for their walk. Zeb led the way, using an old map to trace their progress and keep them on track to meet the co-ordinates specified by Xavier's contact. They gradually turned to the north-east, leaving the centre of the old town behind them. As the land rose they crossed a sloping hill and at the peak, they stopped and took in the view.

In the distance was an expanse of blue water. Unlike the river estuary in the west, filled with brown mud-stained water, the sea on this side of the island was like an oasis of blue calm. Sunlight glinted off the crests of waves that stretched on to the horizon. The land sloping down towards the water was green pasture. Somewhere further back they had crossed the city walls without realising it and entered the ring of arable land which had helped feed the city before the war. It was now an overgrown meadow.

Gabriella pulled out her rifle and aimed towards the water, peering through her scope. She swept backwards and forwards across the horizon, methodically covering the vast expanse. She paused and refocused. 'They're coming,' she said.

Danny followed the direction her rifle pointed towards. Bobbing up and down on the water, leaving a small wake behind it, he saw the small black dot trawling through the waves, heading for the coast.

The harbour was old and disused with crumbling walls of thick stone that were slowly eroding under the constant barrage of rolling waves. A long forgotten mole stretched out into the sea, creating a barrier that sheltered a stony beach. Anchored by ropes to the leeward side of the mole was a boat. It was not a big vessel, nor did it look particularly sturdy as it rocked from side to side on the incoming tide. It was a fishing trawler from a bygone era and still carried the rigging of its past life. A wheelhouse sat in the middle of the deck and to the rear were two large mechanical winches. Behind the winches were two large net-drums, around which tattered blue-green nets were tangled with dirty orange floats attached. The black hull was mottled with patches of brown rust. The deck and wheelhouse had once been white, but the paint had flaked off to reveal dark rotted timber underneath. A large beam was stowed on one side, rusted from exposure to the sea air. Hanging along each side, grimy green fenders prevented the hull from hitting the side of the mole.

The crew of the fishing boat were on the beach, attempting to organise a group of citizens. Several people were bartering with the crew, trying to secure a place onboard the vessel before it departed. The crew members called for calm among the clamouring group, assuring them that there was room for everyone. Children ran up and down, stopping to throw stones into the sea. Some removed their shoes and paddled into the water, delighting in the cold waves as they lapped against them. For many who had lived their entire lives behind the city walls, this was their first sight of the sea. While they made new friends with each other, their parents begged to be allowed onto the rusted boat that could take them to a new life. Each had their reasons for turning their back on the city, for finally wishing to be free from the war.

Lucas was unable to contain his excitement and dashed off towards the water, beckoning Jenny and Eilidh to follow him. The others found a spot on the edge of the beach where bigger boulders provided seating and dropped their heavy backpacks. A loud whistle and shout drew their attention across the water. Out of the trawler a large black man emerged, jumping onto the mole and making his way towards them, waving his arms in greeting.

'Stay alert,' Gabriella told the others. She knew better than to trust a pirate, even one they had done business with before.

Zeb led Danny and Gabriella across the beach to meet the oncoming man. The ship's crew watched the meeting with caution, weapons held in readiness. Xavier strode towards them, his dark forehead glistening in the sun. His hair was styled in tight braids, creating stripes along his head and tied in a knot at the back. He wore a tight t-shirt covered in dirt and grease, combat shorts and heavy black boots. He opened his arms wide and a broad grin burst across his ebullient face.

'Wey, wey. Look wha' we got 'ere, man.'

'Xavier,' Zeb opened his arms in return and the two giant men embraced.

'Issa good ta see yon all.' Xavier gave Danny a forceful embrace. Gabriella he left until last. She didn't respond when his broad arms encircled her. 'Ah see yon haven't chilled since wa last meet,' he smiled at her. His accent was a curious mix, much like his heritage. Wrapped up in his bulky frame there was lineage from the African Union and the European Union. The language of the State was not his birth tongue and he had learned to speak his own version of it.

'Wa done non bisiness fo' thy last year or two.'

'We haven't needed your services, don't take it personally,' said Gabriella.

'Don' ya worry. Ah know ah give thy best service 'ere' Xavier beat his chest with a clenched hand. 'Imagin' ma delight won ah arreve 'ere an' they toll ma tha' ma ol' bud Zeb wa' asked fo' ma. It gon' fill ma heart wi' joy.' He punched Zeb on the shoulder. 'An' then ah asked ma'sell, wha' could ol' Zeb be wantin'?' He looked at Gabriella. He knew from previous encounters that she was the one in charge.

'We have cargo that needs to get to the European Union safely.'

'Wey, tha' may cost ya?'

'We've got some money. You know we can be trusted.'

'Ya certain' can,' he gave a deep, enthusiastic laugh. 'An' wha' cargo you wanting ta ship?'

'Four bodies,' Danny said. He pointed towards Lucas, Jenny and Eilidh at the water's edge. 'The boy, his mother and the girl.'

'An' who else?'

'Me.' Danny said.

Xavier raised the eyebrows on his expressive face and whistled. 'Vey wey. Ah don' blame ya. Wa got two hour befo' thy tide turn. Ya all join ma fo' some food?'

The seafood was delicious, like nothing available in the city. Food supplements that supposedly replicated the taste of fresh fish were hopelessly inadequate by comparison. It reminded Danny of the fresh water fish he had survived on during his time in the wilderness, but Xavier's cook had the upper hand on him when it came to culinary skills. They sat on the boat's deck with the crew, enjoying the meal.

'Cod, halibut an' red snappa" Xavier told them when Kyle asked what fish they were eating.

'I've never tasted anything like it,' Verona spoke with a mouthful of food.

'Fresh caught on thy wey 'ere dis mornin" beamed the boat's captain, 'an special prepared ba ma main man 'ere.' He waved the ship's cook over. The old man, stooped and weather worn, hobbled over to them. 'Loris, tell tham wa' special secret ya use ta cook da fish so good.'

Loris smiled and winked deferentially at the group and said a few indecipherable words in his native tongue. Xavier roared with laughter and clapped his cook on the shoulder, sending him away again.

'He say he neva tell any 'is secret recipe.'

Danny watched Lucas tucking into mouthfuls of the mixed cubes of white meat. 'Be careful what you eat,' he cautioned the boy.

'He can eat as much fish as he wants,' Jenny explained. 'No carbohydrates.' No carbohydrates meant Lucas's blood glucose levels would not be affected significantly.

'Dey say thy Indie's dey leavin', runnin' away.' Xavier said after the meal had been finished. The crew drank from a bottle of spirits, while the others had water. Jenny, Lucas and Eilidh had gone back onto the beach to play, and Hassan and Tyrell had gone with them. The citizens on the beach who had secured a berth on the crossing now sat patiently on the rocks and bade farewell to friends and relatives they were leaving behind.

'We heard that,' answered Zeb. 'We didn't see any troops on this side of the city.'

'So, why ya gettin' those people away?'

'The boy is ill,' Danny answered. 'They say they have a cure in the European Union.'

'Sure, sure. Good life in thy Europa. Wise,' Xavier nodded his head. 'Thy rest of ya? Ya no' go wi' 'im? Ah always got room fo' friends if ya want to go.' He looked at the others. They had not known about Danny's decision until he had announced it on the beach.

Gabriella answered for them. 'Maybe one day soon. Perhaps the fighting will end now.'

'P'haps,' shrugged the big captain. 'Ah word o' advice tho', don' go back to west coast o' thy city.'

'Why not?' Danny asked.

'Ah hear dey State Forces are leavin'.'

'The State Forces are pulling out of the city?'

Xavier nodded, 'I hear thy Indie's is plannin' to flood thy city befo' they go, an' thy State, dey gonna let 'em.'

'Why would they let the Independents destroy the city they had just won back?'

'Ha, don' ask ma to try an' understand how ya crazy people think over 'ere. But ah hear it true enough fro' ya friend Quasimo.'

'Quasimo? You've seen him?' They still had a bone to pick with Quasimo for revealing the location of their forest camp.

'Nah, man, but he speak wi' Julius o'er there. Ya know Quasimo can't help but talk.' Xavier picked up a piece of fruit from a crate and began slicing pieces off with a small knife, slipping them into his wide mouth and chewing as he continued to explain. 'He say to Julius tha' a top, top general in the Indie's found 'im. Pay 'im good money to pass on information to the State Forces. Plan details an' everytving.'

'Can we talk to Julius?' Gabriella asked.

'Sure, sure. He down on thy rocks.'

Julius was the complete opposite of the ship's captain whom he served. He was small, slight and quiet, with a nervous smile and squint. He tried as hard as possible not to make eye contact with Danny and Gabriella as they spoke to him by the water. He had been enjoying a relaxing drink by himself, watching the seabirds circling in the clear autumn sky, when he had heard the crunching footsteps approaching along the pebbled beach. His pale brown skin, dark hair and deep brown eyes gave the appearance of a northern African Union citizen, but when he spoke in the State language his accent had the clipped pronunciation of someone who had been born and bred in the Capital City. He explained that he had been in the old town the previous day, acting on Xavier's behalf as his contact for those wishing to travel on the boat.

'I met Quasimo yesterday evening. I had stopped for food before making my way here. We knew each other before the war and he recognised me and invited me to share his food. He had found a family who wanted to leave the State and he knew I could help them. We made a deal and I told him the time and place to send this family to.

'He had been drinking a little too much. He was in a good mood because he had had a good day, made a lot of money. I asked him how he had done that. He went on about taking opportunities where you could find them in the war, finding the gaps between either side and making the most of them. Then he moved close, started whispering. He said he had received a message from someone high up in the Independents who was betraying them. He had information to pass on to the State Security Forces. It sounded like drunken nonsense to me, but he kept talking. He was desperate to share the information, like he had to get it off his chest. He said the Independents were retreating, but there was something else. The leaders of the Independents were planning to blow up the dam in the west and flood half the city so that the State couldn't get their hands on it.'

'Did he pass this information onto the State?'

'I asked him that. He laughed and said of course he had, but that's the strange thing. He told someone in the State military about the plot to blow up the dam late yesterday afternoon, and by this morning all the State has seemingly done is start pulling their own Forces out of the city. There's been no word of a unit heading to the dam, or an airstrike, or any sort of response.'

Julius wandered off, heading back to the ship to prepare for departure. He left Gabriella and Danny standing together, staring after him.

'They wouldn't sacrifice the whole city, would they?' wondered Danny.

Gabriella thought for a moment before replying. 'Think about it from their point of view. The west is a wasteland. The cost of rebuilding will run into trillions, the entire infrastructure needs built from scratch, every single building needs demolished and rebuilt. Then factor in the energy and food supplies required. What better way to wipe the slate clean than have most of the city disappear. Less people, less energy demand, less food demand. At the same time, the flood water cuts off the north and provides a barrier that leaves any rebellion stranded.'

'But there are still people there. Half a million, a million? They wouldn't kill all those citizens and sacrifice their own military bases and airstrips.'

'Wouldn't they?' Gabriella looked at him. 'You remember how the First Strike War started?'

'That was an accident, they didn't deliberately kill their own population.'

'But they massacred the citizens of other countries around the world in order to cover it up and create a war that suited their own ends. And our State went along with them. They lied to their own citizens.'

'You really think they would be capable of doing this?'

'You know what they are capable of. They would kill their own citizens' children to solve a population crisis. This time they don't have to lift a finger. They let the rebels do it for them. Then afterwards they can claim to have been ignorant of the plot and blame it all on

Phillips. Any lingering support for the rebels would wither away. The population crisis is over, the energy demands are permanently lowered and the land around the flood could still be used to harvest food, without an entire city to feed.'

'What about Phillips? Would he really do this?'

'He would do it if he believed it was the only strategic option left. I know him, he is a military man.'

They fell silent and stood facing the water, staring out of the harbour. The rain had held off all day, the sky remained clear and the sun was still providing a breath of autumn warmth in the air. The crew of the boat were making final preparations on deck. The passengers were boarding, being directed below.

'Someone has to stop him,' said Danny. 'If the State won't do anything, then someone else has to try.'

'I know what you're thinking, but you're leaving, remember? The rest of us can try and stop him.'

Eilidh, Lucas and Jenny were walking across the beach towards the large concrete steps that led up to the mole. Eilidh waved as she saw Danny staring over at them.

THE WANDERER

He was not used to spending so long in one place. He didn't like it. If he wasn't moving it gave his mind time to conjure up images he did not want to see. Confusion returned, the faces jumbled together and harassed him. He began to lose focus and found himself scratching at his head, pulling at his mangled hair, trying to get them out. The women merged into a demonic Valkyrie. There was Maxine, the dead journalist, the blood-spattered martyr, murdered, a pawn used to start a war. She would have her revenge on those who had torn her apart. There was the Chancellor, controlling all from her ivory tower in the south, toying with her puppets, for her pleasure. There was the assassin, the one who had taken everything from him, who had killed his father, who he could have killed, who could have killed him. She had left him on the cold floor. She had spared him in order to mock him, leaving him to live with his own cowardice, his own failure and weakness. She had created this weak tramp, set him on his aimless journey, wandering through hell while his mind slipped away from him. They were all in his head. He had to get them out, he had to silence them. He could not sleep while they haunted his nightmares. He needed sleep. His eyes would close and they would reappear. They would never leave him in peace.

Why did he stop here? There was a reason. He fought the images in his mind and found a moment of clarity. He saw the dam and heard the water. There was the small boat, a mirage on the grey-brown sea. That's why he had stopped here. The soldiers had gone, the land was empty. There was just him and the dogs and the birds. So why were they here? These men in the boat that reached the edge of the water. He tracked them. He stumbled and fell and got up again and in the woods he heard them and found them. And he saw their leader emerging from the forest. The agent. Once they had worked together. More faces flashed through his mind. Danny was there. He had tried to help Danny. And Phillips, the agent for whom he had betrayed the State. The man he had believed in.

The ghosts were tearing him apart. Why was Phillips here? Had he come to torture him? Was he a figment of his imagination? He dared not get too close. He saw their camp and fell back to a safer distance. He waited and watched and resisted the urge to keep moving. He tried to gather facts: Phillips led the rebels, Phillips should have an army with him, the State should be fighting him. Instead he was hiding in the wilderness. The fighting was in the east, the Independents were in the east. Something was not right.

The rain had stopped and the clouds had cleared. The next storm would roll in soon enough. He watched them. They stayed in their camp and didn't venture out. He couldn't get any closer. He saw them looking at the skies. He saw them watching the water. He saw them watching the dam. He saw weapons. He tried to think like his old self. Like a policeman. Collect the facts, put them together, build a hypothesis.

Nightfall darkness descended. He crawled down the tree and found shelter in the forest. When he slept the faces appeared again. They mixed together in his own private newsreel of the war, his war. The violence, the victims. Women, children and men. Bodies piled up, strewn across his streets. His world caved in.

His dream scared him. The nightmare woke him and he ran away. He was weak, a coward. He had been running all his life, scared of stronger men. His father. Phillips. He ran and the spirits that haunted his mind ran with him, mocking him, tormenting him, driving him into the shadows.

But he could not outrun the demons in his head. He could not outrun the demons in the forest. They saw him. They chased him. They caught him. He was bound up and blindfolded. They took him to their camp. The Phillips in his head merged with the Phillips standing in front of him. The noise became unbearable. He wanted to scream. He wanted to make it stop. He wanted it all to end.

13

'Found him shivering under some bushes. When I woke him, he started running, screaming like a madman. Had to tie him up just to get him to stop.'

Phillips looked at the wreck of a man huddled on the ground in front of him. Tangled patches of hair hung from an exposed scalp. Tattered clothes covered his body, stick-thin legs appeared from the end of ripped trousers. Phillips covered his nose and mouth as he bent down and removed the blindfold. Terrified eyes stared out from sunken sockets, the gaunt face was covered in dirt, contrasting with ghostly white skin. The cheekbones were hollows and blotches and areas of skin were covered with boils, with yellow pus leaking from open sores. He scrabbled around on the floor like a skittish animal, looking at his captors in a nervous panic.

'You should have shot him,' said Mitchell, 'put him out of his misery.'

Kruger had discovered the tramp while reconnoitring the perimeter of the camp. 'We need to make sure he's alone and hasn't betrayed us.'

Mitchell laughed, 'You think he's part of some crack State Force hit squad?' He flicked a boot out and kicked the emaciated man, who scrambled away from him.

'Enough,' said Phillips, 'Kruger is right. Better to make sure he is what he looks like and not anything more.'

He bent down and placed a hand on the man's shoulder and tried to hold the gaze of his wild eyes.

'Do you have a name?'

The tramp looked at him, eyes flicking from side to side before settling on Phillips's face. The mouth opened and Phillips recoiled. The teeth were almost all gone, those that remained were black and rotten, the gums were yellowed. The blotchy pink and black tongue was uneven and cancerous and had been bitten away in places. His breath was foul. He was trying to answer the question, but all that emerged was a thin, strangled whisper. The words were indecipherable, but the eyes pleaded in desperation.

'He can't even speak.' Mitchell said.

'Okay, take him a distance away and kill him.' Phillips issued the order without compunction, satisfied that this was no State agent in disguise. He was doing the wretched person a favour.

'Sir,' Kruger resisted.

'We don't have time for distractions, Kruger. Just get rid of him.'

As he admonished her, he looked at the infected face in front of him. The man had stilled on hearing his death sentence. He was staring at Phillips now. A vague hint of recognition triggered in the buried depth of Phillips's memory. He looked closer. He tried to picture those features in a different state – clean-shaven, fuller, the hair cropped short in a military style. Mitchell and Kruger watched. The silence grew awkward as their commander and the tramp continued to stare at one another.

It dawned on Phillips. 'Henrik?' he whispered. The man didn't move but his eyes welled up. 'What happened to you?'

Phillips stood, breaking the momentary bond. 'Take him down to the water. Clean him up. Find him some fresh clothes, shave him and cut his hair. When you've done that bring him back to me and bring food and a warm drink for him.'

'We're not his carers,' exploded Mitchell.

'Do it,' snapped Phillips, 'that's an order.'

Kruger leaned down and pulled the staggering vagabond to his feet.

It was an hour before they returned. Phillips sat in his tent and tried to get some rest. The day had passed achingly slowly. The weather was still and the water had calmed. Finally, out to the west over the sea, the sky was beginning to darken and threatening clouds were forming. As had been forecast, a storm was brewing. It would arrive in the early hours of the next morning at the same time as high tide.

With no men to command and no plans to be drawn up, Phillips was at a loss. He was so used to being occupied with the war: looking at maps and battle plans; gathering and interpreting intelligence; or devising and ordering responses. All that lay ahead was one final task. Everything else could wait until the completion of that task. It took him back to his early days in the State Army, when he was merely an infantryman whose fate lay in the hands of his superior officers. All he had to do was what they commanded him to do, all he had to think about was the next fight. He wasn't responsible for anything or anyone else. He missed the simplicity.

They had taken it in turns to watch the perimeter of the camp around the forest. Giesler had checked, re-checked and then checked his ordnance again, pouring over his calculations for the hundredth time since the recce of the dam. He would allow no mistakes. Phillips had wandered down to the water and back. Even though his body ached from the enforced march of the previous day, he longed to get on with the task. Everything was in place, they now just waited for nature to join them in readiness.

Despite his unease he was convinced their presence had gone undetected. There had been no sign of any State troops and the sky had been empty of any surveillance drones. They had not seen or heard any trace of other human life or technological equipment since they had set up camp. Any nagging doubts about his team were gone, he was convinced no one had betrayed his plan, even though Kruger thought it extreme. The analogue radio had been disabled, an extra precaution in case any of the team had a change of heart and wanted to warn the city or the State about the flood that was coming.

He thought about the wretched man who had been caught spying on them: Henrik James, the former Chief Commander of Central City's police force. They had known each other only briefly, brought together by the assassination of City Consul Donald Parkinson and the subsequent hunt for his killer. When Gabriella and he had returned to the State from their exile abroad, they had few friends in the city who would risk their own position in order to help them overthrow the Party. Henrik had been one of those few. Phillips knew Henrik could not abide the corruption that existed at the heart of the State. Henrik's father had been part of it when he too had been the Police Chief. When Phillips and Gabriella had been forced to flee and Danny Samson was surviving in the wilderness, Henrik had stayed and worked his way up to take his father's place, but he was a very different man from his father. Henrik wanted to protect the citizens of the State and free them from the tyranny of the Party. Phillips had used him for information about the city and the State and Henrik had done his best to inform Phillips about the State Forces and their plans. When the war came, Henrik was one of the first victims. The day Maxine Aubert was killed, the Chief Commander of the State City Police Force had disappeared. He had been presumed dead, a casualty of the ensuing chaos, though his body had never been found. Now Phillips knew why. Henrik James had managed to survive. For three years he must have been scavenging and sheltering in his beloved city, tortured as it was destroyed brick by brick in front of him. And now, the day before Phillips was set to deliver the final blow that would wipe Central City from the face of the earth, the ghost of Henrik James had reappeared.

He was sure Henrik could not be working for anyone, especially the State Forces, or he would have never have appeared in such a state of decay. So why had he arrived at this time? Was he some sort of avenging angel? A martyr come to beg for his city to be pardoned?

Footsteps approached and the tent door flapped open. Kruger pulled the skeletal figure in behind her and pushed him to the ground. Phillips dismissed his lieutenant and looked at the poor man sat before him. The long hair was gone, as was the dirt. His head was crudely shaven and his skin mottled and blotchy. He had been dressed in spare clothes, probably Kruger's t-shirt and trousers. Even though she was a slight woman, the t-shirt still hung from Henrik's bony frame like a tent and the trousers were held up by a belt pulled tight around his waist. On his feet he wore a pair of Kruger's boots.

Jarrod entered bringing in a bowl of stew and water in a canteen. He placed them in front of Henrik and left. Henrik did not touch them, but looked at Phillips.

'Eat,' Phillips said.

A frail hand warily grasped the fork which shook in his unsteady grip as he took a mouthful.

'Be careful. If you have been malnourished you may make yourself sick,' cautioned Phillips. Henrik took two more mouthfuls, then slurped water from the canteen and wiped his mouth with a skinny forearm. Phillips watched until the last drop of food and water had disappeared. Henrik held out the bowl towards Phillips with pleading eyes. 'In a minute,' Phillips answered his look.

It was hard to imagine that the wretched individual begging for more food had once been the commander of the Central City police. Henrik had risked everything to help Phillips at one time and his appearance now was in part due to the minor part he had played in helping the rebellion begin.

'What happened to you?' Phillips asked.

Henrik's eyes were rheumy either from tears welling up or his general poor condition. When he opened his mouth a hoarse whisper emerged. Each word was separated by a sharp inhalation of breath. 'I betrayed the State.'

'You could have come to me for help. You could have joined us.'

'Gabriella,' Henrik gasped.

'Gabriella and I went our separate ways.'

'Left me for dead.'

Phillips shook his head, 'If Gabriella Marino wants someone dead, they end up dead.'

'I killed your men.'

Phillips knew what Henrik was referring to. He had sent soldiers to protect a Central City police forensic officer, Cassandra Ford, another insider in the State Force he had used. When they had arrived a panicked Henrik James had just discovered her body. A State hit squad had got to her first and tortured and killed her. Henrik ran into the street and shot dead the rebels, thinking they were State Security officers. It was a survival instinct.

'That was unfortunate, but I would have forgiven you.'

Henrik sucked in a deep breath and managed a full unbroken sentence, 'I sold my soul.'

'That is your problem, Henrik. You have a soul. A war is no place for someone like you.'

Phillips took the empty bowl and stepped outside. He returned a moment later with another helping of stew and sat it in front of Henrik, who began devouring it. Phillips watched him in silence until he had scraped every last morsel from the bottom of the dish again.

'You've been hiding ever since the war started?'

Henrik slugged from the canteen of water. It spilled over his face and down his front. He nodded. 'Had to,' he rasped once he had swallowed. 'I was wanted for betrayal.'

'No one would help you?'

'I didn't ask anyone. I deserved to be punished.'

'Many would see you as a hero, Henrik. A hero of the rebellion. One of the few who stood up to the State and the corruption you saw.'

Henrik shook his head in disagreement.

There was nothing more Phillips could do for him. Guilt had eaten away at his mind as well as his body. There was no point in trying to recruit him to the cause.

He had nothing to offer. He was too weak to fight in both body and spirit.

'What were you doing near our camp,' Phillips asked.

'I saw your boat at the dam and followed it.'

'You weren't sent by anyone? No one knows you're here?'

Henrik shook his head.

'You haven't told anyone that you've seen us?'

'No, no one. I'm alone.'

Phillips believed him. Henrik had been a traitor to the State, they would have executed him if they had found him.

'You stumbled into something you shouldn't have. You will stay here, tied up and under guard. When the moment comes, I will release you. You will be free to go where you want, but you will be on your own. You don't follow us north. The city will be gone. It's up to you what you do. Understand?'

Henrik nodded.

'You helped us once, for that I owe you. For that reason I will let you live. After today I never want to see you again.'

Henrik nodded again. Phillips looked at him and then whistled sharply. Kruger appeared at the tent door. 'Tie him up securely. He doesn't pose a threat, but he is not to be allowed to leave under any circumstances. Once the mission is complete, he will be free to go.'

'You're letting him go?' Kruger looked surprised.

'He once did me a favour, the rebellion owes him.'

Kruger found this hard to believe, looking at the poor wretch on the floor in front of her.

'You understand my orders?' Phillips didn't like having to explain decisions to his soldiers.

'Yes, sir,' snapped Kruger. She picked up the frail man and marched him out of the tent.

Phillips followed them to the entrance and looked out. The shadows cast by the trees had grown longer as the sun moved west across the sky. The cloud bank that marked the approaching storm front had moved another few kilometres closer. He could do nothing but wait. The hour for action was drawing nearer.

14

They stood on the lee side of the harbour wall. A breeze had picked up, signalling a coming change in the weather.

Strands of Eilidh's sand-coloured hair flicked across her face. Danny swept them aside with his hand, feeling her smooth skin. He looked into her eyes. She had learned to draw up barriers and hide feelings. Each waited for the other to talk first. Eilidh knew why Danny had taken her aside. He would not be leaving with them after all. She had heard about the rebel's plan to flood the city and she knew he would stay and try to stop them. He had a duty to fulfil that he could not give up.

'When it is over I will try to find you,' Danny said, trying to sound convincing.

'Will it ever be over?' Eilidh replied.

'Hassan will travel with you, I have spoken to him,' said Danny, ignoring the question.

'We will manage on our own.'

'He has been in the European Union before. He knows some of the language and has a few contacts who can help. He will be more useful to you than I would be.'

'Very well. Once we have settled, he can return and bring word to you.' It was not Danny's usefulness that Eilidh was thinking about at that moment.

Danny sensed her disappointment in him, 'You do understand why I have to do this? He is going to murder thousands of innocent people.'

'We could start a new life together. We could be happy.'

She was right. When they had been together in their small village in the wilderness, Danny had found a peace he never imagined he would experience again after Rosa. They could find that happiness again, but Danny no longer trusted that such a feeling could last. Experience had taught him the reality of life. This State had conspired to steal it from him before and was doing so again. It would never allow him to be happy.

Eilidh read his thoughts, 'You don't owe this place anything.'

He couldn't disagree with her, but if the city was destroyed then what had the last three years been for? If the citizens were killed, then what had his previous life in the State police been for? He had sworn to protect this city and its people from harm. If he left now, it would be another failure. His conscience was telling him what he had to do. He had suffered when he had fled the city before, turning his back on the citizens. He could not face doing so again.

'It's my choice,' he said. Eilidh looked away. She had lost him, and there was nothing more to be said.

She brushed the hair away from her face herself this time, along with the moisture gathering around her eyes. 'You will have to tell Lucas.'

'I will come and find you,' Danny promised. He meant it, even if she did not believe it. She looked at him with cold defiance. He embraced her and kissed her lightly on the cheek. She let him, and returned the embrace, but not the kiss, then broke away from him.

'Thank you,' she said. He had saved her son three years ago and rescued him from the hospital. She would always be grateful.

Eilidh turned and walked away from him. Danny watched her until she reached the boat's gangway, where she stopped and turned. He waved. She nodded her head in return towards the beach where Lucas was still throwing stones in the water with Hassan and Tyrell. He understood. She stepped onto the deck and disappeared from his view.

Hassan and Tyrell embraced and said their farewells. Tyrell would head back to the wilderness. He would warn the village to expect more arrivals in the next few days as the rebels vacated the city and the State Forces returned. The numbers in the refugee camp would swell again. Danny and Lucas watched them. The atmosphere was solemn as Tyrell hefted his pack onto his back, gave a wave and set off on his lone journey. Hassan turned to Danny and the boy.

'Aren't you going back to the village too?' asked Lucas.

Hassan glanced at Danny, 'No. I'm going with you and your mother on the boat. I'm going to help you when we get to the European Union.' He shook Danny's hand, exchanging an unsaid oath between them. Danny had entrusted him to look after Eilidh and the boy in his absence, he knew Hassan would not let him down. Lucas watched the handshake and his eyes followed Hassan as he walked across the stones towards the boat.

'You're not coming with us, are you?' the boy asked.

Danny turned and bent down, bringing his face level with Lucas's. 'I have to stay.'

'To stop them flooding the city?'

'That's right.' They were still for a moment, looking at each other. Danny straightened up and they both turned towards the water. 'You understand why I have to do that?'

'I guess so.'

'A lot of people could die if we don't do anything.'

'Then I suppose you have to do it.'

'You be good for your mother. Help Hassan look after her and Jenny.'

'Will we ever see you again?'

'I'll come and find you. Just like your mother promised she would come and find you in the city.'

'She loves you, you know,' the boy said.

Lucas's innocent words punched Danny in the stomach.

'I wish it could be different.'

'Me too,' Lucas said.

Danny put his arm around the thin shoulders of the boy. 'It will be better for you now.'

'I hope so.'

'You better get going. Don't want them sailing off without you.'

Lucas turned and circled Danny's waist with his thin arms, his head buried into Danny's chest. Danny bent his head forward and placed his cheek on the soft, warm hair. Lucas broke away from him and ran along the beach. Jenny was waiting for him further along the shore. She waved at Danny as Lucas joined her. She embraced him and they walked away. Danny watched them go.

The boat set sail in the early evening. They watched her depart from the mole of the harbour, following her until she became a dot on the horizon. Gabriella was itching to get moving, but she understood that Danny needed time.

'You're sure about this?' Gabriella asked.

Danny nodded and turned away from the sea. 'Let's go,' he said. All that was left now was a clear mission and they had no time to delay.

Gabriella nodded and gave a sharp whistle. Verona, Kyle, Lachlan and Zeb gathered up their backpacks.

"Kyle out front, Lachlan at the rear.' Gabriella instructed. 'If we hustle through the night we should make it in time for high tide.' On cue, the wind whipped up from the sea. 'The weather is going to deteriorate, so let's make the most of it before the storm hits.'

And then they left, jogging off the beach and onto the cracked tarmac path. They would follow the old coastal road west for the first part of their journey. It would bring them back to the city walls eventually. No one spoke as they marched. All held their rifles in readiness, but there was no sign of any other soul along the deserted track. They followed the weak autumn sun as it set on the other side of the State. Soon the darkness closed in along with the storm clouds. As they reached the city walls the heavens opened and a deluge thundered down upon them.

They found a burnt-out building to shelter in around midnight. The rain battered them constantly and showed no sign of relenting. They had covered thirty kilometres, which left another twenty to cover before morning. It could be achieved, but it meant they would have to fight without any rest or food beyond the meagre rations they shared just now. The atmosphere was solemn, as it always was when they embarked on a mission. Lachlan stood sentry on the other side of the wall from them. Danny felt strangely at peace after the conflicted feelings of the last few days. It was like it had been many times before, like it had been a week ago when they had been preparing to blow up the arms factory. A lot had happened since then.

'Do you think we can do this?' Verona asked.

Gabriella shrugged, 'It will be a fight between two small teams, both well trained. We will have the element of surprise on our side. That puts the odds in our favour.'

'What if we are too late?'

'Then we'll drown,' said Gabriella bluntly.

'If Phillips dies then the rebellion is over,' said Kyle. He still wished to see the State defeated, even though he had deserted the Independents.

'Perhaps.' Gabriella hid her true feelings. She had been waiting for the opportunity to face Phillips since the start of the war. She saw his face in the car that sped past her, almost knocking her over as she leapt out of the way. She saw him in his military lieutenant-colonel uniform, ordering her to guide in the missiles. She knew better than to let her personal feelings cloud her judgement, it might compromise her decision-making, but this was personal. They had been a partnership, a unit, comrades in arms travelling around the globe together, hiding from the State. She had helped him return to Central City and plan his uprising. He had used her, hidden the truth from her and betrayed her. He had not changed from the officer who had ordered the death of the civilians in Idyllwild. She had been a fool to think a person could change. And now this diabolical plan. She wanted him dead.

'What happens after?' Verona said.

No one answered. Maybe the war would carry on as it had before, moving northwards. They could move with it. Someone else could carry on what Phillips had begun.

'Maybe we could all go with Danny to the European Union,' laughed Zeb, trying to lift the sombre tone.

'You'd all be welcome,' Danny smiled. The brief levity didn't last. None of them knew what the future held. They would go on fighting, caught between both sides of the war, because that was what they had become used to. It was all they had.

'Tomorrow will take care of itself.' Gabriella stood up, 'Tonight, we focus on the mission in hand. I am not letting that bastard murder thousands of innocent citizens. We stop him, no matter what it takes.'

'Hell, yeah,' Zeb rose too.

'We keep going through the city until we hit the river, then we'll work our way along it towards the dam. The storm will give us cover.'

The rest of them got up and they set off into the night once more, the rain whipping into their faces.

They pounded onwards, skirting round buildings, debris and vegetation. Danny managed to keep pace with the others, but he could feel his leg muscles tiring and the strain on his back and neck from his heavy pack. He lost his footing on several occasions while the others seemed to glide over the rough terrain. Unlike them, he was not cut out for physical exertion like this. Even Verona, who had never been in the army, outperformed him. She had youth on her side, while Danny, heading into the wrong side of middle-age, was the oldest of them. It was with his mind that Danny had forged a career in the police force, promoted to detective thanks to his ability to think analytically and outside the normal procedures. Those same mental abilities were the reason he had survived in the wilderness and through the war, not through his physical prowess.

The rain blinded him and he slipped and slid with every step. He hated the cold and the wet. Somehow, he managed to stay with them, though they did not make it easy for him. They would not slow down to accommodate him.

To spur himself on, he pictured Phillips and the dam exploding. He pictured citizens drowning before they even knew what had hit them. He pictured Rosa, tied up at the bottom of the river, her life draining away from her as water filled her lungs. He pictured Hanlen and Isla and their memory drove him on harder. He didn't believe in an afterlife or souls living beyond death. No one was looking down on him and urging him to sacrifice himself in order to save their city, but he still felt that he would be failing them if he let Phillips destroy it.

The only sounds, apart from the constant patter of rain, were made by stray dogs and foxes in the alleyways they passed. There were no soldiers to concern them and no checkpoints or look outs. Both the State and the rebels had abandoned the place they had been fighting over for so long. Inside the remains of the white cubes that had once made up the houses of the city, citizens huddled together, seeking warmth, shelter and an end to the war they had been forced to live through. Watchful eyes glinted in the night as the silent unit swiftly passed them.

They reached the west of the city as the first glimpse of daylight followed them from the east. Passing through familiar streets each had memories of their past life. They saw one or two people through smashed windows, and faces withdrawing as soon as they were spotted. The entire city was crouched in fear, as though aware of the imminent danger that threatened it. Following the sloping streets downwards, they met the river that cut through the megalopolis and regrouped. Gabriella gave the instructions.

'Two teams. Danny, Kyle and Lachlan: cross the river and approach from the south. Zeb, Verona and I will work our way along the north bank until we reach the dam. We don't know exactly what they are planning so use caution and cover each other. We'll use flashlights to communicate across the river. Remember, surprise is our main advantage. Use fire power only if necessary, silencers and knifes are preferable.'

Danny recognised the glint in Gabriella's eye. It was the look she had when they were about to undertake a dangerous mission. She thrived on it.

They split into their groups. Gabriella, Verona and Zeb disappeared out of sight heading along the river on the north side. Danny and Kyle rested while Lachlan scouted along the river bank. He returned in less than five minutes, shaking his head.

'No use, they're gone.'

He was referring to the two small craft they had used when they had destroyed the arms factory. It had been a long shot, but it was worth checking if the dinghies had remained anchored to the river's edge. There was no sign of them, by now they were probably drifting somewhere well beyond the coast.

'Okay, the bridge then.' Danny said and they set off back upstream for two hundred metres. There they found a solid abutment, matched by another on the far side of the river. The bridge that had once joined these two structures had disappeared. Its arch had once been a landmark of the city skyline. It was from this bridge that Danny's father, Franklin, had chosen his way out. It was from this bridge that Rosa, suffering from the loss of their children, had tied her feet together and jumped into the freezing water on a cold winter's night.

It was gone now, but the remains of its supports provided them with a chance to cross the river. Kyle stepped forward and aimed a piton gun at the abutment on the far side. Debris from the fallen arch littered the roadway that abruptly ended with a sheer drop into the water below. Kyle fired and the metal spike flew across the gap with a thin black cable attached to it. With a metal clang it landed on the other side and Kyle pulled on the cable. They heard the metal dragging across the tarmac until it fell into the water without finding an anchor point. Kyle patiently retrieved the entire length of cable and reloaded the gun. Then he fired again and repeated the process. This time when he pulled the cable the spike dragged along for a metre or so before there was a small thud as it caught on a boulder. Kyle pulled the cable tight and yanked it sharply a few times to test it was firmly anchored.

'Seems secure.'

The cable spanned a fifty metre gulf between the two sides of the bridge. It swayed around in the wind, which had started to pick up as the threatened storm finally arrived. The rain was still falling incessantly, and becoming heavier by the minute. Kyle tied his end of the cable to a damaged metal support.

'One at a time. Good luck,' Danny patted Lachlan's shoulder as he set off. Without pausing to look at the stirring waters beneath him, Lachlan ran forward and grasped the wavering cable with two hands. He walked forward, until the land beneath his feet fell away. Then he pulled his legs up and wrapped them around the cable so that he was hanging with his face upwards and his back pointing downwards to the water below. Efficiently he put one hand in front of the other and pulled himself along the cable. His extra weight caused the cable to sag and once he was at the midpoint of the gap the waves whipped up by the increasing wind were hitting his back. The cable was buffeted by the gale, sending Lachlan from side to side like he was on a swing. He was forced to stop until the cable had settled. Then he resumed and without further drama he reached the far side, swinging his feet down onto firm ground. Danny and Kyle waited while he located the piton and tied off the other end of the cable to a huge chunk of masonry, ensuring the cable was secure enough for them to follow him across.

'You next,' Danny waved Kyle forward. The younger man followed in the same style as Lachlan and passed over the void in less than two minutes. Kyle took over from Lachlan, who moved ahead, scouting out their route along the river. Kyle signalled to Danny to start crossing.

His years spent in the wilderness had brought back a decent level of fitness and leanness to Danny's body, but he knew this would be a test of his ability. He stepped out to the edge of the abutment, where the last piece of roadway overhung the brown, choppy water below. He took a breath, gripped the cable tightly with his gloved hands and pulled himself along, letting his feet dangle for a moment before pulling them up and wrapping his ankles together around the thin black rope.

He shuffled himself along, as fast as he could go without rocking the cable. The wind had increased and waves cast spray over him as he reached halfway. He had to stop as the cable swayed viciously and pull himself up so the waves did not engulf him. His arms ached and his hands burned from gripping so tightly. The combination of the falling rain and the sweeping waves soaked him. His gloves, with the grip pads on the surface, began to lose purchase on the slick cable. The distances he managed to cover before he had to stop and rest grew shorter. Each time he looked towards Kyle on the far bank he was sure it was getting further away from him instead of nearer. Gradually the slack on the rope began to lessen, and the final metres were in front of him.

Just as he began to relax, he heard Kyle screaming at him and waving frantically to the side. Danny looked the way he was pointing. At first he did not notice anything, then he realised that the river had become a wall of water that was rushing towards him. He had no choice but to pull himself tightly into the cable and hope that it would hold and he could resist the power of the wave. He closed his eyes, took a breath and waited for the impact.

The wave smashed into him with an awesome power. The cable was pulled away from his feet and he felt it go slack as it snapped. Danny was thrown to the side and the breath was knocked out of his chest. He gasped and gulped, swallowing a lungful of water in the process. The storm wave passed and Danny opened his eyes. He was holding the cable, which was still attached on one side of the river. Above the frothing water he made out Kyle calling him. He had scrambled down the bank beside the abutment and was stretching out a hand towards Danny. Kyle was pointing again as another huge wave hurtled towards Danny. The currents underneath the surface were pulling Danny down. He clung to the cable that tossed and turned in the flow of the river. Finally it swung round and brought him close to the bank. Kyle managed to grab onto his outstretched hand and hauled him out of the water. They staggered up the steep bank as fast as they could, the water lapping at their heels, threatening to pull them back into the fast-moving current.

Danny collapsed and coughed up water. He muttered his thanks to Kyle.

'Thought that wave was going to sweep you away,' Kyle smiled. 'Twice in a week, that river really doesn't like you.'

'It really doesn't, but it hasn't got me yet.' So much of Danny's life had been taken from him by the river, he did not want to become another victim in its waters. It seemed like fate was determined for him to join the others he had lost in the murky depths of the river.

Danny checked his weapons. The rifle that had been slung over his back was waterlogged and probably useless. He threw it aside. He would have to rely on his sidearm. Zeb had all the spare weapons in his holdall. He pulled the handgun out from its waterproof pocket. 'Come on.'

They climbed up the rest of the slope, back on to the roadway and began following the walkway along the edge of the old docklands. Lachlan was waiting for them a hundred metres ahead.

'What happened?' he asked, looking at Danny's sodden hair and clothes.

'Never mind. All clear?'

'No sign of anyone about.'

'Okay, you take the lead. Kyle bring up the rear. Let's go.' Gabriella and her team would already be a kilometre ahead of them. The sun had risen now, although its impact was minimal behind the blanket of low, dark clouds that the storm had swept across the sky. They knew that Phillips could blow the dam at any moment now, they had no time to lose. They set off into the storm, towards whatever fate lay in store for them.

15

'We go now,' Phillips said.

'High tide is in another hour away,' Giesler cautioned.

'An hour will make no difference, look at the height of those waves.'

Phillips didn't have the patience to hold back any longer. The calmness of the previous day had been replaced overnight by the building wind and rain clouds. Now the storm was in full cry. Further out to sea rumbles of thunder followed flashes of lightning. He wiped the lenses of the binoculars and stared out across the wild storm waters. Ten metre high waves rolled in with the tide and smashed into the solid edifice of the dam. If all went to plan, in an hour or less, those waves would carry on, passing over the remains of the concrete structure and continuing inland.

Something bothered him, an instinct that something wasn't right. It was the lack of any opposition. He had planned well and taken precautions, only those with him at that moment were aware of his idea. He was sure none of them would have betrayed him, even Kruger with her humane misgivings. He was sure Henrik was a lonely, broken individual rather than a spy. But he could not believe there had been no sign of a State response. There had been no surveillance drones or border patrols along the city walls. He kept expecting to raise his binoculars and see a battalion of State troops and heavy artillery lined up along the dam, or a row of SuperTanks wheeling their way along the highway. No fighter planes crossed the clouded sky and no battleships charged through the stormy waves towards them. It made Phillips uneasy. The war had been a continuous battle against the onslaught of the superior State Forces. Now that they had conceded the city and retreated, he found himself facing no opposition. It didn't feel right, but he had no choice except to continue as planned.

Each of the soldiers set about their tasks. Jonas and Mitchell, the two who would secure the bombs underwater at the base of the dam, stripped to their underwear and put on thick black neoprene diving suits. Casper packed the explosives, checking and re-checking the connections, timers and fuses. Kruger and Giesler loaded and distributed ammunition. Casper and Jarrod went down to the water and uncovered the two grey dinghies they had moored and camouflaged. By the time they returned, manoeuvring the vessels along the shoreline, the rest of the unit was lined up ready to embark.

They had been briefed exhaustively and each knew the role they had to perform. Nothing more needed to be said. Phillips and Jonas boarded the boat that Casper steered towards them. Giesler, Kruger and Mitchell joined Jarrod aboard the second craft. The two vessels split up, heading in different directions. Jarrod steered his boat away from the shore, out into the deep water and began to cut across the rolling waves. Their journey to the far side of the dam was the more dangerous and challenging, which was why the more experienced Jarrod piloted their craft. Meanwhile, Casper continued coasting along the calmer water's edge, heading down the bank towards the near side of the dam. The roar of the crashing waves and the constant drumming rain on the rubber boat made conversation impossible.

Phillips felt better now that they were in action. Nervous tension dissipated, overtaken by the adrenaline that coursed through his body. They were well-drilled and dedicated, nothing was going to stop them now. He kept a close eye on the other boat as it disappeared through the waves. It did not matter if the other boat failed. Giesler had assured them that even if only one of the explosives was discharged successfully, it should be enough to bring about the collapse of the dam. Having four points of attack was extra insurance. Phillips liked a plan that had built-in safeguards, it was why he had hardly ever failed. Casper brought them to the edge of the dam and secured the boat to the side of the wall with a rope. The disembarked and scaled the slope onto the highway that ran across the top of the dam.

Mitchell's stomach lurched as they were thrown from the crest of a wave into the trough that followed. The large orange air tank strapped to his back unbalanced him. Unlike the streamlined military equipment he had dived with in the past, this cylinder had been requisitioned from an abandoned lifeguard station by Giesler. It tipped him backwards, pulling him away from the grab line he clung to. Jarrod steered their small craft into the oncoming waves and down the other side, moving diagonally across the water towards the far side of the dam. The shoreline behind them was out of sight, as was the other craft carrying Phillips, Casper and Jonas.

Thoughts raced through Mitchell's head as the spray from the waves crashed into him. He had done all he could, but he cursed himself for not doing more. He should have risked more to put a stop to this madness. He had managed to get word out of the camp in the east before they had set off, when Phillips had first told them of his intentions, but it had been a rushed effort. The mercenary Quasimo was the only person he had been able to contact. Quasimo was like any other mercenary in a war zone, he was only interested in what he could gain for himself, he had no particular concern for one side or the other, and he held no sympathy for the citizens caught in the middle of the carnage. But if there was no city for him to operate in, then Quasimo would lose out just like the rest of the populace. That thought, and the chance to earn a substantial financial reward from the grateful State were all Mitchell had to convince Quasimo to take his warning to the State Forces. They had left the base camp before Mitchell had been able to confirm if Quasimo had done as he had promised, but there had been no sign of any State Forces in the time they had spent camped by the water. There had been no sign of surveillance, human or artificial, no drones had flown over. If Quasimo had delivered his warning then the State were doing a good job of remaining discreet about their response. His hopes faded. When they had stepped onto the boats and left their camp behind he knew no one was coming. He was on his own.

Again he cursed his lack of initiative. He should have sabotaged the explosives, but Casper did not let them out of his sight. He could have turned on Phillips, pulled a gun and killed him on the spot. The leader of the rebellion deserved to die. Ever since Teddy Davies had selected Mitchell for his mission, placing him within the ranks of the Independents at the start of the war, he had dreamt of taking out the rebel commander. He had worked his way up, insinuating himself into the inner circle of the rebel command. Once he had become a trusted officer he had found ample opportunities when he was alone with Phillips where he could have killed him. One shot at close range to the back of his skull and it would all have been over, but that was not what State Security wanted. They knew Phillips, he had been one of them. Replacing him with someone else would not have helped their cause. What they wanted was for Mitchell to continue to report back to them and remain undetected, poisoning the rebellion from within.

He felt like a coward as he clung to the side of the boat and the dam grew nearer. He should have killed Phillips at the camp. He had been alone with him, sharing his foul alcoholic drink. It had made Mitchell ill, sharing a toast with the man he despised. It had been the culmination of years spent hiding his true feelings, lying, saying things he knew the rebel soldiers liked to hear, but which he completely disagreed with. He was sure the strain would swamp him several times or reveal his true identity to the rebel leaders. The pressure to act against his true feelings tore him apart. He had to keep telling himself he was doing it for the greater good. He had fought against his fellow State soldiers who he longed to help by destroying the rebellion. He had killed his comrades in the State Forces and begged for forgiveness alone in the days and nights that followed each battle.

Killing Phillips would not have stopped the mission though. There was Casper, Kruger and Giesler, all of them dedicated fanatics to their cause. They would have killed Mitchell before he could get away and then they would have carried out Phillips's plan anyway, in honour of their fallen commander.

Mitchell had made one final effort before they had set off on the boats. When Phillips had ordered him to cut loose the poor wretch who had stumbled upon their camp, Mitchell had told him everything. The tramp, shivering and pale, had stared at him with hollow, uncomprehending eyes as Mitchell told him what they were about to do. He had grabbed him by the shoulders and shaken him, slapped him on the face, trying to make him understand. In the end he had disappeared into the forest and Mitchell had little hope that he would do anything.

Mitchell had no option left now. He would have to act on his own. He had to be ready for any opportunity that occurred.

Kruger grimaced at him from across the boat. While he had no compunction about killing Phillips or Casper, he would feel some guilt about Kruger. They had been together for much of the war, they had risen through the ranks of the Independents together, serving alongside each other in battle. They had kept an eye out for each other. He had thought about confessing his true identity to her several times, but he knew that Kruger was committed to the cause of the Independents. She disagreed with Phillips and she disliked the reckless disregard he showed for civilian lives, but she would follow her orders for the good of the cause. Mitchell knew if he had confided in her at any point, her loyalties would lie with the rebels.

A strong surge of water threw the boat forward. They flew over the final metres into the side of the dam, careering into the sheer concrete face. For a moment the dinghy teetered on one side, threatening to capsize. Giesler threw himself across the boat, adding his weight to the side that Kruger sat on and the craft righted itself.

'Grab the hook!' shouted Jarrod above the howling storm. Mitchell saw the piece of metal sticking out from the wall and thrust out a hand. He felt his body being pulled apart by the force of the swell as one hand held the hook and the other clung to the grab rope. Giesler appeared and wrapped a tie rope around the hook. Now anchored, the sea level was high enough to allow them to reach up and pull themselves from the moored boat onto the top of the dam wall. Waves continued to roll in, crashing over them.

'Come on,' cried Giesler. He led the way, pulling himself onto the ledge. Kruger followed, then Mitchell struggled up, weighed down by the cumbersome breathing apparatus on his back. Kruger had to help hoist him up and Jarrod pushed him from behind. Jarrod was the last out. As he stepped away the loose knot that Giesler had tied slipped from the hook and the boat was torn away from the wall, heading back out into the swell.

'Leave it, we don't need it anymore.' Giesler shouted. Mitchell checked his timer. Fifteen minutes until detonation.

They passed the wreckage of the arms factory on the opposite side of the river. Constant rain had dampened down the fires that had smouldered the last time they had seen it. Now it was just a pile of rubble, like any other part of the city that had been ravaged by the bombs and missiles of the war. Gabriella ordered her team to halt and rest for a moment. Verona and Zeb crouched beside her. She watched the far bank until she caught a fleeting glimpse of a black shadow dodging between the large boulders that the fallen towers had strewn across the ground. Now that the other team had caught up with them, she raised her hand and waved Verona on ahead. Zeb followed and Gabriella brought up the rear. They were heading straight into the driving wind and rain which checked their progress with constant gusts. It was not ideal. When they arrived at the dam the elements would not be in their favour.

Danny saw the dam loom up ahead of them. It was still intact. Whatever Phillips had planned, they hadn't done it yet. He had expected to see more activity, but there was no sign of anyone on this side of the wall. If someone wanted to blow the dam it would make sense that they would be working on the other side of it, using the force of the sea beyond to help them. Lachlan and Kyle were waiting for him at the foot of the wall where they were sheltering from the storm that had battered them along the river bank.

'Anything?' he asked as he joined them.

'Nothing,' Lachlan answered. 'No sign of anyone and no sign of any explosives down here.' The water at the foot of the dam was calmer. The huge metal sluice gates built into the structure were jammed closed, as they had been since the war had started. It was here that Rosa's body had been recovered, washed up along with the flotsam that had travelled down river. Danny had not seen her until she was in the morgue. It was here too that Tania Childe's body had surfaced, the assistant to the murdered Consul, who was killed for helping Danny with his investigation. No one had ever been caught or punished for her death. Danny knew the State was responsible, a hit squad had slit her throat and thrown her into the water. She had been found jamming one of the huge sluice gates open. Too many memories.

A flashlight signalled from the other bank. Gabriella and the others were opposite them, taking shelter against the foot of the dam just as they were.

Lachlan deciphered the code of flashes, and replied with his own flashlight. 'All clear on the other side too,' he translated for them. 'Proceed as agreed.' He finished tapping out their response. They had no option but to continue. They had no idea what they might be walking into at the top of the dam.

On either bank each team now moved along the foot of the dam until they met the sloping road that would take them to the top. Once they were out from under the cover of the dam, they would be in the open and exposed. There was no cover on the highway that ran up the dam and traversed it. If Phillips had planned his operation properly, he would have someone covering the approach on either side, with a clear shot at any oncoming enemy. They could be walking straight into a kill zone and they were relying on good fortune alone as they jumped from the river bank onto the cracked tarmac of the road and began darting up the slope.

He had to get the heavy oxygen tank off his back, he could hardly move with it weighing him down. Kruger and Giesler were kneeling in front of him readying the explosive packages. Jarrod was standing close by, scanning the area for any sign of the State Forces. Mitchell unbuckled the harness and slipped the canister down, placing it on the ground. No one had noticed. He moved quickly now, ripping open the pocket of the wetsuit that held his gun. Jarrod turned just as Mitchell brought the weapon up to point at him.

'What…?' The bullet hit Jarrod's chest. His eyes bulged as he staggered backwards, a look of confusion on his face. Before he had hit the ground, Mitchell turned to face Kruger and Giesler. The howling storm and crashing waves had helped to conceal the noise of the shot.

Giesler had turned round, but Kruger was still crouched over the explosives.

The engineer saw Jarrod land on the ground, then Mitchell bringing the gun round to point at him. He raised his hands in a gesture of surrender.

'What are you doing?' he shouted.

Mitchell pulled the trigger again. The bullet smashed through Giesler's forehead, spinning him round. He was dead before he hit the ground. Blood and brain matter sprayed outwards, hitting Kruger as she reacted, jumping up and drawing her own gun. Mitchell would have liked the chance to explain to her, but there was no time. Mitchell realised his mistake. He should have taken Kruger out first. She was a trained killer, the most dangerous of the three. Their eyes met briefly as they both faced one another. Both guns discharged at the same moment, both of them were hit at close range and fell backwards. Mitchell felt instant searing pain in his chest as the bullet tore through his wet suit and continued through skin, muscle and bone. Mitchell's hastily aimed shot hit Kruger in the shoulder, spinning her round as she fell.

The sound of the bullets echoed away through the storm and Mitchell felt the world go still. He lay on his back, the rain drumming on the ground around him. He felt the blood seeping out of his chest and gathering inside his wet suit. He moved a hand, searching for the wound. He found the hole in the right side of his chest, at the base of his ribcage. He took in a breath and wheezed and spluttered. The bullet had penetrated his lung. He tried to pull himself up, but the effort was too much. Above him the threatening grey mass of clouds swirled. A shape moved into his line of vision. He blinked away raindrops. The shape came into focus.

It was Kruger's face. She stood over him, one arm hanging limply by her side, the other pointing her gun at his face. She kneeled over him.

'You traitor,' she spat at him. She pushed the end of the gun barrel into his forehead as she leaned over him. He saw the look of hatred in her eyes.

The gunshot exploded. Kruger froze above him. Her face changed from anger to shock. She looked down at the hole in her chest where Mitchell had shot her, then she toppled backwards, disappearing from his view. Mitchell dropped his gun, feeling his strength seeping away. He had failed. There was no one else coming to stop Phillips and the other team. He was no longer thinking straight. He grimaced and managed to roll himself over. He crawled over Kruger's inert body and pulled himself towards the two black packages that contained the explosives lying on the tarmac. The countdown timers had not been activated. He would take the explosives and get rid of them. There was nothing more he could do.

Phillips, Casper and Jonas were arming their explosives when they heard the echo of gunshots from the other end of the dam.

'That bitch Kruger, I knew it,' Phillips shouted. He turned to Casper. 'Go. We'll finish up here. The plan stays the same.'

Casper picked up his sniper rifle and started running without hesitation, heading for the maintenance tower that stood at the end of the dam, rising up above the highway. It provided the highest point on the dam and was a perfect position for a sniper to provide cover. He reached the base of the tower and shot out the rusty lock that secured a metal door with his handgun. He kicked the door and the rusted hinges moved a few millimetres. He took two steps back and threw himself at it, putting his whole weight into the effort. The door gave way and he pushed through it. Metal stairs led upwards. Casper took them three at a time and reached the top. In the roof of the tower was a hatch. He used the butt of his handgun to break off a metal bolt that locked it, then battered his shoulder into it. The hatch flew open and Casper pulled himself up onto the roof of the tower. He replaced the cover over the opening and moved over to a turreted wall. He placed the long sniper rifle through a gap, flipping out the two short legs under the barrel and placing the butt into his shoulder. He put his eye to the scope and scanned the highway across the dam where the other team should have been positioned. He gauged the distance. Eight hundred and fifty metres. For Casper it was a manageable distance, he had hit targets further away than that before, but the conditions were against him. The rain did not trouble him, although it made the gun and the wall he balanced it on slippery, and droplets clouded the lens. He wiped them away with his glove and reset. The strong wind would cause him some difficulty as the gusts would affect the flight of the bullet. It did not deter Casper. He had first learned to use a rifle in the wilds off the coast of the mainland, he was used to shooting into crosswinds.

He scanned the highway and saw three bodies on the ground. Next to them was the orange air cylinder that Mitchell should have been wearing. He adjusted the magnification on his scope and the bodies became larger. He recognised Giesler despite most of his head having disappeared. Further away he saw Jarrod. He was still alive, making feeble movements lying on the ground. A third body lay on its back, looking up at the sky. He had to wipe his lens again, then focussed in on the inert shape. It wasn't Mitchell. Long black hair gathered round the face. It was Kruger.

Casper swept the area surrounding the bodies. Possible scenarios ran through his head. Had Kruger betrayed them and killed Giesler and Jarrod? Had Mitchell then taken her out and was now attempting to set the explosives himself?

It took him a moment to pick out the dark wet suit against the grey background of the highway and the storm. Mitchell was on his feet, staggering slowly away from the bodies, heading down the slope that would take him off the dam. He was carrying the explosive packages. He wasn't trying to set them to detonate, he was taking them away. It was Mitchell who had betrayed them.

Casper flipped the safety switch and began the same routine with which he approached every shot. He calmed his breathing, settling into a steady rhythm and stilling his body. He made an adjustment to the scope and centred the crosshairs on the slow moving target. Then he pointed the rifle away to the right, allowing for the wind that would swerve the bullet back towards its intended target. He felt nothing, his movements and thoughts were like a machine carrying out a dedicated task. He did not suffer haunting memories of those he had killed before. There were too many now, ever since he had killed Maxine Aubert and started the war.

The shot cracked through the storm. Casper absorbed the recoil from the powerful weapon and remained still. A split second later he saw the bullet hit Mitchell. He had judged it well, although it had come in a little low. It hit Mitchell in his lower back, throwing him forward. The explosives were thrown out of his hands and landed on the edge of the highway. Mitchell didn't get up. The shot was good enough.

Phillips looked up at the sound of the rifle being fired. The sloped curve of the highway meant he could not see who Casper had hit, but he trusted that his young lieutenant had done what was required. He turned back to Jonas and made some last adjustments to his harness.

'Set?'

Jonas, his breathing regulator in his mouth, replied with an 'okay' gesture using his free hand. In the other he held the bomb, securely tethered to his wetsuit.

'Once you've set the bomb in place, get out of there if you can. Meet us back at the rendezvous point.'

Jonas nodded. They both knew his chances of making it out in time were slim, but Jonas had agreed to take on the task of delivering the underwater bomb. Phillips helped him walk over to the edge of the dam. There was a sheer drop into the swell below. Jonas used Phillips's shoulder to lever himself up on to the top of the wall.

'Good luck,' Phillips shouted. He had no idea if Jonas heard him.

Jonas shuffled forward and dropped off the edge into the raging water below. Phillips leaned over and caught sight of him bobbing amongst the waves, the orange tank on his back separating him from the dark water that engulfed him.

He didn't have time to stand and watch Jonas's progress. He ran back to the remaining bomb and picked up the rope and grapple he would use to abseil down the face of the wall in order to position the explosive in the correct place on the fault line that Giesler had specified.

He set off towards the point a hundred metres further up the slope from which he would descend.

16

The shots had come from just ahead of them on the highway, further up the slope. Danny lay with his face pressed against the tarmac. They waited, straining to hear anything else over the noise of the storm. They couldn't just lie there all day. Danny pulled himself up and ran forward in a low crouch. He tapped Kyle and Lachlan as he passed them, urging them to follow him. It was reckless to charge ahead without knowing what they were running into, but they had little choice and no time.

The first thing he noticed when he crested the top of the dam was the incongruous bright orange cylinder sitting in the middle of the road. Then he saw the three bodies dressed in black lying near to it, and another further along the highway, lying with his arms thrown forward and his face down. Pools of blood mixed with puddles of water. He didn't recognise any of them.

Lachlan arrived next to him, 'Is it him?'

Danny shook his head, 'Not Phillips.'

'The air cylinder?'

'Check the sea, maybe there are more of them.'

Kyle inspected the body that lay apart from the other three. 'These were lying next to him.' He held up the two black packages.

'Explosives?'

Kyle nodded, 'A lot.'

'What happened to them?' Danny gestured to the bodies.

'Some sort of fall out? Kyle guessed.

Lachlan shouted to them from the wall. He was pointing into the water beyond the dam. Above the storm they were able to make him out. 'There's a boat drifting in the water,' he called out.

'They must have been planning to detonate bombs under water.'

'They were until something went wrong. We need to find Gabriella.' They stood up. Danny shouted across to Lachlan, telling him to leave the boat and follow them.

Lachlan took two steps towards them, then stopped in his tracks. The sound of the gunshot arrived fractionally afterwards. Danny saw the fountain of blood spurt out of Lachlan's chest as his hands reached up to cover the wound. He stumbled backwards, slumping down to the ground, his back against the wall. Kyle shouted his name and dropped the explosives onto the ground. He dashed across the highway towards his fallen comrade before Danny could stop him.

They kneeled down next to Lachlan. They knew there was nothing that could be done for him. Kyle pressed against the wound, trying to stem the flow of blood. Lachlan's face turned pale as life ebbed away from him. He turned to Danny.

'Go,' he rasped. A trail of blood dribbled from his mouth.

Danny answered him with a resigned nod. He pulled Kyle away from Lachlan. 'Come on, he's gone.'

'He's still alive,' Kyle cried. He stumbled backwards, unbalanced by Danny's efforts to pull him away. As he did so there was a thud against the wall where a moment earlier Kyle had been leaning over their stricken friend.

The bullet dislodged a piece of the wall which landed on the ground next to them.

Danny grabbed Kyle firmly. 'Move,' he screamed. If the sniper had time to get another shot at them, they would end up like Lachlan. Dragging Kyle alongside him, they stole back across the highway, crouching until they found cover beside a metal barrier which separated the lanes in the middle of the road. As they kneeled together, there was a metallic clang on the other side of the metal. The barrier had stopped a bullet entering Danny's head.

'We have to keep moving. Keep low, use the barrier as cover. We need to get to the other side of the dam and meet up with the others.'

Danny turned and Kyle followed.

Gabriella arrived on the highway as the sniper rifle barked for the second time. Like Danny, she had stopped when the first gunshots had been heard and then had continued with caution after a moment of silence. She scanned the road. At first it seemed deserted, then she made out the dark figure running along the side of the dam in the rain.

Another rifle shot rang out. This time she was able to locate the source of the sound. It had come from above them. She turned and saw the tower. The sniper was up there, it was the perfect vantage point to protect both ends of the dam. They had been spared because the sniper was concentrating on something on the other side of the dam, which meant they must be up there alone without anyone to watch their rear.

'Zeb, the tower,' Gabriella shouted decisively, 'Verona, with me.' Zeb headed for the foot of the tower, Gabriella and Verona crossed the highway and sprinted in pursuit of the figure they could see running along the dam.

Phillips found the point on the dam that Giesler had pointed out to him. He stepped back and fired the piton gun at the wall. The metal spike dug into the concrete. Phillips gave the rope a sharp tug to make sure it held. He took the loop of rope from his shoulder and unravelled a length of it, wrapping it around his waist and tying it securely. He crouched down and opened the control panel on the explosive package. The timer was set for ten minutes, enough time for him to plant it, pull himself back up the wall and get off the top of the dam before it detonated. He hit the square red button that armed the device. The timer started to countdown. As he stood up he felt the point of the gun in the back of his neck.

'Slowly,' the voice cautioned him. Phillips recognised it straightaway. 'Drop the package.'

'I really don't think you want me to drop it.'

There was movement behind him, then a girl appeared in front of him. She was slight and could not have been older than twenty years of age. She had a gun trained on him and looked him straight in the eye.

The gun pressing into his neck nudged him. 'Give it to her.'

Verona reached out and took the bomb from his hands.

'On your knees,' Gabriella ordered him. Phillips was calm and followed her instructions. He just had to be patient, he knew Casper could make a shot at this distance. He watched as the girl placed the package on the ground and opened it.

Verona looked up at Gabriella as she saw the red digits of the clock ticking down, 'It's armed.'

'How long?' Gabriella asked.

'Less than ten minutes.'

'Can you stop it?'

Verona shook her head, 'Only if we had more time. It's tamper proof.'

The gun pressed harder into the base of Phillips's neck.

'How many more devices?' Gabriella demanded. Phillips said nothing. He felt the pressure ease as the gun was pulled away from his neck. The metal butt smashed into the side of his head, sending him sprawling onto the ground. 'Dammit, Phillips, how many more?'

Lying on his back and looking up into the storm, Phillips saw the devil standing over him. She had changed. Her hair was wild, clinging to her scalp and face in the rain. There was a patch over one eye, surrounded by pale, scarred skin. The ear on that side of her head was deformed, the remaining green eye bore into him. The look on her face was one of fury. She had come for vengeance. Phillips felt a shiver of panic run through him. Why had Casper not shot her?

From the tower roof, Casper tracked their progress along the road, tucked behind the metal safety barrier. He kept the scope focused on them, waiting for a split-second opportunity to present itself. All he needed was one of them to raise their head a fraction and he would have an easy kill shot, but they kept themselves hidden. There was a gap in the barrier about halfway along the road. He took his eye away from the scope to see how far away they were from it. He could take them out when they reached there, they would have no cover.

That was when he noticed Phillips below him, lying on the ground, a soldier standing over him, pointing a gun at his head. Casper switched target in an instant, pulling his rifle round and simultaneously judging the distance of the shot. It was a simple target, even with the steep angle involved. He took a deep breath and drew the crosshairs onto the head of the target. His finger applied the first hint of pressure to the trigger. From behind him he heard the rattle of the trapdoor flying open. He pulled the trigger sharply and got the bullet off before turning to face the giant man leaping through the hatch and hurling himself towards him. The bullet missed its target by centimetres and buried flew unnoticed into the sea beyond.

Zeb had needed both hands free to lift the hatch so did not have his gun drawn as he burst onto the roof, but he did have surprise on his side as he barrelled towards the sniper. He also had a height and weight advantage. It should have been easy for him to take out the young man, but in his haste he had not assessed the dangers of close combat in a confined space. Casper was agile enough to take a step to the side as Zeb rushed towards him. He didn't make it fully out of the way of the oncoming Zeb, but it was enough to avoid the full force of the initial charge. Caught off balance, Zeb hit the low sidewall and had to recover his footing before he toppled over the edge of the platform.

Now they turned and faced each other, both soaked by the rain. The confined space gave the smaller Casper an advantage. Zeb couldn't make his superior bulk work in his favour. Casper had practiced and honed the martial arts techniques he had learned as a young boy. They had come in useful during the war, and now they were ideally suited for the fight he faced. Zeb threw a huge punch towards Casper's head. Casper ducked under the swinging limb, neatly stepped to the side and twisted Zeb's flailing arm underneath him. There was a sickening snap of bone as a flash of lightning illuminated the sky.

Danny and Kyle made it to the gap in the barrier. They could see Gabriella standing over a man. As the scene was lit by the lightning flash, Danny peered out around the barrier and looked towards the tower where the rifle shots had been coming from. He saw two men locked together in combat. The large silhouette could only be the distinctive form of Zeb. He was grappling a smaller man. Danny knew it would be Casper, the boy he had once known in the wilderness who had come to the city and become a rebel. He was renowned as the Independents' most lethal sniper. It was he that had shot and killed Maxine Aubert. For the moment he was occupied in fighting Zeb and their path was clear.

'Get to the tower and help Zeb,' he ordered Kyle, who nodded and ran through the gap towards the base of the tower.

Danny ran towards Gabriella. Verona was with her. He waved his hands and screamed as loud as he could, trying to make himself heard over the thunder that rolled around them. 'Check the water, they have diving equipment!'

Gabriella heard him approach and looked up. She saw Danny wildly gesturing over the side of the dam to the sea. The message reached her. They had men in the water.

'Watch him,' she shouted to Verona.

Verona pointed her gun at the prone Phillips. She held the bomb in her other hand. 'Eight minutes,' she shouted, glancing at the countdown timer.

Danny arrived next to Gabriella at the wall. 'They had a boat and diving equipment, they might have another diver here.'

Gabriella loosed the rifle she carried on her back and balanced it on the top of the wall. Together they scanned the water. The waves churned up the surface. Not far away, underneath them, tied to the wall, they saw a second inflatable dinghy.

'If they've gone under already we're too late,' cried Danny.

Gabriella didn't reply, but continued to search the surface of the water. It was impossible to track anything in the constant turmoil of the storm waves.

Then she saw it. She put her eye to the scope and swivelled the rifle round. Danny saw her action and looked in the direction that the rifle pointed. A huge wave rolled away and in the valley behind he saw what Gabriella had spotted. On the surface was a bright orange air cylinder. Now he focused on it, Danny could see the human shape attached to it. Legs were kicking forward and arms were pulling through the water. The diver had not yet submerged, they were still swimming to get into the right position, and seemed to be struggling against the stormy current that surrounded them.

Gabriella balanced the rifle on the ledge and blocked out the chaos that surrounded her. It was not a great distance to shoot, less than a hundred metres, but she was shooting a moving target being tossed about in unpredictable waves and firing through wind, rain and spray.

The diver stopped kicking and began treading water. 'They're about to go under,' she heard Danny shout. She exhaled. The weapon was not her preferred sniper rifle, which she had reluctantly left behind. It was too cumbersome to bring on a mission like this. She double-checked her scope. The diver raised themself up, ready to bend over and push down beneath the surface of the water. Gabriella pulled the trigger lightly and felt the kick as the butt recoiled into her shoulder. She let off ten rounds in quick succession. The first two hit the water near to the diver. She used them to guide herself in. The remaining bullets found their target. The head of the diver was thrown backwards and red spray emanated from the stricken head before a wave swamped over the body. As the wave rolled away they spotted the orange air cylinder floating in the water. It rolled over, disappearing under the surface and throwing skyward the inert body of the lifeless diver still attached to it. They watched as cylinder and human slipped under the waves.

'Got him,' Danny said. They stepped back, turning away from the water and then froze.

Phillips stood behind Verona, holding her in an arm lock, a serrated hunting knife pressed against the jugular of her throat. A trickle of blood ran down her neck where the knife had slit open the skin. She still held the explosive device in front of her.

'It's over,' Gabriella shouted. 'Let her go.'

'It's never over, Gabi, you know that,' Phillips snarled at her. 'I've still got a bomb here, and it's going off in five minutes, there's no way of stopping it once the countdown has been triggered.'

She hated being called Gabi. Only her mother had called her that name. Phillips knew that.

'What good will it do?' Danny shouted. 'Killing all those people? It won't help your cause.'

'Those people deserve to die. If they had risen up this war would have been over by now. We could have won. We could be living in a new country, free from the Party. Instead they did nothing but stand aside and watch all hope drain away.'

'You blow this dam and you lose the war.'

'Still so naïve Danny, that was always your problem. This dam blows and the city is destroyed. No one wins, but the State loses an entire city and her citizens. The State loses the invulnerability that protects it. We have support in the north, they will see that the State can be defeated. They will rally to our cause.'

Phillips started to back away from them, pulling Verona along with him. As he stepped backwards Danny and Gabriella moved forwards, maintaining the distance between them. Danny and Gabriella had their guns raised and aimed at Phillips. One opening and they would not hesitate, but the knife stayed planted against Verona's neck.

'Will you tell them it was the State that destroyed the city?' Gabriella asked, 'the same way you told them it was the State that killed Maxine Aubert?'

'You know what they have done, they killed millions in a fake war. They killed their own children in the name of protecting their own people. They rule by corruption and lies, yet you still defend them.'

'You've become just the same as them.'

'No,' Phillips snarled. 'I used to do their dirty work. You know that Gabi, you were there. Remember? They ordered me to slaughter innocent people in the name of a false war.'

'They knew about your plan, Phillips,' said Gabriella. 'They knew you were going to blow the dam up and they stood by and let you go ahead. They've evacuated their troops out of the city, they know you will lose the war that way. The citizens will turn against you. They want you to destroy it so they don't have to rebuild it, so they don't have to care for the citizens you kill. You're doing their dirty work for them again.'

Phillips paused, 'You're lying,' he said uncertainly.

'How do you think we found out about your plan? Someone leaked it, I'm guessing the same person who took out your team on the other side of the dam. They know what you are doing and they haven't sent anyone to stop you. You said it yourself, the Party will do anything to stay in control and protect the State as they see fit, including letting a whole city die if it is to their advantage.'

Phillips kept moving backwards. He risked leaning to the side to look over the wall on the edge of the dam. Below him he saw the boat still moored to the side.

'It's too late,' Gabriella tried one last time, 'blowing the dam will achieve nothing.'

'You're wrong,' he cried, as a ferocious gust of wind buffeted them sideways. 'It doesn't matter if they want it to happen or not. It doesn't matter if their troops are there or not. The rest of the world needs to wake up to what has happened, to the lies that their leaders have told them. We have all been betrayed. There was no First Strike. They killed millions. When the world sees a State willing to let a city full of its own people die, then the world will finally realise they cannot trust those in charge.'

'Four minutes,' shouted Verona.

Phillips let go of her arm but kept the knife pressed against her throat. With his other hand he took the explosive from her. He waited for the right moment. He still had time, if he could get into the boat and manoeuvre it into the right place by the dam, he could anchor the bomb and get just far enough away before it detonated.

'You can never beat them,' Danny yelled. 'Even if you do, they will be replaced by more of the same. Power corrupts, you know that, even those with the best of intentions.'

'You should have joined me,' Phillips replied, stalling them. 'We could have won this war already with both of you with me. But I knew you would never have the guts to do what needed to be done.'

Lightning lit up the sky, blinding them for an instant as it sprang out of the gloom their eyes had become accustomed to. Phillips seized the opportunity. Before Verona could react, the knife had left her throat and she felt sharp pain as the blade cut through her hamstrings. Her legs gave way and she fell to the ground, screaming in pain. Phillips leapt over the wall and disappeared. Danny and Gabriella fired simultaneously, but they were too slow. Their bullets flew harmlessly through the air and out into the sea beyond. They rushed forward. Gabriella reached Verona first and ripped her shirt off wrapping it round the wounds to stem the gushing blood. She couldn't tell if the femoral or popliteal arteries had been ruptured, but either way Verona would bleed out in minutes.

Danny leaned over the side of the wall. He saw Phillips below. He had landed in the boat and had released the rope that had anchored it to the wall.

'He's still got the bomb,' he called to Gabriella as he jumped up onto the ledge.

'Let him go,' shouted Gabriella. 'He's not worth it.'

'I can't let him blow the dam.'

'Wait,' cried Gabriella, but it was too late. Danny leapt from the wall and disappeared, plummeting to the water below.

Both were bloodied and bruised. Enclosed on the top of the tower, neither could retreat. Casper was cut badly on his forehead, blood flowed into his eyes. He was beginning to feel the effects of the unrelenting barrage of heavy blows that Zeb delivered. He fell to his knees, and had to pull himself up using the low wall.

Kyle burst through the hatch at exactly the wrong moment. He came up between them, with his back to Casper. Casper seized his moment and grabbed Kyle around the neck. With his other hand he snatched the handgun out of Kyle's raised hand and pointed it at Kyle's head.

Zeb froze, 'There's no way out of here. Put the gun down and you might live.'

Casper looked round. He couldn't see Phillips below, only a woman bandaging an injured soldier. He had to get away. It was a twenty metre drop to the ground, just over four storeys. He put his chances at fifty-fifty.

Zeb guessed what Casper was thinking. 'Don't do it,' he cried, stepping forward.

Casper turned the gun on Zeb and fired. Kyle instinctively knocked Casper's firing arm. The shot clipped Zeb on the shoulder, enough to halt his charge. Before Kyle could turn, Casper placed a hand on the low wall and vaulted over the side.

He fell through the rain, trying to turn his body so he would land on his feet and protect his vital organs. He hit the ground hard and rolled forward. He felt the snap in his left leg. Despite the agony he had to keep moving. He stood up and began limping away, taking his weight on his right leg, dragging his broken left leg behind him.

Kyle looked over the edge of the tower. He wasn't going to follow the sniper by the same route. He checked on Zeb, who was sitting against the wall, holding his wounded shoulder.

'Let him go,' Zeb advised, 'he won't get far.'

Kyle pulled the big man up by his good arm and helped him towards the hatch.

Danny landed on the boat as the engine coughed into life. The boat kicked into gear, sending him rolling forward. Phillips set a course along the dam wall, ignoring Danny as he flailed around the front of the boat. Waves crashed into the side of the dinghy, threatening to capsize them with every blow. Phillips needed to get fifty metres along the dam and he could place the bomb against the wall. It might still be enough to damage the top of the fault line. Giesler had assured them that one successful explosion in the right conditions could break the dam. He had thought it would have been Gabriella who would have followed him over the wall, not Samson. Phillips held the serrated knife in one hand, the tiller in the other, ready for Danny to approach.

Danny regained his balance on the swaying deck and faced Phillips. The bomb lay on the deck between them. Their eyes met, then both of them leapt forwards. Danny felt the knife enter his stomach as they collided. The bomb slipped away from both of them, sliding across the deck as the boat was rocked by another wave. Phillips twisted the knife, grabbing Danny and pulling him onto the blade. Danny felt the cold metal slide deeper inside him, gouging through his intestines.

'You should have run away again,' Phillips hissed in his ear, their faces close together. 'Now you're going to die and while you bleed to death you can watch your beloved city drown.'

The knife pulled away and then plunged into Danny's stomach again. He gasped with pain, his life draining away. He looked up at the storm clouds as he was tossed around by the waves. He hallucinated, fragments of his life flashing before him. He saw Hanlen and Isla as he imagined they would have been, six years old and smiling and laughing. He saw Eilidh and Lucas as they stepped off the boat, ready to start a new life. He saw Rosa, waiting for him to join her somewhere out there under the water.

The knife withdrew again, the sharp blade ripping at Danny's skin. Phillips raised the knife once more, ready to strike a final blow across Danny's stomach, gutting him.

The boat was hit by a huge wave and rocked violently. They toppled apart and landed sprawled on the deck. The knife fell out of Phillips's hand. As he scrambled to retrieve it, Danny found the strength to pull himself on top of Phillips and hit him across the face. He pinned him down with his body. Blood broke out over Phillips's face as Danny pummelled him. The adrenaline and anger gave him strength. How long until the bomb detonated? Were they too close to the dam?

He saw the knife rolling around on the deck, just within reach if he stretched for it, but he couldn't keep Phillips pinned down at the same time. He went for the knife, throwing himself across the deck and grabbing it. He spun over onto his back, anticipating Phillips following him. As Danny landed, he thrust the knife up into the air. Phillips landed on top of him. They both froze for a moment.

Phillips staggered backwards on his knees, looking down at his chest. The handle of the knife stuck out, the full blade was inside him, it had gone straight through his heart. He feebly grabbed at the handle, but his arms had no strength, his hands wouldn't do what he asked them to. He felt strange, weak. He stared down at Danny, lying on the boat in front of him.

'You bastard,' he muttered. His voice was lost in the noise of the waves swirling around them. He tried to stand and fell back further and his foot hit the edge of the boat. With a gentle sway he toppled over the side and into the raging water.

Danny hauled himself up. The bomb still sat on the deck. He had to get it away from the dam. He pulled himself along to the tiller and wrenched it round, steering the boat out to sea. The engine strained against the current, the dinghy kicked in protest, but gradually it cut through the water. He reached for the package and saw the timer. Thirty seconds. The whole fight with Phillips had lasted less than two minutes. It had felt longer. He looked behind him at the receding dam. He was sure he was far enough away now. He let go of the tiller and picked up the bomb. With his last remaining reserve of strength he managed to throw the package over the side. It submerged beneath the waves. He tried to count down the seconds as he grasped the tiller and manoeuvred away from the bomb.

Gabriella propped Verona against the dam wall. She needed proper medical help if she was going to survive. Kyle and Zeb came running from the tower. She looked out across the water and saw the boat with one person in it. She couldn't tell if it was Danny or Phillips. Suddenly a huge roar exploded above the sound of the waves and the wind. A mushroom of water was thrown into the sky, showering them and the surrounding area in a fresh deluge. The bomb had detonated. They all ducked and shielded their eyes, then Gabriella rushed forward and looked over the wall at the dam. There was no sign of any damage, the bomb had been too far away. The boat was still in the water, it had survived the explosion too. No one was steering it, it was swirling round, out of control and being tossed around by the storm.

'Casper?' she looked to Kyle and Zeb, noticing Zeb's bullet wound.

Kyle pointed along the highway, 'He got away.'

Gabriella saw the limping figure hobbling away from them. 'Get Verona up, we need to get her to the hospital.'

She left them and walked back to the rifle that sat where she had left it on the wall. She picked it up and then lay on the ground, propping the gun up on its stand. She put her eye to the scope. She settled her body. She calmed her breathing. She judged the distance. She adjusted the scope.

She paused. 'For Maxine,' she said.

The final gunshot cried out through the storm. Casper's head exploded in a red mist. His body stood for a moment, then crumpled to the ground.

Danny lay on his back, staring up at the sky. The storm eased. The swirl of the boat became gentler, soothing him as he lay dying.

Had any of it been worth it? His years in the State Police? Parkinson? Phillips? The war? Had he achieved anything worthwhile? Would saving the city from flooding make a difference to life in the State? He had to believe some of it had been worthwhile. If nothing else, he had done what he believed was right, that must count for something. It was for others to decide what happened next. He had saved his city and the lives of those that survived there. Perhaps one day they would find happiness, and unbeknown to them they would have Danny Samson to thank for it.

He knew this was the end. He could feel the life seeping from him. Spots of rain fell onto his face. When he tried to wipe them away he found he could no longer move his arms. He was ready for whatever came next. He had never believed in anything beyond life, no one in the State did. Yet, now that he was close to the end he imagined another world to which he could journey.

He pictured a different body of water, and a different boat. It anchored in a harbour and from it stepped a woman with tousled brown-blonde hair. Her arm was round the shoulders of a young boy. They stepped onto a new land that promised them hope and a new life. Danny smiled as he thought of Eilidh and Lucas. Should he have gone with them? It didn't matter now, it was enough to know they were safe and they had a future full of the possibilities that precious life and freedom can bring. That was something he had achieved.

The clouds lightened, a bird flew across the sky, gliding effortlessly on the current. He felt weightless as the pressures and strain of life left him.

He was in his wooden cabin in the wilderness, the one he had built with his own hands. He stood on the porch as sunshine lit the meadow around him. The dream was familiar. He turned to face her, knowing she would be there beside him. Rosalind. Rosa at her most beautiful, with her long dark hair and glowing olive skin. She had not aged, she was frozen as he remembered her. The wide, hazel eyes looked at him, her mouth curled up into her infectious smile that was always on the verge of breaking into a joyful laugh. Her thin arms circled his waist and she kissed him on the cheek. He felt the sensation of her soft lips on his skin. He wrapped his arms around her and they stood holding each other, staring into each other's eyes. He would give anything to see those eyes again, to feel that embrace, to kiss those lips one last time.

From the meadow they came shouting and laughing through the long grass. Isla and Hanlen, now aged six or seven, full of mischief and joy. They chased each other, running through the soft flowers. He wanted to reach out and join them, but he could not. They had never existed like this in life, only in his mind. That was the only place where he could keep them, where they were safe and protected from the evil in the world. They had lived on within him for as long as he had lived, now he could let them go. If there was anything beyond this cruel world, he would find them there and they would be together again. His only regret was that he did not save them in this life.

He was wheezing, struggling to suck air into his lungs, his breath was shallow and rapid. There was not long left. The boat bounced off something and tilted as a weight hit the deck next to him. He could not move his head to see what was happening. He felt hands grab at him. A face came into view, a woman. One green eye looked down on him. She had olive skin too, but some of it was burnt and scarred. Her hair was short and dark. She said his name.

'Rosa,' he answered. The face leaned closer to him. It wasn't Rosa, it was Gabriella, she who had haunted his dreams and his nightmares alongside Rosa. Now they joined together, becoming one blurred image, representing everything he had cared about in this world: Eilidh, Gabriella and Rosa. Isla, Hanlen and Lucas.

He stared up at her. She sheltered him from the drizzle of rain yet a drop of water fell, a single tear.

'Rosa,' Danny said again, trying to make himself heard. 'Did I save Rosa?' he asked.

Gabriella looked at him, clutching his hand. She knelt down beside him and propped his head up on her lap.

'You did it, Danny. You saved her. You saved them all. The city is safe.'

Danny smiled weakly and felt the last breath leave his lungs. His eyes closed and his head went limp in Gabriella's arms.

17

The Chancellor hated travelling outside of the Capital City. It had been Harris Ellroy's idea. The Field Marshall had warned her the State troops were unhappy with the order to abandon the city just as they were on the verge of capturing it from the rebels. Rumours about the retreat and the subsequent reversal had started to spread. The idea that their political masters would throw away the city which the soldiers had risked their lives to regain did not go down well. A visit from their Commander-in-Chief, Ellroy argued, would put a stop to any insurrection in the ranks. If the Chancellor stood before them and proudly announced her joy at defeating the enemy and regaining Central City, then the situation could be salvaged.

Románes stepped from her private aircraft onto the tarmac of the military base. Ellroy was there to meet her alongside Teddy Davies. They all got into a military car. Ellroy spoke as they drove through the streets of the war-ravaged city, but Románes didn't listen to him. She had lost interest in hearing from her military advisors. She had told them to finish the rebellion in the north, she didn't want to hear the details. The First Strike War was over, the civil war would end soon. She was looking forward to ruling a State that was not at war for her last few years in office. A new era could begin once this unpleasant business was put to rest.

The destruction on the streets that they sped through did not shock her. She had seen the images in detail during her security briefings. The roads along their route had been cleared in preparation of her arrival, no obstructions or debris slowed their progress. Some citizens stood by the side of the road, staring at the passing cavalcade of vehicles. One or two children waved, while the adults only stared. They looked wretched, Romános thought, not like the clean and healthy people of Capitol City.

'We've gathered a few hundred citizens in the square to hear your address,' Ellroy told her. No doubt they had been given little option but to be corralled into the centre of the city. 'And the troops will be there in force. Your decision to come personally and speak to them has galvanised them exactly as we hoped it would.'

'Let's just get this over with as quickly as we can,' she snapped. Not for the first time, she wished Phillips had been successful. It would have solved so many problems.

The only consolation was knowing that Phillips was dead. Davies had been the one to break the news to her. He had watched the events play out live from an overhead satellite and showed her the footage – the two boats approaching the dam, two teams making their preparations. It was hard to decipher looking from above what actually occurred, but it appeared that one team started shooting each other before a small tactical assault team arrived and took out the rest of Phillips's men. Then there had been a final struggle aboard one of the boats. Davies had managed to freeze the image and magnify it so that they could identify the two men on the boat. Phillips had tipped over into the water and didn't resurface. The other man lay on the boat, looking straight up at the camera twenty thousand kilometres above him.

They had identified him using facial recognition. Daniel Samson. The name rang a faint bell. Davies filled her in: the police detective who had uncovered the clinical trial on unborn children, wanted for murder when the civil war had broken out and a former ally of Phillips.

They didn't know why Samson had stopped Phillips, some old vendetta between two former comrades perhaps? Románes didn't much care what the reason was. They were both dead now, which was one less thing for her to worry about. But Central City still stood and her plans would have to be adapted. She had done that more than a few times in her fifty years as Chancellor, she could do it again. Once they had sat down and studied it, she was sure they could find some way of turning the rebuilding of the city to their advantage. There were always opportunities, even without war to fall back on. Large scale redevelopment and infrastructure plans could be just the sort of thing the Party needed to reassert its control over the people.

They said it was over. They were wrong. It wasn't over. The troops came back. He knew they would. He made sure he was selected when they started rounding up citizens. In the crowd, pushed and cajoled, no one resisted. The rebels were defeated and had fled. The State was in charge again, ready to show their power once more. They took anyone they found on the street. That wasn't enough, so they went into the buildings and found more citizens, dragging and pushing them out. They corralled them like cattle into the main square. The rubble had been cleared away. On the steps of the parliament building, a platform had appeared with banners behind it. The State crest flew, the bull and the dove waving on flags. The soldiers surrounded them and held them in a pen. How many?

Four hundred, five? Enough to look convincing on the cameras. The last time citizens had gathered here the war had started, now it would end.

His mind was clear now, clearer than it had been since the war had begun. He had seen them on the dam. Instead of running as they had told him to, he had watched from the forest. One of them had told him they were going to blow up the dam. He should have gone to the State and warned them. He couldn't. The State would not believe him, he had betrayed them before. They would kill him for sure. He saw the boats leaving the camp and heard the gunshots and saw muzzle flashes. He saw through the storm. He had seen her, the fury that haunted his nightmares. She was burnt and scarred. She stood over her enemy like she had once stood over him. He saw Danny, his ex-partner and Phillips. Fate had brought all of them together again. Phillips went into the water, dead. An explosion. Danny had not stirred.

The avenging warrior Gabriella had sprinted along the dam and leapt into the water. She swam to the second boat that was drifting free. She drove out to get Danny. He watched her collapse next to him and he knew Danny was gone. Rest in peace, partner. The rain stopped at last, the water stilled. Gabriella picked up the lifeless body and brought him ashore. There were others injured. One had to be carried, her legs bandaged. Gabriella carried Danny. At the other end of the dam they collected another body and then left. He was alone again.

He crept out and walked along the bank to the dam. He found the youngest one first. The back of his head was gone and a leg was twisted unnaturally. He remembered him from the camp, the quiet one who had said nothing. Further along pools of blood lined the wall and the drying tarmac. Across the other side of the dam more bodies lay on the road. He recognised them. One had given him food and helped wash him. One was the engineer he had seen poring over his plans. The woman was there, he bent down and brushed her dank hair away from her face. The yelp of two dogs fighting disturbed him. He looked up and saw them. They were biting at another body, each trying to claim their carrion.

He ran at them, waving his arms, chasing them away. It was the one who had given him clothes and cut his hair, the one who had spoken to him as he set him free. He remembered what he had told him. They were going to blow up the dam and the State were not doing anything to stop them. They were going to destroy the city and kill them all. His city and the people he swore he would protect.

He had been too weak to do anything. Instead, Danny had stopped them. Danny and Gabriella. They had done what Henrik had not been able to do. They had done his job for him. They had sacrificed themselves for his city.

Further on, on the side of the highway, he saw the black packages lying where the dead man had dropped them. He thought it might be food, but they were not. They were the explosives that were supposed to have blown up the dam. An idea formed. Something he could do. He only needed one. The other he threw into the deep water, weighed down with rocks. It sank beneath the surface. The tide had turned, the water level had dropped, the waves had calmed. The storm was over.

Now he stood in the crowd with the bomb wrapped under his jacket. The Chancellor was coming. No one was being searched. He just needed to get close enough to her.

The procession pulled up in an alleyway, behind the remains of the parliament, bordered on each side by crumbling walls. Románes remained in the car while her security detail exited and formed a protective perimeter. The lead agent opened the door for her and she stepped out. Davies followed her. Ellroy got out the other side and joined them.

'This way.' The Field Marshall went first. They climbed some stairs and walked across an uneven and cratered floor which had once been the interior of the city parliament. Internal walls still stood in place. A path had been cleared for them to walk through until they reached the back of the huge banner that hung from scaffolding. They stopped behind it. If there was a crowd gathered on the other side, Lucinda Románes could not hear it. There was only an ominous silence, broken by a cough or the bark of a wild dog.

Ellroy left them and walked round the banner. There was a squeal of feedback over the primitive sound system as he got to the microphone. He started his address, introducing her to the crowd. After he announced her name there was only silence. It didn't bother her, she didn't need them to adore her. She needed to reassert the control of the Party and the State and to tell them everything would get back to normal now that the rebels had been defeated.

She stepped forward and looked out onto the crowd of citizens gathered in the square. She saluted Ellroy and shook his hand, he stood aside and left the podium to her.

Ten minutes, she thought, and it will be over. She would be back in the car heading to the airstrip. In two hours she could be back in her office overlooking Capital City, leaving Ellroy to deal with mopping up the remains of the rebellion. She looked at them, her citizens, shuffling around against the backdrop of ruins. They looked pathetic, she thought, hopelessly lost and defeated, the opposite of the image of a successful nation the Party wished to project.

Ten minutes she reminded herself, as she stepped in front of the microphone, and she could leave this cursed city and never visit it again for the rest of her life.

There she was. Her familiar dark hair and grey piercing eyes. The Chancellor. It was all because of her. She had others who helped and schemed with her, but it all ultimately stemmed from her. She was the cause of everything: his father's death, the wars, his own downfall, all those dead citizens. She ruled the State, she owned the State, she had corrupted the State.

She started speaking. He heard the same words the politicians always used: victory; rebuild the city; make the State great again; rise from the ashes of war; mission accomplished; heal the divisions. Meaningless soundbites.

The citizens were restless. They were hungry, weak and dispirited. Words could do nothing to console them. They had all heard the rumours during the war: the child killing, illegal nightclubs for the rich and powerful, the fake reasons for the First Strike War. Some believed these rumours more than others, but no one thought the Party was entirely innocent any longer. Then came the recent rumour. State Forces had left the city because they wanted it to be destroyed. They wanted the citizens to disappear. Henrik knew it to be true, he had seen what had happened.

He caught some more words ringing from the podium: Kept you safe. Protected you during the war. We won for you, our precious citizens. It is you that make the State great.

The first cry of dissent rang out.

'Liar!'

It came from somewhere in the crowd. Románcs ignored it with a brief pause and carried on. Just get through the speech and get away, she thought, but when she tried to continue, more voices called out from below.

'Murderer!', 'Criminal!' Emboldened they increased in volume. Raised fists appeared. The crowd of oppressed victims took on a menacing form.

She tried to continue. 'We have protected you. We have saved you, rescued you from the threat of the rebels.' She was not used to competing to be heard. She was not used to insubordination.

There was a surge forward, the mass moved as one towards the foot of the steps. Ellroy stepped forward. Románcs was happy to let him take control of the situation.

He shouted a command to the troops that surrounded the people, calling them to arms. 'Form a barrier and push them back.'

The soldiers did not move. Románcs saw the look of uncertainty on her Field Marshall's face.

He repeated his shout, 'Dammit, push them back.'

'Why aren't they doing as you command?' Románcs cried out. The crowd surged forward again. They were at the foot of the steps now, only twenty metres away from them.

Ellroy looked at her. He saw the hint of fear on the Chancellor's face, a look he had never seen before in all their years together, through the First Strike War, the assassinations, the energy crisis and the food shortage. Now she knew what it felt like to be directly in the firing line like one of her soldiers. He turned and marched down the steps, his imposing stature giving him the air of invulnerability that surrounded all good commanders. He grabbed a staff sergeant by the shoulder.

'Get these men to follow their orders. Charge on these citizens and push this mob back. Protect your Chancellor.'

'They won't do it, sir,' the sergeant informed him.

'What do you mean they won't do it?'

'They won't charge on their own people, sir. The civil war is over. These people are not rebels.'

'They are threatening your Commander-in-Chief,' Ellroy yelled above the noise.

'With due respect, sir, the Commander-in-Chief ordered us to abandon these people to their death less than a week ago. She ordered us to desert the city. A lot of us lost friends in this war, a lot of us have had to kill fellow citizens, only to be told it was worthless in the end.'

'You will not protect your leader?'

'Will she protect us?' the sergeant snarled back.

'You are dismissed, sergeant. You will pay for this insurrection, as will every single one of these troops.'

The sergeant squared up to Ellroy, 'I really don't think any of them will give a damn.' He spat on the ground in front of Ellroy.

The citizens nearest to them saw the confrontation between the officer and the sergeant. They cheered and pushed forward again. The soldiers let them pass.

It took him a moment to realise what had happened. The soldiers were standing aside. The Field Marshall ran back up the steps. Then citizens were swarming after him. He saw the Chancellor as her security detail surrounded her. The banner picturing the State crest was ripped down.

This was his opportunity. He wouldn't reach her if he followed the crowd. Think Henrik, he urged himself. It was his city. He knew what way they had come. He had seen the streets being cleared. They would go back the same way. If he was quick enough he could intercept them. He tucked the package in tight under his arm and started to run.

Románes did not appreciate being manhandled by her security detail as they dashed back the way they had come to the rear of the parliament building. The car engines were already whirring, ready to go. She was bundled in by unknown hands and righted herself in the seat, adjusting her suit jacket and trousers which had been pulled all over the place. Davies and Ellroy made it into the car with her.

'Move it,' ordered Ellroy to the driver.

'The other cars, sir,' the driver protested.

'Forget about them, just get us out of here.'

'Yes sir,' he replied and pulled out from the middle of the motorcade. Out of the rear window as they accelerated away they saw the other cars being swamped by marauding citizens.

'I want them punished,' Románes said. Her steely calm returned now that she was out of immediate danger.

'We'll identify the ringleaders,' Davies assured her.

'I don't want anyone identified, Teddy, I want them punished. All of them, every single one of them. I will show them what it means to threaten the Chancellor of their State.'

'Understood, Chancellor.' Teddy Davies saw the anger in Lucinda Románes's face. There would be severe reprisals for the citizens after what had just happened.

'Back to the airstrip,' Ellroy instructed the driver, 'call ahead and make sure the Chancellor's aircraft is readied for immediate departure.'

New found energy came from his definite purpose. He had to make it in time. He knocked over a woman and didn't stop to help. He had one chance to save the city, like Danny had done. He would save the State, avenge the dead and the voiceless. He broke free from the crowd, and leapt over rubble, taking a shortcut down an alleyway to cut over one block. He came out of the alley into the main road. The street was empty, had he missed them? There was a screech of tyres and the car appeared round the corner. He unzipped his jacket and hit the red button that armed the bomb. He gripped the dead man's switch tightly. He stood in the middle of the road as the car accelerated towards him.

'Sir?' the driver pointed in front of them. Ellroy looked ahead at the citizen standing in the middle of the road.

'Run him over. Whatever you do, do not stop.'

The car was not slowing down. They would run him over. The explosion wouldn't work if he was outside the car, the armour plating would protect her. He had no other option, it was all he could try. Maybe it would be enough.

The crowd poured out of the alleyway into the road. They had followed the lone man who had dashed off to intercept the car. The driver swerved to avoid hitting the mass of citizens who suddenly filled the street.

'I ordered you to keep going,' Ellroy cried in vain. It was too late. The car skidded and stalled and stopped in the middle of the road. 'Secure the doors,' he shouted.

The crowd swarmed around the car, rocking it from side to side. The driver tried to restart the motor but it would not power up. Fists, rocks and bats hit the roof and windows of the impregnable vehicle. The driver panicked. He was not a soldier, he was a chauffeur. He reached for the door and pulled it open.

'Don't,' shouted Davies, 'we're safe if we just stay inside!'

It was too late, the door opened an inch and was yanked aside by the angry mob. The driver was pulled out from his seat.

Románes froze. She had no idea what to do. The mob would tear her to shreds if they got their hands on her. She shrank into the footwell of the back seat.

Ellroy pulled his gun out and fired shots through the open door. It was enough to make the crowd back away. Davies saw the opportunity and dived to get into the driver's seat. Ellroy fired another volley of shots. The motor engaged and Davies began to edge them forward. Ellroy yanked the door to close it. They were going to get through this, they were almost clear.

He fought through the crowd. A group were beating up the unfortunate driver who had been pulled from the car. The driver's door was still ajar. He dived forward and stuck out an arm and got a grip of something. The car started moving, breaking free of the crowd. The door slammed on his arm, crushing it, but he held on. He was being dragged along. He just had to get the bomb inside. He pulled himself forward and got his head and shoulders inside the door. He was punched in the face. A gunshot just missed him. He felt blood in his mouth and nose as he was punched again. He held on and heaved himself forward with one final effort. He was inside. The car was moving fast now. Another shot from the gun. The bullet hit his leg. He felt pain and then the struggle stopped. He lay on his back, across the person who had been punching him. He realised why the man had stopped attacking him. His coat had been ripped open. They were staring at the bomb strapped to his chest.

'Bomb,' shouted Ellroy, falling backwards from the intruder who had fought his way in through the open door. He landed in the backseat of the car. He saw the Chancellor cowering on the floor. He knew this was the end.

He saw her from the front seat. She was on the floor. She looked weak and scared. He had no sympathy. For one second he looked at her, forcing her to look at him, to acknowledge him.
  'Do you know who I am?' he asked.

Lucinda Romános looked at the bloodied, sneering face staring at her.
  'Should I know you?' she yelled with a last ounce of defiance.

Of course she didn't know who he was. He would be the last face she looked at upon on this earth. He was not just Henrik James. He was Danny Samson. He was Gabriella Marino. He was Phillips. He was every State citizen of the city who had died in the war. He was every person who had been murdered in the First Strike War. He was every child she had ordered killed. He was vengeance, he was justice. He let go of the dead man's switch.

The citizens heard the massive explosion. The car driving away from them erupted in a fireball. They felt the heat as pieces of metal bodywork flew across the street. The entire vehicle lifted into the air and crashed to the ground. Debris at the side of the road was blown apart, a crater opened up in the road into which the burning wreckage settled. No one made an effort to help. They could not approach due to the heat. Anyone who had been in the car was dead. They simply stood and watched, listening to the crackling flames as they licked upwards from the burnt out shell.

Realisation dawned on them slowly, as if they were awakening from a bad dream.

The Chancellor was dead.

EPILOGUE

The clean, white walls and shiny floor reminded Lucas of the hospital, when he had first arrived there. He stayed close to Jenny as they followed the immigration officer who had collected them from the processing hall.

The hall had been noisy, with officials waving people forward, directing them into various queues, ensuring everyone was in the right place. Different languages had circled around them as they stood in line. Eilidh spoke to the man behind the desk. Lucas saw her hand the note to him, the note that Xavier had given her. The man read it, looking up at Lucas halfway through reading, then at Eilidh, Hassan and Jenny in turn. He typed something into his TouchScreen and directed them to wait in some chairs that were behind him.

They sat watching the clerks processing the people. Most of the people were smiling as they made their way through and went onward, into the European Union. There were some arguments for those less fortunate. Several imposing security officers stood around the hall carrying large guns. One individual, a distinguished-looking man wearing a smart suit created enough disturbance to earn a visit from two of the security officers. He was dragged through a door at the side of the hall. Then a kind looking woman had arrived and asked them to follow her.

The woman stopped now in front of a door. There were several identical ones lining the bright corridor. She showed them into a private room and asked them to take a seat. There were no windows, the walls were white, and there was a table and four plastic chairs. No one spoke. Hassan got up after a few minutes and paced around the room. Eilidh sat next to Lucas and put her arm around him, Jenny stared at the floor. Had they made a terrible mistake?

***

When the abandoned harbour on the coast of the State had disappeared from view they had been shown below deck by Xavier. Entering the interior of the vessel it was apparent it was not an old fishing trawler. The deck and exterior were a disguise. Below deck the boat was sleek and modern. Xavier showed them into one of several cabins.

'I hope you will find this comfortable for the duration of the voyage,' he smiled at them. The accent he had spoken with on the beach had disappeared, now he spoke the State language perfectly. 'Please excuse me while I go and change out of these clothes.'

There were four bunks in the room, all with fresh sheets and a selection of food laid out on the sideboard. Jenny gave Lucas an insulin injection and they began eating. They felt the boat cutting through the water faster than an old trawler could ever have run.

'What's going on?' Eilidh asked Hassan.

'I guess our friend Xavier is more than just a common people smuggler.'

After eating, Lucas and Jenny lay down on the comfortable beds and the smooth motion of the boat sent them to sleep. Half an hour later there was a knock at the door. Hassan answered it. It was Xavier, now dressed in a naval uniform. He beckoned Hassan and Eilidh to join him in the corridor.

'You will have some questions.' He gave them a broad, warm smile. 'Please be assured there is nothing to worry about. Follow me and I will explain.'

He took them to the wheelhouse, which was no longer the dilapidated mess they had glimpsed while in the harbour. It had been transformed into a modern boat's bridge. Computer monitors flashed with various charts and information, chrome controls had been revealed in place of the dirty, greasy metal that had been there before. The old-fashioned wooden wheel at the front of the boat had disappeared. The men on the bridge, also wearing uniforms, saluted Xavier as he entered. Eilidh recognised the cook, Loris, and Julius. Both had shaved and changed clothes.

'You will understand that we have to be cautious when we are dealing with the State,' Xavier told them after he had returned the salute of his crew. 'You are now aboard an official vessel of the European Union Navy. Such vessels are not permitted to enter the seas around the State.'

'What will you do to us?' Eilidh asked.

'Relax, please,' Xavier's huge hands waved in placation. 'Nothing has changed for you. We will take you to the European Union as you wish, but we are not illegal smugglers. We are part of an official task force set up by the European and African Unions to stop illegal people trafficking. Instead of letting criminals profit from the desperation of those in need, our leaders decided to help refugees who wished to flee war by rescuing them from within your borders.'

'The State would never allow you to take her citizens,' Hassan objected.

'Precisely, that is why it is a covert operation. An official mission to expatriate those who wish to leave the State would never be sanctioned by your government. However, a small fishing boat smuggling people abroad does not set off enough alarms to trouble your Party. The State Forces had other problems to worry about. Early on they did try to intercept our boats, but since the first year of the war, we have been left to our own devices.'

'Do Gabriella and Danny know you are a naval officer?'

'No,' grinned Xavier, 'to them I am a pirate, out to make a profit. It is better that no one in the State knows the truth.'

'What will happen to us when we reach the European Union?'

'You will be processed at a border facility and given official papers. This will allow you to live legally within the European Union. You will be given a choice of settlement and be given accommodation there until you can stand on your own two feet.'

'And the boy?' Hassan asked.

'I have messaged ahead. Once the paperwork has been done, he will get the care he needs. It is true what you have heard, there is a cure for his condition now, still in a trial phase but they are hopeful.'

Eilidh and Hassan returned to the cabin. Hassan fell asleep after they had spoken about the revelations they had discovered. Eilidh tried to close her eyes but her mind was racing. She was torn between joy and fear about the future. Were they swapping one authoritarian State for another? She was willing to risk it in order to cure Lucas. They could always run again, there was wilderness in the European Union too. She had heard that communities outwith the major cities were allowed in the European Union. They were given the same assistance and benefits as those citizens in the city. If they had the choice, she would request they live in one of those places. Perhaps it would be like the village she had lived in before, where Lucas and she had been happy. She thought of Danny, wondering if she would ever see him again. She had a feeling she would not. He belonged to the State and the city. She had always known that, even when they had shared those few months together in the village.

They sailed through the night and arrived at the modern harbour on the northern coast of the European Union in the early hours of the following day. Once the ship had docked, the passengers walked ashore, setting foot on the new continent. Xavier waved them off, his bright, broad smile wishing them well. Once the last passenger alighted, the gangplank was withdrawn and Xavier shouted a command to his crew. Before the refugees had left the harbour, the boat was already setting sail back out to sea, perhaps heading to take onboard another load of State citizens seeking to escape.

They were met with water and food and given the chance to wash and change into fresh clothes. Then they were transported by train to the processing facility. The landscape they passed through did not look much different from how the State had once looked, although the signs were in a different language. The land was flat, and the fields were covered in vast swathes of agriculture. Occasionally there was a herd of cattle or sheep. A highway ran parallel to the monorail, filled with the grey coupé cars that used to drive through Central City.

***

It seemed too good to be true, thought Eilidh, but then she had heard that the State had once been like this too. She had never lived within city walls, never experienced life under the control of the State. They had housed everyone, made sure everyone had food and power and an income. There had been a good side to the Central Alliance Party before the First Strike War, overpopulation and the climate emergency had changed everything. The borders had closed and the State had cut itself off from the rest of the world, expelling immigrants and allowing protectionism and fear to rule. The thought of being processed and becoming a documented citizen for the first time made Eilidh uneasy, but for Lucas's sake she had no choice and she would do whatever it took to see him cured.

She looked at her son sitting next to Jenny. Neither of them had spoken since they had entered the building. Hassan continued to pace around the room. He was a good man. Forced together by circumstance, she knew Hassan would stay with them until he knew they were safe. Perhaps he would settle with them. He had nothing to return to in the State, no family waiting for him, no one dependent on him.

She smiled at Lucas when he looked up and saw her staring at him.

'It will be alright now,' she said. 'We're together, that's the main thing.'

He nodded.

The door opened. A thin woman entered. She took the chair that Hassan had vacated and powered on a TouchScreen.

'Welcome to the European Union. I'm your settlement agent, Monica Németh, I will be processing your applications and looking after you until you are fully settled.' She tapped the screen. 'It is all four of you who wish to settle here?'

Eilidh looked to Hassan. He nodded.

'Yes,' Eilidh replied, 'all four of us.'

'Excellent,' the woman smiled. 'Please be assured you will all remain together. We do not separate families.'

No one objected to her assumption, they were a family now.

Monica Németh turned to Lucas. 'And I understand you have type-1 diabetes.' Lucas gave no response. Her look was one of understanding and sympathy. 'Well, we must see about getting you cured.'

Eilidh saw the face of her son change. His eyes grew wide as he looked at the woman and then at Jenny next to him. Jenny squeezed him tightly with her arm around his shoulder. A smile spread across his face, a smile Eilidh hadn't seen since he had been a much younger child playing in sunlit fields.

***

Gabriella sheathed her knife and inspected her handiwork. She was no engraver, but it would do, it was symbolic, not a lasting memorial. She placed the stone on the ground, pushing aside some leaves to make a space for it. She was not sentimental, but this had felt like the right thing to do. She knew Danny would have appreciated it. It was comforting to imagine him reunited with his family in some way. Without an afterlife, the small collection of inscribed stones would have to do.

Danny had told her about the three white squares in the city Memorial Park, although he had not visited them in the years of the war. It had taken her a couple of hours to find them. The memorial park took up a large space that had once been a green area next to the river. There were no graves, just row upon row of white square plaques laid out neatly on the ground. Each had an inscription on it representing a citizen of the State who had died. Neglect through the war and the recent storms had meant she had to wipe the plaques clear of leaves and mud before she could read the names on them. She knew they were together in a row: Rosalind Samson, Isla Samson and Hanlen Samson. Now she added the grey stone she had brought with her, upon which she had carved out the name Daniel Samson. She did not know his exact date of birth, so she had only added the date he had died. She stepped back and looked down at the memorial.

They had burned his body, together with Lachlan, on a pyre they had made in the forest overlooking the city. Kyle and Zeb were with her. They had left Verona at the hospital, staying long enough to ensure she was discovered by medical staff and taken inside. She would survive. Gabriella had bandaged up Zeb's shoulder, it was a flesh wound that would heal with time.

The flames had died down and the final ashes drifted away over the valley. They bedded down for the night.

The path of the civil war was uncertain. With Phillips dead it remained to be seen if the Independents would die with him or if someone would pick up his mantle. Perhaps it would be Zeb and Kyle. Zeb had decided to head north and rejoin the rebels, Kyle had agreed to go with him. They had asked Gabriella to join them. She declined their invitation. She didn't disagree with the aims of the rebellion, but she was too used to the life of a loner now, too used to questioning authority and acting on her own. She could only exist outwith the official organisations that made up a State or an army.

The following morning they had bade each other farewell and the two men had left on their journey north. Gabriella wished them luck. She stayed in Central City, waiting to see what fallout came from the death of Phillips and the return of the State Forces. She saw the citizens emerge from their crumbled dwellings and occupy the streets again. The storm weather relented and there was a final late autumn surge of cool sunshine. The State Military returned. She saw them erecting banners in the remains of the main square. She had been on the roof of a building two kilometres away when the Chancellor had come to deliver her speech. When the crowd had begun to riot she had sat and watched. She heard the explosion of the car, only later did she learn that Lucinda Románes was dead. Some deranged loner with a bomb strapped to his chest had jumped in front of her car and fought his way inside. Teddy Davies and Harris Ellroy had also died.

Things moved quickly. After a leadership contest that lasted only a week, Johnathan Sadiq was elected as the new State Chancellor and leader of the Central Alliance Party. He was seen as young and fresh enough not to be tainted by the controversy surrounding his long-serving predecessor. He promised a fresh start, transparency and fresh elections to the Senate. The circle of history was revolving once again. Would it ever break free from its repetitive cycle?

In Central City, the citizens set up their own local committee to run the city. They agreed to work with the

State in the Capital City to hold free elections. The Central Alliance Party could stand candidates if they wished, but it was soon apparent that they stood no chance of winning any seats in the northern megalopolises. Where it would all end, Gabriella did not know. Perhaps she would be back one day to fight in another civil war. Perhaps the Central and HighLand cities would break away from the rest of the State and form their own country, just as Phillips had envisaged, but through a peaceful, political process. The State Forces had not so far pressed north to take on the remains of the Independents. Instead the rebels had entered into constructive talks with the Citizen's Committee of Central City. Gabriella wondered if Zeb and Kyle were leading the discussions.

She felt like she should say something to mark the moment, standing over the memorial to her friend. History would quickly forget Danny Samson. There would be no statue to him, no one really knew his story, no one would write it down or sing songs about him. The citizens who walked about the city owed him their life, but none of them knew who he was or what he had done. She thought of the boy, Lucas, and his mother, Eilidh. Apart from her, they were the only ones who would remember Danny. Perhaps that was enough.

She could not think of anything to say, she was no good with words or speeches. She turned away from the plaques and slung her rifle over her shoulder. She walked away and left the Memorial Park behind.

She had no set destination. The First Strike War was petering out around the world, but she was sure there would be a fresh outbreak of war somewhere soon. Until then she was quite happy to be on the road, seeing the

world and all it had to offer. [...]
America when she had visited [...]
she would return there. She [...]
more of the African Union.

As she left the cemetery [...]
first snow of the coming winter [...]
her hood up and hunched her shoulder[...]
bracing cold and carried on walking, turning away [...]
the city.

A familiar song flickered through her memory. She had not sung it for a long time. She remembered it from when she was a little girl, hearing the different generations of her family singing it to her. The words meant nothing to her, but the sounds and melody brought back the comforting memory of the past, a past long buried, and one that she would never return to. She remembered the title: *Casta Diva*. It translated as something like 'pure goddess'. It was a prayer to the moon in heaven for peace on earth. The words came back to her as she walked away:

> *Casta Diva, che inargenti*
> *queste sacre antiche piante*
> *a noi volgi il bel sembiante*
> *senza nube e senza vel…*

Her voice trailed off. That was all she could remember. Perhaps more would return to her one day. She hummed the tune as the moon began to rise and the cold chill of winter settled across the land. The drops of snow soon turned into a flurry, covering the harsh remains of the city with a fresh, white blanket.

...hite plaques of the cemetery disappeared ...he snow, along with the grey stone placed ...hem.

THE END

THE STATE TRILOGY: MAIN CHARACTERS

CENTRAL CITY

Daniel Samson: ex-State police officer who fled Central City after discovering evidence of State corruption while investigating the murder of City Consul Donald Parkinson.

Franklin Samson: Daniel Samson's father (deceased).

Rosalind (Rosa) Samson: Daniel Samson's wife who took her own life after the death of their newborn children.

Isla Samson: Daniel Samson's daughter (deceased).

Hanlen Samson: Daniel Samson's son (deceased).

Henrik James: Formerly Daniel Samson's partner, then Chief Commander of Central City State Police.

Lars James: Henrik James's father, formerly also Chief Commander of the Central City police before he was killed by Gabriella Marino.

Cassandra (Cas) Ford: State Police forensic pathologist, friend of Daniel Samson.

Janette Michaels: Former Superintendent and Chief Commander of Central City Police, now Chief Commander of the Capital Police.

Archie Cancio: State Police Detective.

Gabriella Marino: ex-State soldier turned assassin, hired to kill City Consul Donald Parkinson. Aliases: **Helena Myers; Phillipa Young**

Elisabeth Sand: Nightclub owner who learned of a State trial to euthanize unborn and newborn children in order to control overpopulation in the State. She hired Gabriella Marino to kill those responsible, including City Consul Donald Parkinson. Killed by a State hit squad. Alias: **Symington**

Donald Parkinson: Respected Central City Consul with links to State high office, killed by Gabriella Marino.

Phillips: ex-State soldier and former State Security Forces agent. He helped Daniel Samson and Henrik James in their investigation into the assassination of Donald Parkinson. Leader of the Independents.

Montana (Tania) Childe: Junior assistant to City Consul Parkinson, who aided Daniel Samson in his investigation. Killed by State hit squad.

Doctor Leroy: Doctor who assisted Donald Parkinson in his euthanasia trial.

Jenny: Orphan and friend of Lucas (see below) at the city hospital.

Verona, Zeb, Rodrigo, Kyle, Lachlan: Mercenaries who join Gabriella and Danny during the Central City civil war.

Kruger, Mitchell: Soldiers in the Independents army and Phillips's trusted lieutenants.

Giesler, Jarrod, Jonas: Soldiers in the Independents army.

CAPITAL CITY

Lucinda Románes: Chancellor of the State.

Ishmael Nelson: Former Defence Secretary of the State, murdered by Agent Phillips.

Patrick Donovan: Former Vice-Chancellor of the State, murdered by Gabriella Marino.

Johnathan Sadiq: Candidate for Chancellor of the State.

Edward (Teddy) Davies: Current Head of State Security Forces.

Field Marshall Harris Ellroy: Senior Officer in the State Military

John Curran: Veteran Journalist at The Star Tribune.

Byron (Buzz) Mayfield: Veteran Editor at The Star Tribune.

Maxine Aubert: Reporter at The Star Tribune.

Horace Frinks; Timothy Pigeon; Kelvin Mothersby: State Media Reporters

NORTHERN WILDERNESS

Rona; Bruce; Hansel; Jia Li: Village elders.

Hassan: Raiding party leader.

Matthias; Tyrell; Tia: Raiding party soldiers.

Eilidh: Member of the village who befriends Daniel Samson. Later tracks Samson down seeking his help in Central City.

Lucas: Son of Eilidh, suffers from type-1 diabetes. Daniel saves his life by taking him to the hospital in Central City.

ISLAND WILDERNESS

Skylar: Cult leader.

Casper: Young member of the Cult, who becomes Phillips's protégé in the Independents.

THE EUROPEAN UNION

Xavier: The captain of a boat, a people trafficker

Julius, Loris: Members of Xavier's crew

For Caden Daniel and Chloe Dawn

ABOUT THE AUTHOR

Iain Kelly lives in Scotland. He works as an editor in the television industry and is married with two children.

For more information visit his website:
www.iainkellywriting.com

Follow on Social Media:

facebook.com/iainkellywriting
Instagram: @with_two_eyes
Twitter: @iainthekid
linkedin.com/in/iain-kelly-writing

ALSO AVAILABLE

A JUSTIFIED STATE
Iain Kelly

Book One of The State Trilogy

The future.

The socially reformist Central Alliance Party rules unopposed.

Poverty and homelessness have been eradicated, but overpopulation, an energy crisis and an ongoing war jeopardise the stability of the country.

When a local politician is assassinated, Detective Danny Samson finds himself at the centre of an investigation that threatens not only his life, but the entire future of The State.

Praise for 'A Justified State':

- 'the action is pacey and exciting, the characters fleshed out, nuanced and believable, the mystery…is genuinely intriguing and alarming.'

- 'the writing brought to mind Phillip Marlow, Do Androids Dream of Electric Sheep?, the world of George Smiley, and Robert Harris' Fatherland'

- 'This is a superbly well written fast paced, suspenseful mystery. A page turner as the action…makes you gasp'

ALSO AVAILABLE

STATE OF DENIAL
Iain Kelly

Book Two of The State Trilogy

Election time in The State, the citizens prepare to vote.

A journalist from the Capital City heads north to report on growing resistance to the powerful ruling Party.

An ex-police detective returns to the City he once fled.

Together they become entangled in a burgeoning opposition movement.

Soon they learn the Party will do whatever it takes to remain in power, and one life is all it takes to spark a revolution.

Praise for 'State Of Denial':

- 'Well paced and full of drama. A great sequel.'

- 'Well written, the plot flows effortlessly… A gripping sci-fi that is a little bit horrifying and a lot entertaining.'

- 'Get lost in the pages…through passages that may have you holding your breath.'